WOLF CHILDREN

WOLF CHILDREN

PAUL DOWSWELL

BLOOMSBURY

LONDON OXFORD NEW YORK NEW DELHI SYDNEY

Bloomsbury Publishing, London, Oxford, New York, New Delhi and Sydney

First published in Great Britain in August 2017 by Bloomsbury Publishing Plc
50 Bedford Square, London WC1B 3DP

www.bloomsbury.com

BLOOMSBURY is a registered trademark of Bloomsbury Publishing Plc

A CIP catalogue record for this book is available from the British Library

ISBN 978 1 4088 5851 6

Typeset by RefineCatch Limited, Bungay, Suffolk
Printed and bound in Great Britain by CPI Group (UK) Ltd, Croydon CR0 4YY

1 3 5 7 9 10 8 6 4 2

To DLD, with a big hug

CHAPTER 1

Late Spring, 1945

It was a chilly night for the end of May. As he crouched, hidden behind the rubble, Otto could see his breath glow in the moonlight as it curled towards the starry night sky. Helene had noticed too and tapped him gently on the shoulder, then pointed to his ragged black scarf. The scarf was full of holes, from moths, from wear and tear, but he couldn't bring himself to throw it away. It was the only one he had, and his mother had given it to him. Now everything she had given him was precious, and it was just the thing to stop your breath giving you away on a bright moonlit night.

Helene was peering over the perimeter of a large crater a stone's throw from a Soviet supply depot in Kreuzberg, a district south-east of the centre of Berlin. Otto took a look too, despite the fact that he had been taught that only one person should look out from a hiding position at any one time. All the Hitler Youth boys had been told that – it was basic military fieldcraft. Helene knew it too. He had told her himself. She tugged on his collar to pull his head down.

It was vital that they were not seen. At this time of night, breaking the curfew, they could be shot on sight. But neither

1

of them, nor the rest of their little gang, had eaten that day. And ahead of them was a treasure trove. Otto's stomach turned over at the thought of it. Piled up by the depot perimeter were tins of juicy spam: succulent, spicy processed pork from America, and a mainstay of Soviet military rations. He had a small rucksack on his back and if he could fill that up, none of them would be hungry for several days.

His empty stomach let out a loud gurgle and as the sound of it drifted across the night air a couple of the Soviet guard dogs began to bark. They set off the Siberian ponies and camels, and a strange braying echoed across the Berlin ruins. The Russians used the camels as pack animals. 'Kuznechiks' he'd heard they called them. They were Bactrians, shaggy two-humped beasts; Otto remembered that from school. It was bizarre, seeing them out there in the street, rather than in Berlin Zoo, and Otto had quickly learned they were not as friendly as they looked. Their minders were even worse. When he had approached a camel to pat it, in the days after the Russians had arrived, a soldier had cuffed him so hard he had knocked him to the ground.

They heard footsteps in the distance. This, almost certainly, was the perimeter guard. Helene lay still, her face pressed against the rubble. Otto did too, trying to breathe as slowly and quietly as he could.

The footsteps were almost upon them now, and this was the awful moment when you never knew whether the guard could see you or not. He might be pointing his rifle at them at this very moment.

But the sound of footsteps continued, even though the guard had been close enough for them to smell harsh tobacco smoke as he passed. Otto stretched out his arm to look at his watch. It was one his father had given him as a fourteenth birthday present, two years ago. He had been careful to keep it well hidden whenever he had been anywhere near the Russians. Those soldiers were fascinated by anything mechanical, especially something as small and delicate as a wristwatch. In the first few weeks of the occupation it had been common to see Russian soldiers, of all ranks, with three or four wristwatches glinting on each arm. They just took them at gunpoint from any German civilian foolish enough to still be wearing one.

Now Otto and Helene waited. Two minutes passed, then the footsteps began again, echoing faintly in the distance. After they passed by, Otto mouthed, 'Two minutes and thirty-five seconds,' to Helene. She nodded and held up three fingers of her hand. This was a familiar routine. Give the guard three circuits. The first time they tried this, at a supply depot on the far side of Görlitzer Park, they had timed the guard there at three minutes and then nearly got themselves shot when he returned in under two. When they talked about it afterwards they guessed he must have stopped somewhere for a chat or a piss that first circuit. Anything could delay a guard on his path, so it was always best to time several circuits to be sure.

This one was almost as regular as clockwork. Each time around, two minutes twenty or thirty seconds. That gave them plenty of time to nip across the perimeter and grab a few tins of spam.

As the footsteps receded for the third time, Otto's heart began to beat faster. This was it. No time for hesitation. They both stood, crouching low, and gingerly crept across the small area cleared of rubble by the camp perimeter. Lit by intense arc lights, their shadows trailed stark behind them. If anyone was awake and watching they would be shot in an instant. This was the most terrifying moment: when you first stood up. It was even worse than being in the middle of a battle. There you went from one horrendous scene to another – the whole thing like the blur of a bad dream where you were watching something happening to you rather than making rational decisions. Here you were completely calm and safe one second, in mortal danger the next.

They reached the depot perimeter in a few moments. Now they hugged the shadows of tents and makeshift corrugated-iron huts. A thin barbed-wire fence surrounded the depot, but it was easy enough to squeeze between the strands. The tins were piled untidily in an old canvas tent, easy enough to see through a tear that flapped lazily in the thin wind.

Helene carefully placed a hand through the gap and quickly picked out tins, one at a time, handing them to Otto to put in his rucksack. They were chilled by the wind and it almost felt like she was taking them out of a refrigerator. Every little clink of metal on metal made them flinch. When he had filled his sack she rolled hers off her shoulder and gave it to him, along with two more tins. Otto glanced at his watch. 'One minute, at the most,' he whispered.

They heard a voice, drowsy but full of indignation. Someone was inside that tent, most likely a guard who had fallen asleep.

Instinctively they both fled back to the rubble, Otto ripping his shirt on the wire and dropping two of the tins Helene had just given him. The tins clattered to the ground and set off the dogs and camels. Harsh voices shouted across the depot. Otto hugged his rucksack close to his chest as he ran to try to stop the tins rattling together. As they dashed past the crater they had previously been hiding in, a shot whistled past, splintering a concrete wall in front of them.

Further ahead were more derelict buildings. If they could reach them they might be able to hide there. Several more shots rang out. Otto heard a cry as Helene fell to the ground. His legs went weak. A jet of bile lodged at the back of his throat. He looked around, expecting to see her with blood seeping from a wound. But there she was, rolling over and crawling forward, obviously uninjured. There were no more shots. The Russians must have seen her fall and now they would be coming out there to retrieve her body. They were not out of danger yet. He kept running.

Just to the south a flash lit up the sky. A moment later the sound of an explosion rolled over, followed by a cascade of falling masonry. Otto recognised the sound from the scores of air raids Berlin had endured. Another bomb had gone off – probably one with a faulty fuse. Maybe it had been lying there since the last air raid in March. But there was no time to think about that now.

They scrambled on, keeping to the shadows, until they reached a shattered apartment block, burned out with not a single windowpane still in place. Helene and Otto peered back over the wasteland, trying to keep their breathless gasping from giving them away. The depot was settling now. The animals were quiet. No Russians were coming out to investigate further. It was as if they had shot at a dog and thought no more about it. Otto and Helene stood in the darkest part of the building and waited until their breathing returned to normal and their hearts stopped thumping in their chests.

Otto was desperately relieved to see that Helene was safe. She had lived with his family for a while because her mother had been the Roths' housekeeper in the last year of the war. It had been a phenomenal stroke of luck finding her queuing at the same water pump in the week after the Russians arrived. The moment they realised they had both survived the final catastrophe was one he would remember for the rest of his life. He hadn't recognised her at first. She had come up to him, plainly delighted to see him still alive. When she'd heard the stories about the Russian soldiers molesting every woman they could lay their hands on, she had cut her hair short and looked instead like a beautiful boy.

In the Hitler Youth they had taught them that girls were meek creatures fit only for motherhood and homemaking.

He knew now that was nonsense. She was a wiry girl, and the bravest person he knew. Before the Russians came, when Helene had a shock of blonde curly hair, he had thought she had something of a young lion about her. Now she had hands with cuts all over them, a dirty face and a few curls at the back of her neck. But she was the same Helene. Always thinking of others, and often smiling, despite everything.

'I thought they'd got you back then, when you fell over,' he said. He wanted to reach out for her and hug her close, and was surprised to feel his throat tightening up as he spoke. She didn't notice.

'That was nasty,' she said. Then, briskly, 'How much have we got?'

Otto laid out his stash carefully on the floor. There were twelve. Not bad for a night's work. The gaudy blue tins, with their American words, seemed like objects from an unimaginable other world of plenty. A world where people were safe to go about their everyday lives and always had enough to eat. For a moment he was struck with a deep longing to be somewhere as safe as that in the world. To wake up in the morning and know his life was not in danger and he would have enough to eat for the day. Where was like that? America, certainly. Canada, Australia? He had been born in the wrong place and at the wrong time.

As he carefully placed them back in his sack he noticed the Cyrillic lettering stamped to the bottom of the tins in red ink, identifying them as Russian property. Those letters would condemn them to death if they were caught carrying them. The Russians would know at once they had been stolen.

'Let's go home,' Otto said.

'Home' was on Skalitzer Strasse in an abandoned derelict hospital with a basement room where the rain only came through in manageable drops rather than a deluge. Back there they would keep their stolen supplies in a stash far enough away from that room to make it plausible they knew nothing about it. Some Russian soldiers had been there once before, but that time all of the gang had been surprised by their kindness. The officer had given them two tins of corned beef, and left with a smile. Otto shook his head at the memory. That was the problem with the Russians: they were completely unpredictable.

'You're right,' said Helene. 'We need to get back. I'll carry the food.'

'No, let me. It's OK.'

She looked at him fondly. 'Come on, we said we'd take it in turns. We've been through this!'

'Honestly, I don't mind.'

She took the bag off him. 'No further discussion,' she said in that prim voice she used when she pretended to be a strict school teacher. Then she softened. 'I'm not having you take any risk I'm not prepared to share.'

They had agreed to take it in turns. If they were caught, one of them could deny all knowledge and only the other would be shot. It seemed like a good idea at the time, and when they had been out earlier that week, Otto had carried the three loaves they had seized from the field bakery at Kottbusser Strasse and carried them home.

The room grew darker as clouds blotted out the moon. That was good.

'Let's get this over with,' said Helene. 'Make the most of these clouds.'

Peering round the broken entrance and making sure no one was coming, they dashed over to the next shattered ruin. This was the way to get home. The journey would take them ten minutes in the daytime, but at night they might be home in an hour, if they were lucky.

They worked their way back south. Every building along the way was a burned-out husk. Not a single one had escaped the fighting, or else had been destroyed in the bombing campaign that had blighted the city over the last two years. Otto and his brother Ulrich had been angered by how the Yanks and the Tommies had ruined their beautiful city with their bombers, but when the Russians came they had taken something that had been pretty beaten up and completely pulverised it. In the first few days of the battle for Berlin, Otto had been angry with them for this city-wide vandalism. But now he was beginning to realise it was the Nazis who were really to blame. They had been the ones who had ordered the army to fight on stubbornly when everyone knew the war was lost. It was the Nazis who had hanged German soldiers – many of grandparent age, or boys – from lamp posts with the words 'Traitor' or 'Deserter' on a sign round their necks. When Otto saw this, all the Nazi phrases and beliefs that he had heard since childhood began to make no sense. The spell that Hitler had cast on him since childhood began to fade. Now he wondered if that was what had happened to his father. In the week before he went missing, Dr Roth had made no secret that he saw no need to defend Berlin to the last. It had been almost a month now since Otto had seen him, working behind the front line with injured soldiers. Maybe they had done that to him, too? The thought of it made him feel sick, and instead Otto tried to imagine the moment he would be reunited with his father and he could show him the watch he had kept from the Russians.

Helene pointed to a house in front of them, on the other side of the street. That would be their next hiding point. Otto stared at it through the dark. Although it remained upright, and still had a roof, the whole facade was peppered with machine-gun bullets. Those windows, too, were charred and there was black soot around the burned-out frames. Otto shook his head. He could imagine what had happened there. He guessed it would have been a strongpoint for the *Volkssturm*, the militia of youths and older men enlisted by the Nazis to defend the homeland. He could imagine frightened old men and boys his age, crouching behind that window frame with their First World War rifles, and maybe a *Panzerfaust* anti-tank rocket launcher, waiting for the Russians to appear in their street. Their lives would have ended in a hail of machine-gun bullets and flying splinters of glass, followed by the cruel jet of a flamethrower. Even now, three weeks after the last of the fighting, there was a good chance that a house like that might still contain the remains of the fighters who had died to defend it.

So they crept instead into a shop with a smashed-in front, broken glass crackling under their feet like ice on top of snow. There was a terrible smell in there. It wasn't the smell of death – that sweet, sickly odour which hit you like a wall and made you want to throw up. This was more of a sharp excremental whiff, mixed with stale decaying fabric, like a dirty dishcloth. Almost certainly, there were people in here. Living people. Otto's first instinct was to run, but Helene held him back. In the distance, further up the street were boisterous voices. The language was Russian. They had been drinking and were braying like camels, and had that mad, deranged laughter that warned anyone who heard it that they would make extremely dangerous company.

Helene pulled Otto back into the shadows and both of them started when they saw something move in the corner of the room. Was it a rat? Or a stray dog? There were still some left that hadn't been killed for food. The shape made a grunting noise. The kind of sound someone makes when they are asleep.

The drunken voices were growing nearer. The soldiers were singing. Otto and Helene flinched when they heard the sound of breaking glass. Now the men were directly outside their shop window. There were seven or eight of them. Holding on to each other for support, they moved

11

down the street like a strange beast of many arms and legs. One of them stooped down to pick up a half-brick and lobbed it towards a window on the other side of the street, where a small pane of glass remained unbroken.

The noise made the creature in the corner shift some more. The men outside shouted at each other and then a fight began between them. The shape froze. Whatever it was, its instincts told it to stay still and silent. The men outside began to abuse each other angrily, then just as suddenly they were laughing and pushing each other about. One of them fell straight into the shop. Otto felt a cold shiver run through him. There he was, carrying twelve tins of Russian spam. If they found him they would shoot him on the spot. Why had he not left his bag a safe distance away?

The soldiers were so close he could smell the alcohol coming off them. Two others barged into the shop to lift the third up by his arms. As one of them bent down, a terrified Otto found himself staring straight into his face. The man made a hissing noise. The sort you would make to warn a cat off a dining table. Then they were gone. Otto could barely bring himself to move. He knew his legs would not support him. He and Helene gripped each other's arms.

Now the shape in the corner moved some more. It was stirring into life.

CHAPTER 2

'Who are you?' came a thin voice. Helene felt the tension ebbing out of her. The voice belonged to a terrified child. She stepped into a pool of moonlight so the child could see her.

'Hello, my name is Helene,' she said gently. 'I'm here with my friend Otto. Who are you?'

A tiny shape emerged from a black bundle of woollen blanket. There before them was a spindly little girl with curly blonde hair, crouched ready to spring. She was caked in dirt and held a small kitchen knife in her shaking right hand.

Helene tensed up again when she saw the knife. Even a child could do serious damage with that. 'Easy now,' she said, holding her hands open to show she was no threat. 'We won't harm you.'

The girl stared at them with a sullen defiance.

'How long have you been hiding here?' asked Helene.

'I don't know,' she said, in a pitifully weary voice.

'Are you here on your own?'

The question seemed to pierce the little girl. The knife came down to her side.

13

'My Mutti and Papa have disappeared. They told me to wait here for them, and . . .' She began to sob.

Helene moved towards her. The girl recovered herself and held the knife in front of her. 'Don't come any nearer,' she said, trying to sound tough.

'What's your name, *mein Schatz*?' said Helene softly.

'Hanna,' came the wary reply.

'Well, my name is Helene. Hello. When did you last have something to eat, Hanna?'

'Ages.'

'Will you come back with us?' asked Helene. 'We live in a little basement not far from here. You can stay with us if you like?'

'Helene,' muttered Otto in a low voice. He sounded cross but she waved her hand for him to shut up. She could have guessed he was going to object. To tell her they had enough mouths to feed already. That was all true but she wasn't going to leave this little girl here alone.

'But then Mutti and Papa will never find me.'

'We'll leave them a note, a big note, telling them where you are,' said Helene.

The girl sank down to her knees, deep in thought. Helene sensed this was the moment she was giving up on the idea that her parents were going to come back, and that she would, in all likelihood, never see them again. She felt a sob rising in her throat. Her own father was dead and her mother had disappeared in the chaos of the final battle. She was always hoping she would see her somewhere on the streets of Berlin.

'Go away,' Hanna said defiantly.

Helene got down on her knees so she was nearer the same height as the girl.

'Hanna, you can stay if you want, but you'll be safer with us. We'll look after you. Won't we, Otto?' she added, a little pointedly.

He nodded, reluctantly.

Otto would come round to it, she thought. He was a decent boy and she just knew he would be haunted with guilt if they left her there. Of course they had to bring her home. She would die here on her own. He would see that.

Helene reached out a hand and the girl shrank away from it. Helene was so weary now, but she had to be patient with the scared little girl. 'OK, how about we sit here for a while and have a chat, so you can get to know us?' she said.

The girl nodded.

The first glimmers of dawn were lightening the sky, and Helene could see more of her surroundings. Hanna had a stubborn, hostile expression on a face that was thick with dirt.

'How did you end up here?' asked Otto softly. Helene could tell by the tone of his voice he was going to let her take Hanna home. He had crouched down too, although she sensed that made the girl even more uneasy. She was still acting like a cornered animal. Helene waved a hand behind her back, urging him to back away.

She was desperate to get home to Skalitzer Strasse. It was the only place where she felt safe, although she knew there was no logical reason to think that. She was anxious too about leaving Otto's younger brother Ulrich to his own devices for too long. Ulrich needed watching, which was difficult as he often went out alone, not telling anyone what he was doing. He was always up to something that might get them killed. But they couldn't rush Hanna into trusting them.

In a flash Helene formulated a plan. 'Here's what we'll do, Hanna. Me and Otto are going to have a rest. We'll probably go to sleep for a while. Now, you can do that too, and know we're here to look after you, or you can sneak off while we're asleep. You'll know. We're both terrible snorers.'

The girl let out a little laugh. Helene sensed she was winning her round.

Helene sat back against the hard concrete wall and curled up, resting her face on her knees. 'Come on, and let me lean on you,' she said to Otto. That was often how they slept when they were away from their home – shoulder to shoulder, heads resting on heads. She liked the feel of him, warm against her.

'I just need to put this bag away from us, somewhere in a corner,' said Otto. 'If the Ivans find us . . .' He didn't need to say any more.

'Good idea,' she said. He was clever like that, was Otto. Sometimes he thought of things she didn't. They were a good team.

Within a few minutes Otto was sitting beside her, snoring softly. It was as soothing as a purring cat. She drifted away moments later. But when they woke up it was fully light, sunshine pouring into the derelict shop. Both Hanna and the bag were gone.

CHAPTER 3

Judging by the angle of the sun streaming through the broken window, it was still early in the morning. 'Are you sure you left it there?' said Helene, as Otto whirled around looking for his precious rucksack. He was trying hard to contain his anger. 'Otto, we're not beasts in the field,' she said impatiently. 'We couldn't leave a little girl to fend for herself. She'll die if we leave her here.'

Otto was not going to fall out with her about this, but they had risked their lives to get that food and now they had fallen for the oldest trick in the book. Hoodwinked by an eight-year-old girl.

He sighed. 'She saw us coming,' was all he said.

Helene put her arm around his shoulders. 'I'm sorry too, Otto. This was a piece of bad luck. Anyway, I think we should wait here for another couple of hours. Let the street fill with people. I'm still so tired and it's definitely too early to be out and about.'

Otto patted her hand and agreed. There was always danger out there in the curfew hours – Soviet soldiers, groups of dispossessed prisoners of war, recently freed slave workers. All of them completely unpredictable – like a group of drunks on their way home from a party.

So they waited another two hours in the shop, dozing a little, but it was hard to sleep on rubble unless you were really bone-tired.

Soon there was a trickle of rag-tag people outside. Like all civilians in Berlin now, they wore clothes that had not been washed for weeks, and many were coated with a fine film of dust. Some walked with determination to a specific destination, others hobbled in a daze, eyes glazed and seeing nothing. Otto felt thirsty and went at once to a water pump he knew was still in working order on the corner of Lange Strasse and Koppenstrasse. It was too early for a big queue, one that lasted for hours, but he still had to wait for ten minutes to fill the *Afrika Korps* water bottle he carried on his belt.

Back at the shop, where he had left Helene dozing, he was surprised to see Hanna had returned. She was nestled under Helene's right arm and held it tight with both her hands. In the light he could see how dirty she was, with mud and oil streaked all around her face. She also stank, and – he had to admit – he admired Helene's ability to be that close to her without flinching.

'Hello, girls,' said Otto, trying to look friendly for Hanna. 'Who's thirsty?'

They all took a long draught from the water bottle.

Helene hugged Hanna tighter. 'She's agreed to come back to the hospital with us,' she said with a smile. 'Haven't you, Hanna!'

The little girl searched Otto's face for approval.

'She went off when we were asleep,' said Helene. 'But she got frightened and came back, didn't you, little *Mausi*?'

Helene spoke directly to Otto. 'Your rucksack was in the back of the shop, in one of the drawers under the counter. Hanna put it there. She thought it was too easy to find, where you left it. She also says she's not eaten for two days and could she have a little of what we've got with us.'

'We thought you'd run away from us, Hanna,' said Otto. He was puzzled by her behaviour.

Helene gave him a sharp look. 'She's frightened of strangers – aren't you, Hanna?' she said. 'She decided she can trust us, so she's back now.'

Otto felt light-headed and not a little confused. He needed to have something to eat before they walked home. 'I think we could all have some breakfast,' he said.

The tins of spam had a small key along the side. When you twisted it, a narrow strip of metal came away, and you kept on turning until the whole top came off. Otto thought it was a miracle of simple engineering – but you had to be careful. The tin was razor-sharp along the edge.

The pink, juicy meat was covered in a glistening film of fat. They all looked at it sitting in the tin, their eyes full of longing. Otto carried a small dining knife in his knapsack and he cut the chunk of spam in two and then cut one of the halves into six thin strips.

'Two each,' he announced, and then said to Hanna: 'Just tiny mouthfuls. And chew them at least twenty times. That way you will feel you've eaten more than you have.'

His father had told him that. The slower you ate, the more you chewed your food, the more the body felt it had eaten enough.

Hanna bolted down her two slices, he noticed, completely ignoring his instructions.

By now the streets were crowded enough to avoid standing out and that made it much less likely they would be singled out by a Russian patrol making a chance inspection of people's bags or pockets.

'Let's get back,' said Helene. 'I worry about the others when we're not there.'

It was true that Ulrich and the twins certainly needed them around. And they'd probably be worried themselves about Otto and Helene. 'Will we remember where this place is?' asked Otto.

He knelt down and reassured Hanna that they would come back and leave a notice for her parents, telling them where she was. But first they had to find a pen and paper.

As they stood up to go, Hanna tugged on Helene's sleeve and whispered something in her ear.

'She says there's something for us in the basement,' said Helene.

'Can she show us?'

Hanna shook her head. She looked frightened.

'What is it?' asked Otto.

'More tins,' she said. 'Peaches.'

'So why haven't you eaten them?' asked Helene with a smile.

Hanna shrugged.

'I'll go and look,' said Otto, noticing a descending staircase at the back of the shop he had not seen before.

'Be careful,' called out Hanna.

'Why's that?' asked Helene.

'Wires, big bang,' she said.

Otto stopped in his tracks. 'How do you know?'

'Soldiers came here,' she said. 'Just before the Russkis.'

'Show me,' asked Otto.

She shook her head.

'Don't do it, Otto,' said Helene. 'It's not worth getting blown to pieces for.'

'I'll just go and have a look.' None of them had eaten fruit for weeks. Ever since Otto and Ulrich were small, his dad had said you had to eat fruit every day because it contained vitamins to stop your teeth falling out. Just recently Otto had started to lie awake at night convinced that his teeth were starting to loosen in their sockets. Those tins were worth the risk.

A plain wooden staircase led down to the basement.

Otto went down the stairs one at a time, looking carefully for tripwires. He knew about them. They had been trained to lay booby traps in the Hitler Youth to catch the Russians as they entered the city.

Light from outside illuminated the basement through the small pavement-level window. The room was a catastrophic mess. A pile of rubble in one corner, shattered glass under-foot, and a free-standing set of shelves by the staircase, where there were tins. It was such an obvious place to put a booby trap, but Otto's hunger overcame his caution.

He reached out a hand to pick up a tin.

'Don't do it, Otto, it's not worth it.' Helene had followed him down the staircase. 'Look – I have a candle and some matches,' she said. 'Let's have a proper look. Hanna found it for me. She said she keeps a few in the back of the shop,' she added, answering the question that formed on his lips.

The candle glow cast a dull yellow light behind the shelf.

'Look at that,' said Otto. Sure enough, hidden behind the stacked tins was a small wooden box, and coming out of that was a wire tied in a knot around one of the tins. 'There'll be a grenade in that,' he whispered.

'So which tins can we take?' asked Helene. 'Any of them?'

Otto considered the tins and the way they were positioned. The pictures of peaches were making his stomach gurgle. But he had to be careful. A thin film of sweat formed on his face. He picked up one tin at the top of the pile, lifting it very slowly to make sure there was nothing attached to it. As he handed it to Helene he noticed the shelf wobble a little. All the tins were stacked on the highest shelf.

'Can we disarm this?' asked Helene.

'Not something I know how to do,' said Otto. The Hitler Youth had not taught them how to disable booby traps – only plant them.

'Come on, let's go. This isn't worth it,' said Helene.

But Otto turned back to the tins, their peeling labels promising a sweet taste of life before the war. He couldn't help himself. He grabbed a couple more and as he did so the whole shelf toppled forward.

The two of them ran up the stairs almost falling over each other. There was a loud explosion and some of the shop floor collapsed. Hanna shrieked in terror. A cloud of dust whooshed up the stairwell, covering Otto and Helene, who crouched down, coughing uncontrollably. But the blast and the fragments did not harm them or Hanna. They all gripped each other tight, wild-eyed and breathless.

As the dust settled a crowd of curious onlookers gathered outside. In Berlin, in late May 1945, with the fighting only recently over, these sorts of random explosions meant there could be something worth looting from the rubble. Otto immediately began to fear for his tins.

'We're OK!' Helene shouted at them. 'Nothing more to worry about.'

That seemed to do the trick, and they started to disperse.

'Let's go,' said Otto. He had had enough of this strange little spot.

He held out a hand for Hanna. As she warily rose to her feet to take it, the floor collapsed beneath her weight. She shrieked, and Otto quickly grabbed her hand. He braced himself on the edge of the hole as she swayed beneath him, screaming, her feet dangling into the basement below.

'Quick! Pull her up!' said Helene, leaning in to grasp Hanna's other hand.

Together they hauled her up and she clung tightly to Otto, arms around his neck. Otto could feel her trembling with fear.

'You're safe now,' Otto told her, looking her straight in the eye.

Despite her fear she managed a little smile and for the first time Otto felt a connection. She was starting to trust him.

'Let's go before any more of the floor caves in,' he said.

They hurried out into the street, bags bulging with cans. As they walked away, another explosion billowed from the basement. Something else in there had gone off. None of them looked round but a crowd was already hurrying forward to investigate.

'Keep going,' said Helene. 'And when we're far enough away to stop, you'd better wrap your pullover around these cans.'

They had been caught like this before. Noticing the tins in their canvas bags, a gang of older children had simply stopped them and taken the bags. Otto hurriedly wrapped his pullover around the contents of his bag, disguising the tin-shaped bulges. Really, he could do to wear it in the early morning chill, but he was determined no one was going to steal those tins.

'Is it far?' asked Hanna.

Otto suppressed an urge to snap at her. He realised with some shame that a small part of him still resented her coming with them. They already had enough mouths to feed.

The journey back was so much easier in daylight, although the sight of the city was still enough to lower anyone's spirits. The streets were, without exception, devastated, and almost unrecognisable from their pre-battle state, although the roads had been cleared of rubble in surprisingly quick time, making transit through this husk of a city easy enough. The Russians had seen to that, offering rations in return for labour. It was the buildings either side of the streets and avenues that were far more of a problem.

Bricks and shattered concrete were easy enough to move if they were in small enough pieces, as were the bodies of those caught up in the fighting. They had been cleared away within days of the surrender. Everybody had got used to the strange sight of the dead, wrapped in paper and string, like parcels ready to be posted into the afterlife. They had run out of anything else to wrap them in.

Plenty of evidence of the fighting still remained, though, and the memories at the sight of the wreckage came unbidden to Otto. On Muskauer Strasse a once mighty King Tiger tank stood by the side of the road, its massive gun turret sideways on and leaning against an apartment building, the barrel still pointing forward. Clearly this monster had been stopped by an explosion so great it had lifted the turret out of the body. Looking at the tank now, Otto couldn't imagine anyone inside surviving that.

Even in its dereliction something of the tank's intimidating authority still remained. The great beast stank – of rusting metal and oil and burned rubber, and the lingering stench of rotting human flesh. It was a creature from a nightmare and Helene instinctively picked up Hanna and hurried her past, talking to her to distract her.

Otto remembered seeing a tank rolling towards his barricade during the fighting against the Soviet soldiers. He had been shaking with terror already, wondering if his last moments had come. He and another boy, whose name he could not remember, both instinctively fled to a building behind them, and dashed through the back door. He had lost track of Ulrich at that moment and hoped he wasn't making a brave stand. The boy he was with had been caught in a burst of machine-gun fire and fell dead to the ground. Otto was unscathed. Now, looking back, he shuddered at his close escape.

The tank was not the only extraordinary sight they met on their journey home. Just streets away from their home, Otto turned to face the burned-out remains of a Fieseler Storch. This spindly reconnaissance plane could land and take off in seconds on the shortest of runways – streets even, if they were wide enough. Seeing it remaining still, incongruous in the ruined city, it looked to him like the fossilised remains of some prehistoric flying creature.

Otto thought sadly of the day he, Ulrich and his father had gone to an air display in the great Olympic Stadium and seen this wonder of aviation technology set itself down like a dragonfly. It could almost land in a tennis court, they had been told. He wondered if he would ever find out what had happened to Papa Roth. He felt his father's loss like a physical weight in his chest. He vividly remembered the last time he had seen him, when they had run into each other near the front line. Papa was working with the medics, Otto and Ulrich were both in their *Volkssturm* uniforms, Otto with a First World War rifle, Ulrich with his *Panzerfaust*. Papa had tried to persuade them to hide, wait out the coming Soviet surge in the basement of their house in Charlottenburg. But Ulrich wouldn't hear of it. He was so angry, Otto was convinced he would have shot him if they'd given him a revolver instead of that anti-tank missile.

The streets of Berlin were full of terrifying memories. Just now, as an emaciated horse pulling an empty wooden cart trotted by, he remembered seeing a carthorse caught by artillery fire, lying on its side close to death, its eyes wide with fear. He had bent down to stroke its head and whisper a few comforting words, and he had seen his gaunt reflection in those black staring eyes. The whole scene was like a vision of hell, burning buildings and billowing red and yellow flames, tormented souls running here and there behind him. The horse had died with a sigh, and there he was, still among the living.

CHAPTER 4

The journey was nearly over. They crossed Skalitzer Strasse by Görlitzer Bahnhof and just in front of them stood Skalitzer Hospital. The central facade was a mere two storeys high, but to the left and right of the main entrance were two higher blocks of four floors. The building, with its heavily ornate brickwork, fancy window frames and internal courtyard, was now a husk. Barely a pane of glass remained in any of the windows. The bombing, then the street fighting, had rendered the hospital unusable.

'Here we are!' Helene said cheerfully to Hanna.

As they got closer, Hanna shrank back from the hospital walls. There was something undeniably sinister about this once magnificent building.

'It's fine. Come on!' said Otto. Ahead he had spotted a squad of Russian soldiers and he wanted to get the three of them inside as quickly as possible.

Otto hurried Helene and Hanna into the main entrance. The grand wooden and glass doors had been blown off their hinges and stood at odd angles. Inside, shattered glass and brick debris crunched underfoot on what had once been an elaborate and beautiful tile floor. Immediately in front of them stood a marble staircase and a vaulted ceiling held up by marble pillars. Exposure to the elements had already begun to erode the interior, and fragments of peeling paint hung limply off the walls, ready to float down like stray snowflakes whenever a fierce gust of wind drove through the corridors.

'You can't live here,' said Hanna. 'It's horrible.'

'Wait and see,' said Helene with a friendly smile.

They walked down the wide ground-floor corridor, each room they passed a tableau of picturesque dereliction. A great sunray machine stood battered in the corner of one room, the large ultraviolet light bulb miraculously still intact at the centre of its domelike shade. Beds in wards lay overturned, like toys in a doll's house scattered by the hand of a petulant child.

There had been fierce fighting here and bullet holes and grenade blasts were splattered across the walls. Occasionally a great black stain surrounded a burned-out door frame.

They hurried down bare stone steps to the basement. Here a similar straight corridor ran the length of the building. Even in the gloom, you could see that the whole interior was plainer. This was a place where patients did not go. Only the dead were taken down here. In fact, the room next to theirs was a mortuary, where four stone autopsy tables lay in regimental order, sinister grooves etched into their inclined hard surface, to channel fluids down to a plug at the feet end.

'Nearly there, Hanna,' said Helene, squeezing her arm. 'You'll like it where we are.'

Hanna said nothing, and her face remained a picture of intense trepidation.

As they reached the end of the corridor they came to a door that was miraculously still in place. Otto pushed it open and they stood in a tiny vestibule. There in the gloom a locked door lay in front of them. He took out a key and opened it. Hanna took this moment to flee. Haring down the corridor, she began to leap up the stairs two at a time as Otto and Helene hurried after her after a confused pause

'Wait!' Helene called.

Hanna tripped on the top stair and fell face down into the rubble. Helene grabbed her and lifted her to her feet. She struggled again to break free. 'You're going to eat me, I hate you!' she shouted into their startled faces.

Helene shouted back. 'Eat you? We're just trying to help you!'

Otto had heard those stories too. Children were being hunted and butchered, their bodies sold on the darkest corners of the black market. He had heard about this so often he wondered if it could actually be true.

He wondered whether to just let Hanna go. They already had five hungry mouths to feed and Hanna would just add to their problems. Could they really find enough to feed her too? But then he looked at this frail little girl and he thought of his mother and what she would have done, and in a flash an idea came to him and he knelt down.

'Look, Hanna,' he said, 'here's what we'll do. You can go. You can walk out of here and go back to your shop. Or you can come down the stairs and we'll clean you up and look after you.'

He turned to Helene, seeking approval. She raised her eyebrows.

'You sit here,' he continued, 'and we'll wait down the corridor. We'll come back in five minutes and if you *want* to come with us you can. If you want to go, you'll be long gone by then.'

Hanna abruptly stopped struggling. Helene released her grip and smiled as she wiped away the tears streaking down the little girl's dirty face.

Hanna's eyes darted around in confusion. It was obvious she didn't know what to do.

'Come on, let's go,' said Helene to Otto. She helped Hanna up again and popped her down on a marble seat right by the steps.

'Bye,' she said as they walked off. Hanna looked confused and tearful.

They stood at the far end of the corridor. Helene gave Otto a quick hug. 'Brilliant,' she said, and kissed him quickly on the cheek. He grinned at her.

Almost at once they heard a plaintive cry, and the sound of Hanna scurrying down the steps towards them. 'Helene. Come back!'

'Come on then,' said Helene, carrying Hanna. 'We'll show you where we live.'

Otto pushed through the two doors and they walked into a comfortably sized room that was astonishingly different from the rest of the hospital.

Light poured in from a narrow band of opaque glass, high on the wall by the ceiling. In places, where the glass had been shattered, it had been replaced by X-ray plates of chest cavities and arms and legs. It gave the place a slightly macabre edge, but there was something rag-tag and homely about it.

Helene placed Hanna gently on the floor. 'Have a look around!' she said. 'We live here with three other boys. They must be out foraging this morning.'

Hanna stood staring at her new surroundings. She looked bewildered. Helene picked her up again and gave her a short, fierce hug. 'It'll be nice to have another girl around,' she said.

The floor had been swept of debris and broken glass, and there was a stout broom propped against the wall. Here, before the capitulation, was where the hospital auxiliary staff had whiled away their breaks. The stale smell of cheap cigarettes still lingered in the walls. There was a sink, a draining board, shelves, cupboards, although all were bare.

Hanna went at once to the sink and turned the taps. 'Nothing there,' she announced. Not even a hiss or a dribble.

'We've got water here,' said Helene. 'Look.' She pointed to a row of ten tin buckets lined up on the far side of the room.

On another side of the room were mattresses and blankets, all neatly arranged and folded, all salvaged from the wards above. But Hanna's eyes lit up when she saw the table in the corner. It was a strange vision of respectable normality, an intruder from a world where everyone was safe and parents placed three meals a day on a family dining table. There was even a lace tablecloth on it.

'Pretty,' said Hanna, and she gently stroked the lace cloth between a very grubby finger and thumb.

'We even have a lavatory,' Helene said. 'Come on, let me show you.' She took Hanna to the end of the corridor. Even the toilet sort of worked. You could flush it if you tipped a bucket of water down it (they all dreaded the day it would block). But so far, if you had water collected from a street pump, then it worked fine. All of them knew a working lavatory in Berlin was a rare luxury. One of the consequences of defeat was a modern city of millions of people with no sewage system. On hot days the smell was vicious.

'Shall we get you cleaned up?' said Helene gently, when they returned. 'Make you look presentable?'

Hanna looked sad and nodded.

'We've even got some new clothes, if you want them?' said Helene.

Early on, when they had first come to the hospital they had found a treasure trove of clothes in an upstairs cupboard – leftovers perhaps from the 'Winter Relief' collections made by the Nazis for the 'less fortunate'. Such donations had been particularly helpful for German refugees fleeing to Berlin as the Russians swept in from the east, and for the victims of the bombing campaign.

They went to rummage through the collection, which was in a basement room close to theirs, and found Hanna a blue polka-dot dress that was only slightly too big for her, and some pants and socks. She seemed excited with these pretty clothes and when they found a smart little Fair Isle cardigan that was just the right size, her face lit up.

'Now, before you try them on, we need to clean you up,' said Helene. There was a little soap and a tin bath, water and a sponge. 'And those clothes you are wearing will have to go.'

Hanna looked defiant. 'No,' she said. 'Mummy gave me those. I can't get rid of them.'

'OK, we'll put them somewhere safe,' said Helene firmly.

Otto watched Helene as she cleaned Hanna up and just for a moment he realised time had stood still. She had put on a white nurse's headscarf, taken from the stock of clothing in the basement here, and her blonde hair had grown back a little now. He loved the way that it curled around the scarf, framing her face in little golden wisps. She turned to him. 'Otto, fetch me a little more water, could you?' And the spell broke. He blushed a little, wondering if she had caught him staring at her, and scooped a bowl from one of the larger buckets they kept in the corner.

As Helene sponged the dirt from Hanna's face she turned to Otto and smiled. 'I worked as a nurse in the last few weeks,' she said. 'I was an auxiliary. That means I didn't really have any training. I just did all the horrible stuff – bedpans, bloody bandages.' Helene scrunched up her eyes and stuck out her tongue, pulling a disgusted face that made Hanna laugh. 'But I got pretty good at changing dressings. I spent a lot of time listening to dying young men and writing letters for them to their mums or girlfriends . . .' Her voice caught at the memory and they all fell quiet for a moment.

Helene took Hanna's dirty clothes and hid them at the far end of the corridor. Otto noticed that the little girl had trusted her enough to let her do that. He looked at her sitting there by herself humming a little tune, and began to feel ashamed for objecting to her coming back. He felt grateful too, to providence, for giving him Helene. Since the surrender they had faced death together several times and he could not imagine how he would survive without her. She was someone he would trust with his life, and he hoped she felt the same about him, too. He thought with a shudder about the time they had stolen a tin of canned beetroot from a temporarily vacated sentry post, a week after the Russians arrived. Shortly afterwards a burly thug of a youth who had been watching them snatched it from them. Moments later they were all stopped and searched by Red Army soldiers. The tin was clearly marked with Russian Cyrillic lettering and they shot the boy right there in the street. Otto often thought about that in the small hours when he couldn't sleep.

When Helene came back they opened one of the cans of peaches Otto had rescued at such great risk to his life. Helene took a large serving dish and counted out the contents. 'There are six of us living here now, Hanna,' she said. 'We share out everything, so there are no arguments.'

So the three of them had two peach slices each, and a little bit of the thick syrupy juice. The taste of it was so marvellous Helene and Otto cut up each slice into several smaller pieces, to try to make it last as long as possible. Hanna could not contain herself. Her pieces were gone within ten seconds. Then they scraped up every tiny morsel of juice left on their plates.

In Otto's childhood there had always been enough to eat at home. Back then, during the early years of the war, Berlin had become a gourmet paradise, with food purloined from every corner of the New German Empire. Cheese from France, apples from Poland, wheat from the Ukraine. That had only stopped in 1944. Now here they were, a bare six months later, savouring tinned peaches like they were Russian caviar or the finest Parisian patisseries.

There was a rustling outside and young voices. 'Good, they're back,' said Otto, and they looked up to see three boisterous boys burst into the room. He was surprised how thankful he felt to see them safely home.

'There you are!' said one of them. 'We wondered if something had happened to you.'

'The Russians did shoot at us, but we managed to get some tinned meat,' said Otto proudly. 'And then we stayed in a shop overnight, where we met Hanna.' He gestured at her with a smile. 'She was in Köpenicker Strasse, living on her own, and we thought she might like to come home with us. Hanna, this is Klaus and Erich.'

Two boys in their early teens stepped forward to shake her hand, smiling. They were both blond and fresh-faced – handsome in the German way – and unnervingly identical. Neither tall not short for their age, they were stocky, freckle-faced youths who looked like they enjoyed the outdoor life.

'Hi, Hanna,' they said together.

'As you can see, they are twins,' said Otto. 'And this here is Ulrich, who is my brother.'

Ulrich was fourteen and he stood apart from the others. He looked like Otto but he was fair, like his mother, and several inches taller than his elder brother. He also lacked Otto's amiable character. Now he smiled thinly at Hanna and nodded, but Otto could see at once he was not happy with the newcomer. He could understand that, but he did not want Ulrich falling out with Helene about this. He would have a chat with him about it later.

Hanna gave them all a bright smile, although she snuggled closer to Helene.

'Hanna has brought some peaches with her,' Otto continued. 'We have all had a couple, and we have saved the rest for you.'

'So, boys, what have you been up to?' asked Helene.

'There's a couple of strawberry bushes in the bomb site

by Mariannenplatz,' said Klaus. 'I'm amazed no one has noticed yet. Anyway, we cleaned the whole bush of anything worth eating. Anyone any good at making jam?'

His little joke fell flat. They all knew you needed something to cook the fruit on. The gas stove in the corner was as useless as the taps in the sink. And you needed sugar, and lemon juice. No one had had either of those since the battle for Berlin had begun.

Hanna piped up. 'I know how we can make jam.'

They all turned and looked at her, surprised.

'Back at the shop, where you found me, there's a little wood-burning stove. My Mutti and Papa used to take it with us on picnics.'

'Well, you're a useful girl,' said Erich, 'but I want to eat the strawberries now!'

'Let's all eat a few now,' Helene said. 'One day, if we ever find any sugar, and maybe a lemon, then we'll make jam. That way it'll keep for when we're really short of food.'

While they ate, Klaus and Erich clamoured to tell them about their latest adventure. 'Big bomb last night,' said Erich between mouthfuls, 'in a basement up by Wrangelstrasse.'

'We reckon the Yanks probably dropped it in March,' said Klaus, swallowing.

'Took half an hour to set off with a bonfire,' said Erich. 'But it was worth the wait. Brought the whole building down!'

They both laughed and looked extremely pleased with themselves.

Hanna looked on, mystified.

'It's so dangerous!' said Otto, remembering the earlier booby trap. 'You might get yourself killed. And aren't you worried someone else might get hurt?'

Klaus and Erich shrugged in unison.

Ulrich scowled and said nothing.

Later that day Otto found himself alone with his brother. He knew there was a row brewing and this was the time to get it over with. He also knew they had barely enough food to keep them alive. They had ration books, it was true, but the food allocated to them was not enough. Why else would they risk their lives stealing food?

'What are we doing taking her in?' Ulrich hissed. 'The five of us here barely get enough to eat.'

Otto could understand why he thought that. But he wasn't going to turn a little girl out on to the street. 'We couldn't leave her on her own. She was in a terrible state – you should have seen her, Ulrich. So dirty and frightened.'

'She's a useless eater, Otto. What can she contribute? She's eight if she's a day.'

Otto flinched at this harsh Nazi term. He remembered it well from Political Science lessons at school. 'Useless eaters' was the phrase they gave to the physically and mentally handicapped, because they had nothing to contribute to the National Community.

Otto folded his arms. 'You're wrong. Already she has brought us peaches, and she knows where we can find a stove.'

'I still say she will be a burden,' Ulrich insisted. He stared at Otto, challenging him. 'Why do *you* get to decide who joins us, anyway?'

Otto bristled. 'Why do *you* want to choose people based only on how useful they are? Do you think Mutti would have done something like that?'

'Vati certainly wouldn't have,' Ulrich muttered sullenly.

Otto disliked the tone of his brother's voice, but he didn't want this argument to descend into the sort of rows they had often had when they were younger.

Otto's hand instinctively went to the watch on his arm, and Ulrich noticed.

'I wonder where Father is,' Otto said softly. 'I often look out for him on the streets.'

Ulrich turned away. 'Well I'm not sharing my blanket with her tonight, I tell you that now.'

'Enough, Ulrich!' Otto cried. 'She is here, and we will all share what we have to share.'

Ulrich said nothing, but his glowering face left Otto feeling there would be more trouble. That filled him with foreboding. Ulrich had always been unusually stubborn, and here he was, still clinging to the Nazi ways. Everyone else he knew had stopped believing in Hitler when the war had ended in the total destruction of the capital. But here was Ulrich now, still acting like he was in the Hitler Youth.

Otto had quickly realised that the Russians could be quite as ruthless as the Nazis and he knew that if Ulrich caused them any trouble they would kill him without a second thought. And the rest of them too, if they were unlucky enough to be tangled up in whatever he had done.

Otto was right to worry. That night as they lay in their beds, Ulrich sulked and plotted. The kind of trouble he had in mind didn't involve petty looting or even Klaus and Erich blowing up old shells and bombs. Before the surrender Ulrich had heard about Nazi plans to resist the conquerors if Berlin should fall. Groups of Hitler Youth would form guerrilla groups. They would be known by the code word 'Werewolf'. Every day now he hoped he would pick up clues to lead him to a Werewolf group. The idea excited him so much he couldn't sleep. So far he had heard nothing, although whenever a bomb or a shell went off he wondered if this was the beginning of the resistance. He needed to be patient. One day he would get lucky and then the fightback against the subhumans would begin and Germany would be resurgent.

CHAPTER 5

The next morning they all headed out to search for something to eat. As they walked down Skalitzer Strasse a lone figure watched from behind the shadow of a wall. He was tall and lean with broad shoulders and sharp features. Someone with a keen eye for these things might have guessed from the way he carried himself that he had been a senior officer in the army, or even the SS. And they would have been right. To the Jews and Russians who had witnessed him slay their families and neighbours, and raze their village, he had evil engrained in his bone structure. To others, especially his own kind, he had a handsome *Übermensch* kind of face – the kind that would win the Third Reich an empire to last a thousand years.

As they walked by he didn't really notice the others, because his eyes had been drawn to the fair-haired boy with the closed, determined expression. The stranger knew that face at once and what it meant. He had seen it on boys who had been sent to the front at the close of the war. It was the face of what he liked to call a 'hundred-per-center'. He always knew he could rely on boys like that.

He wondered briefly who the others were. A girl with short hair. An older boy with curly dark hair. Maybe he was this boy's brother. He looked weaker though. He did not have the boy's determination. Then there were twins, and a young girl. He trailed them, keeping hidden, wanting to know what they were doing. He was a master of stealth and could infiltrate an Ivan camp as easily as most people would walk into a department store. The group had stopped and were arguing. His boy was making a point very forcibly. The man liked that, it showed spirit. Then he heard the older boy call his name: Ulrich. A good German name.

How would he lure the boy away from them? He would watch and wait. One day his opportunity would come, and then he would make this boy his. He hoped he would last longer than the last one. He'd had to kill him within a week.

The following day Helene left the hospital early and hurried into a hazy morning along Skalitzer Strasse, her head down, her stride determined. Her hair was still short enough to convince anyone who gave her a casual glance that she was a boy and today none of the Russian soldiers out in the street gave her any trouble. Her destination was Kottbusser Tor U-Bahn, a brisk fifteen minutes west. Kotti, as they all called the station, had been destroyed in the fighting, but it was still a focal point in the area and that was where the *Trümmerfrauen* – the rubble women – gathered to be given their day's work in Kreuzberg.

44

As she approached the ruined station she saw a group of small children playing among the rubble. It can't have been more than seven in the morning and she couldn't understand why they weren't still asleep. One of the small boys adopted the unmistakable swagger of a Russian soldier and marched his way across the fragments of brick over to the group of girls. '*Frau komm!*' he shouted in an exaggerated Russian accent, hefting a broomstick like a rifle. Helene stopped in her tracks. Time stood still. That was a phrase the Russian soldiers had used to summon a German woman when they had first arrived in the city. The Russian soldiers would take the woman away and there would be nothing anyone could do to help her.

The little girl looked sternly down the barrel of the broomstick at the boy. With an unmistakable shooing gesture of rejection she cast the broomstick aside and pushed the boy firmly in the chest. The other children joined in, play-fighting with the boy pretending to be the Russian. In their games these children were able to do what the adults around them had not been able to do in reality: protect each other. Helene found herself choking back tears. She felt a terrible sadness for these children, that they had witnessed such horrors at such an age.

There was already a large group of women waiting at the station, and soon after Helene got there a squad of drab khaki-clad Russian soldiers arrived, accompanied by an officer with his peaked cap and epaulettes. Helene recognised this man, a small pugnacious fellow in his forties, his chest emblazoned with medals. She had worked for him before. He looked stern and spoke abruptly through one of his soldiers who acted as an interpreter, but he made sure his men protected the women as they worked, and he was scrupulously fair in ensuring they had food and drink and a break from their labour.

The day's instructions were barked out. In the entire square around the station only two or three buildings had survived – the rest were piles of rubble. They were to start on a collapsed apartment block, once seven storeys high, now barely two. It was the usual work. Rubble was to be piled as neatly as possible on carts at the side of the road. Any intact bricks were to be chipped clean of mortar and stacked in a pile. Any rubble too heavy to lift was to be broken down into smaller more manageable lumps.

The officer's stern demeanour broke for a moment as his interpreter announced they had a gift for them from the Soviet people. Another soldier came forward with a green canvas bag and emptied its contents on the road. A bundle of padded gloves tumbled out and the women dashed forward to claim them. The soldier stood guard over his precious pile, and insisted on issuing a pair of gloves to each woman. It was a sensible thing to do. Anyone with a morsel of cunning would take as many gloves as they could and sell them to other *Trümmerfrauen* for a cigarette or a loaf of bread. Helene looked at her chapped and bleeding hands and wished they had been given gloves when she'd started this work. Still, better now than never.

The morning passed in a haze of heavy lifting, brick dust and bruised ankles from the constantly slipping debris. But Helene could not say she hated the work. The women, who were mostly older than her, were a chatty bunch. They set about their tasks with a cheerful determination and if anyone grumbled they were swiftly reminded that this was much better than repairing an endless stream of broken sewage pipes. Helene had dressed in her toughest, shabbiest clothes but some of these ladies were in their Sunday-best dresses. You saw sights like that every day – the world turned upside down. A posh frock was probably the only clothing that woman had.

A woman next to her was telling them all about a fat little man who lived along from her semi-derelict apartment. He had been a kindergarten headmaster until his school was destroyed when the Russians arrived, and now he still continued to teach a small group of children in the ruins. The day started with the 'Hitler salute', as it had in all those years under the Nazis. The other women laughed.

'He won't be fat for much longer,' said one.

'He won't be alive for much longer, if the Ivans hear him doing that Sieg Heiling with the children,' said another.

Helene felt angry at his stupidity. All that Sieg Heiling had led to the utter destruction of her city. But the women around her just talked as though it was a harmless eccentricity.

There was only one man among them, a sprightly old buffer who must have been about sixty. He stood in line with the rest of them, joining in with their gossip, as they passed rubble between them.

'I hid in a cellar when the Russians arrived,' he said. 'Six days I was there. Didn't want to get killed fighting with the *Volkssturm*.'

'Understandable,' said the woman next to him.

Helene smiled at that. A few weeks before, such an admission would have had him denounced and hung from a lamp post with a placard saying 'Traitor' around his neck. Now the women clapped him on the back and said they didn't blame him. That was progress.

But he was still taking a risk, coming along to work. Almost every German male between the ages of twelve and seventy had been taken prisoner by the Russians – especially if they had been wearing the uniform of the *Volkssturm*. They had been marched east in great stinking columns, faces stiff with anxiety. There had been many rumours circulating the water-pump queues. It was said they were being taken to slate quarries outside Woltersdorf and systematically exterminated with machine guns. Or they were being put on trains and shipped out to Siberia.

Whatever was really happening it was enough for Helene to insist that none of her boys at the hospital volunteered for the *Trümmerfrauen* work. It was too much of a lottery. Most of the time you could hope not to be arrested. After all, there were plenty of displaced persons floating about Berlin – liberated slave labourers, or waifs from the camps, and the soldiers did not now automatically assume you had been fighting them when they arrived in Berlin. Maybe in a few weeks' time, when things had settled down, she thought as she worked, the boys could come out to help. Perhaps with them all working they would be able to stop worrying about not having enough to eat. But for now, she was the only one who could turn up for rubble-clearing duties and reasonably expect to return home.

Helene's train of thought was interrupted by the arrival of another squad of Russian soldiers. These ones had bayonets attached to their rifles and were waving them towards the women who were working with Helene. '*Frau komm!*' they were shouting, grabbing the youngest and strongest-looking girls. Helen's blood turned cold and she could tell by the frightened faces around her that the other girls were just as alarmed. She looked around for the Russian officer who had always protected his *Trümmerfrauen* in the past, and he was there, across the square, sharing a cigarette and a joke with another officer. He seemed unconcerned. Surely he must know what was going on.

Helene and another nine of the girls were lined up and marched away from Kottbusser Tor. They were all pale with fear and a couple were sobbing quietly to themselves. Whenever one of them spoke a guard would bark at her. Helene kept quiet. She was afraid but her mind was clear. She would try to escape at the first opportunity.

After fifteen minutes, Helene noting all possible routes back home as she marched, they came to a factory on Moritzstrasse and were directed inside at bayonet point.

Helene tensed, ready to run. But as soon as they came to a large loading-bay hatch, she began to relax. It seemed that nothing terrible was going to happen after all. Inside a huge machine room, hundreds of other women were milling around dismantling and loading factory machinery on to Russian army trucks.

The factory work was much harder than the rubble clearing. And your clothes got covered in grease and oil – so much more difficult to rinse out than brick dust. But Helene was pleased to be given an extra slice of cheese and ham along with her bread when the women lined up to be fed at the end of the day. Only that night, as she lay in the hospital basement while the others snored around her, did she allow herself a shiver of revulsion when she thought about what might have happened to her.

A couple of hours after Helene had scurried off to work, Klaus and Erich emerged from the hospital to scavenge for valuables and firewood. It was still cold for this time of year, and they needed wood anyway, for the stove they had salvaged from Köpenicker Strasse. There was something exciting about living in this city on the edge of anarchy. Both of them had fought with the *Volkssturm* – that was where they had met Otto and Ulrich – and both of them had faced death every day during the final battles. Although they had found it exciting in parts, warfare had been a disappointment to them. In magazines and books they had read that battle was noble and exciting, and German soldiers always triumphed. Nobody ever pissed their pants or broke down in hysterical tears, and if they were hit they died quickly and cleanly.

The twins had had so many narrow escapes they thought themselves invincible. Once, a mortar had even landed in the crater where they were hiding but failed to explode.

Now, here at Waldemarstrasse, only three blocks away from the hospital, they had discovered an unexploded shell. Close to the park, there was a whole apartment block that had collapsed in a bombing raid, and although the rubble had been cleared from the narrow cobbled street it was still piled two storeys high at the side. The shell was half a metre in length, and they could see a Soviet slogan in impenetrable Cyrillic lettering daubed along its slender cylindrical body.

Klaus recognised it at once. '25 kilogram, 122 mm,' he said casually.

Erich wasn't quite so impassive. 'Couldn't this go off any second?' he asked his brother.

Klaus shrugged. 'Maybe. But it hasn't so far. Probably fired in early May.' He laughed. 'Hit a building that was knocked down already. Fate certainly had it in for this block.'

'Reckon we can set it off?' asked Erich.

There was a large Santo refrigerator lying on its side nearby, with the door open.

'Let's put it in that,' said Klaus. 'Set a fire underneath it. That'll make a fantastic bang!'

The shell was buried for a third of its length in light rubble and would be easy enough to extract.

'Reckon we can lift it?' said Klaus. 'It's the same weight as a big dog.'

They spotted a Russian patrol coming down the street and immediately stopped what they were doing. One of the soldiers yelled at them in barely understandable German. 'Hey, Fritzes,' he called up to them. 'You can break necks up there for all I care.'

The soldiers laughed and walked on.

Klaus and Erich made an obscene gesture behind their backs.

As Klaus cleared away the rubble, Erich held the shell at its base, so it didn't crash down. It was part of the thrill for them, doing these unbelievably dangerous things. And if it did go off, then they would be blown to pieces in a second. It would hardly even be painful. Both of them had seen that happen so often in the final week of the fighting. A soldier would be there one moment, and gone the next. The twins had long ago decided that was the way to be killed. Bullets, flamethrowers, bayonets – they all promised an agonising death. With a big shell it would be over so quickly you wouldn't even know about it.

They tottered across the top of the pile of rubble, sometimes unsteadily as it gave way a little beneath their feet, one at each end of the shell.

'Quick, Erich, in case another Ivan patrol comes again and spots us.'

The shell was lowered carefully into the refrigerator, and the lid gently closed.

'We'll be back for that, with an audience, I think,' said Klaus.

That afternoon they returned to Waldemarstrasse with Ulrich, and Hanna had come too. Otto and Helene were both out, and the new girl had grown bored alone at the hospital.

'We'll show you something exciting,' Erich had said to her, and her eyes had lit up.

The two older ones would have forbidden it, of course. But Erich liked this little girl. She reminded him of his sister. The one that had been killed back in '43, when the bombing had really started.

They also brought along a teenage girl they knew called Christa, who was around the same age as Helene. She always went round with two small children called Rolf and Traudl – waifs from Berlin by the sound of their accents. They lived in a cellar close by and Christa sometimes came round to sit and talk with Helene. She had come up from the east just before the Russians arrived and had recently told them she was astonished to find an utterly devastated city. There had been nothing on the radio or in the newspapers about Berlin being destroyed by the Allied bombs. Dr Goebbels, the Nazi propaganda minister, had kept the destruction of the capital a secret from the rest of the German people.

While the younger children played in the park opposite the derelict house, the boys began to pile paper, fragments of wood and then substantial bits of door frame or skirting board underneath the fridge.

'Hey, Hanna, can you keep watch for us?' asked Erich.

Ulrich rolled his eyes.

'Yes!' she said eagerly. 'What shall I do?'

'If someone like a policeman or some Ivans come along, then start singing "*An meiner Ziege hab ich Freude*" as loudly as you can, and get the others to join in,' explained Klaus with a wink. 'Then we'll know to hide.'

Hanna laughed. '*An meiner Ziege hab ich Freude*' ('I'm Happy about my Goat') was one of the few children's songs they all knew that was not directly about the Nazi regime.

After half an hour they were ready. They lit the fire with some precious matches, and ran down the piles of rubble to the park, where the others were waiting.

'If the fire keeps burning, it will set off the shell in about ten minutes, I think,' said Erich.

Traudl, the little girl who had come with Christa, looked worried. 'What about if people walk past?' she asked.

The boys all laughed.

'That's all part of the fun,' said Rolf.

Hanna was beginning to look concerned too. But she didn't say anything.

They waited, hiding in a bush in the park with a clear view of the building. Every now and then a pedestrian would walk past, completely unaware of the mortal danger they were in. The children would laugh hysterically as they approached, and hold their breath while they passed.

'It must be more than ten minutes now,' said Rolf. He was getting impatient and cold.

Just then a woman with a pram and two tiny children trudged exhausted up the street. She stopped exactly by the derelict house and sat on the remains of a low wall. She looked half asleep, almost like she could bear to walk no further. Her two children slumped either side of her, and occasionally all three would make cooing noises or take it in turn to rock the pram whenever the baby inside began to make noises.

Christa began to fret. 'You've got to tell them,' she said defiantly. 'That's not funny any more.'

No one was laughing now. Erich sneaked out of the bush and walked confidently to the opposite side of the street, where he called, '*Guten Tag*. Excuse me, *Frau*, the rubble from this building here is always falling down on the street. It is a very unsafe place to sit.'

Then Klaus shouted over, 'And look, madam, there's a fire burning in the building.'

The woman looked up at Erich with a weary frown. For one awful moment he thought she was going to ignore them both. But she waved and slowly stood, and the little family began their journey down the street again.

Erich returned to the bush, but the rest of them were getting restless. Christa, Rolf and Traudl wanted to go, and began to complain.

'Come on, look at that fire,' Klaus chided. 'It's still going strong. Just wait another five minutes.' He wasn't going to let them go. He needed an audience for his explosions, otherwise what was the point?

They all peered towards the fridge, excitement and anticipation just about simmering away.

The sun went behind some dark clouds and Erich and Klaus began to feel foolish. Ulrich chided them. 'I said we needed more wood on the fire. It's just not hot enough to . . .'

His words were cut off by a blinding flash and a colossal eruption. Bricks, splinters and lethal fragments of sheet metal from the fridge shot out at lightning speed. All of them cowered in the foliage, trying to press themselves hard into the soft ground. The blast itself sucked the air from their lungs, leaving them gasping. The sounds around them seemed muffled. A few moments later, rubble hurled high into the air began to rain down. A hefty section of wall, six or seven bricks thick, thudded into the ground close by, burying itself halfway into the park grass. The younger children whimpered in shock and fear. For several seconds debris landed in the area around them, the large heavy pieces first, the smaller fragments later.

Everyone's ears were singing.

Erich let out a whoop of joy. 'How about that!' he yelled.

As the last of the fragments descended to earth, the twins stood up to admire their handiwork. As they did, the ruined building to the left of the explosion wavered and began to sway, crashing in upon itself with a huge cloud of dust.

Up the street a Russian patrol was running fast towards them.

'Play it cool,' said Ulrich to them, nonchalantly brushing himself down. 'We were just playing in the park, remember?'

There was an officer with the soldiers who spoke rapidly in Russian. But they could tell by the tone of his voice that he was concerned for their safety. He made them line up and looked at each of them to ensure they were not injured. Then he sent them on their way with a brisk few words in German. 'Hurry home, *Kinder*. You lucky not hurt.'

They trotted off, barely able to contain their sniggers and began to laugh uncontrollably when they turned the corner and were out of sight. Only Traudl was unimpressed and seemed quite tearful.

'We won't take her along next time,' said Rolf brusquely.

Hanna was pale, and had briefly clung to Erich, but seemed fine. He thought she had enjoyed being out with them all.

Klaus and Erich strutted home like peacocks. This was their best one yet.

CHAPTER 6

Early June

When Helene had come home, drained from work, the twins, Ulrich and Hanna had thought it wisest not to mention the day's excitement to her or to Otto. Instead, the small group curled up with one another in their beds and waited to fall into exhausted sleep. But that evening the usual street noise of foreign shouting and hurried steps gave way to something different. Piano music, beautifully played, floated through the night.

At first Otto thought it was a recording and that someone had found a wind-up gramophone somewhere in the rubble outside. Now and then, though, a note sounded wrong, like the piano was out of tune, or some of the notes were missing. But the skill of the pianist, and the beauty of the music, were undiminished.

Then he remembered there was a piano not far from the hospital. It was one of those strange surreal sights you stopped noticing on the streets of Berlin – like the burned-out tanks and lorries or light aircraft. Certainly Otto had never had the inclination to play a few notes on it or had even noticed anyone else doing so.

Helene was enchanted. 'Let's go out, see who it is.'

Hanna and Erich readily agreed.

They hurried to get their coats on, feeling a shared excitement. But Otto called to them to be quiet a moment. 'Wait a second. We don't know who else is out there.'

They stopped to listen and at once the pleasure they felt in hearing the music faded. Whenever there was a pause in the music, an angry voice demanded the pianist played some more. It was a Russian voice – the accent was unmistakable – but the speaker had some command of German.

'Come on, you SS pig,' they heard him say. 'Play on, or we'll kill you.'

Then the music would start again, beautiful and often familiar, carrying with it memories of a time when music meant dancing, or a gramophone in a warm living room. He was good, this man, but eventually he began to beg them to let him stop. He sounded desperately weary, almost at the point of tears. Shots would then be fired and he would carry on playing.

Hanna began to sob uncontrollably and Helene held her tight, trying to get her to stop. But they all looked wide-eyed with shock. 'This is like some scary film,' said Klaus. Otto shook his head. It was like no film he had ever seen.

Whenever there was silence they all tensed, awaiting further shouting or violence. Otto felt so stiff with fear he felt dizzy.

Far into the night, when Otto's watch told him it was three thirty in the morning, the piano playing stopped.

The shouting didn't come. Instead, they heard a volley of machine-gun fire, and the splintering of wood and the pinging of piano strings breaking under high tension.

They slept late, all of them haggard and pale the next morning. They gathered round Helene as she sat at the table, Hanna in her arms, and without a word they hugged each other. No one wanted to leave the safety of the basement. They all knew what they would find by the piano in the street.

CHAPTER 7

The next afternoon Ulrich and the others returned from foraging. Helene was already back from her shift with the *Trümmerfrauen*, with bread and cheese that she would share out scrupulously. Ulrich hated having to accept food from her. She wasn't his mother. But thankfully, today they'd been lucky themselves.

'We found a vegetable garden in the back of one of the bombed-out houses on Oppelner Strasse,' announced Otto. 'Carrots, potatoes. Just a few, but better than mud and straw.'

Hanna laughed at that. 'And pebbles,' she said. 'They don't taste very nice. Even if you boil them for hours.'

'Crocodiles eat pebbles, you know,' said Klaus.

'And stones,' added Erich.

'No they don't,' said Hanna with a frown.

'It's true,' said Klaus, pretending to chew big mouthfuls. 'Lots of animals do. It helps them digest their food. Grinds it up in their gizzard.'

'I remember that from school too,' said Helene. She turned to Hanna. 'See, *Mausi*, not everything Klaus and Erich say is nonsense.'

'We have enough for soup,' said Ulrich in a loud, flat voice. Why were they teasing Hanna, when they could be eating?

'We'll need some more water for that,' said Helene.

'I'm not doing it,' said Ulrich, throwing himself down on a chair.

Otto glared at him, but Ulrich ignored him. He was always on Helene's side. So pathetic, always wanting to please her.

Klaus and Erich whispered to each other, as they often did, then one of them said, 'We'll go, but Otto and Ulrich have to wash up afterwards. And start the stove fire.'

Before Ulrich could object, Otto agreed for them both. Typical. Just like Otto to think he was in charge of him just because he was the older brother. Older, but weaker.

'Thanks, boys,' said Helene. 'Come on, Hanna, let's clean these carrots.'

The cellar grew dark as evening clouds thickened and rain began to fall in sheets. They lit candles as the room filled with the smell of cooking, then sat round the table to eat their vegetable soup with Helene's bread and cheese.

'I have some important news to share,' said Helene. 'I heard it from the other *Trümmerfrauen*. The Tommies and the Yanks are coming. They'll be here within the week.'

Ulrich stopped eating and looked at her.

'How do you know it's true?' he said.

'Ilse asked the Ivan officer who usually watches what we do. He told her they're coming on the fourth of July.' Helene was beaming as she took a spoonful of soup.

'Is that good?' asked Hanna. She sounded afraid. 'Won't they be horrible too?'

Ulrich opened his mouth to reply but Erich interrupted.

'It's very good,' said Erich, and beckoned Hanna to sit on his knee. When she snuggled up to him he carried on with his explanation. 'The Russkis hate us because we invaded them. And they hate us even more because we have a nice country and they had a horrible country with no lavatories and dirt for roads. The British and the Americans come from countries more like ours. And we never invaded them.'

'Not that we didn't try,' snickered Klaus.

'So they'll be nicer to us,' concluded Erich.

'Well, we have to hope that is the case,' said Helene.

How could they laugh about it? thought Ulrich, with rage simmering in his stomach. Their enemies, who destroyed his city, were now coming to lord it over them all. The Russians were bad enough, but the others, too? Ulrich clenched his fists.

'It's almost like normal, isn't it?' said Otto. 'I mean, sitting here in the dry, having had a proper hot meal. When we do normal things like this I start to believe everything will turn out all right.'

'Yes, it would be nice to think we can all go home one day,' said Erich.

'Where is home for you?' asked Helene, sounding surprised. 'I've never asked.'

'Friesack,' said Erich. 'It's an hour's drive west of Berlin.'

'What happened to your parents?' asked Otto quietly.

'Papa was at Stalingrad,' said Klaus, scraping up the last of his soup with his spoon and not catching his eye. 'We haven't heard from him since 1942. Mutti was still in Friesack when we *Volkssturm* soldiers left to defend Berlin. I'm hoping the Yanks got to Friesack before the Russians. What about you, Helene?'

'Papa died in North Africa,' she said. 'Late '42. Round about the same time as your Papa was in Stalingrad. Mutti helped out with Doktor Roth after his wife died. That's how I know Otto and Ulrich. But I lost touch with her when the Ivans arrived. But I know my Mutti's still alive. She's a survivor, just like us.'

Hanna said nothing but Ulrich spotted tears in her eyes. The child was weak. He didn't cry when he thought of his mother being killed by that bomb. He just promised himself again that he would kill the first American he saw in revenge.

'What are your Mutti and Papa like, Hanna?' asked Erich.

'They are kind, like you all are,' said Hanna slowly. 'And quite old. Like a grandad and a grandma . . . Big glasses and lots of white hair. Always something baking in the oven . . .'

'We'll go back to the shop and see if there is any message for you, Hanna,' said Helene.

'I want to go back home to Sophienstrasse,' said Otto suddenly. 'See what's there.'

Ulrich looked at him in surprise.

'There's no point, Otto,' said Helene gently. 'The house has been destroyed. I've seen it with my own eyes.'

'I know,' said Otto. 'But I want to go and see for myself. Perhaps there's someone there who knows what's happened to Papa. Or maybe he left us a note.'

'He won't have left a note,' Ulrich said. 'But there might be something there that hasn't been looted. I'll come too.' He didn't really want to go back, but he wasn't about to let Otto go without him.

The streets were quiet that night and everyone slept well. The next morning Helene went to sit with her friend Christa on the steps of Skalitzer Hospital. There was a heavy gun platform there, left without its weapon. Now, bizarrely, it was used by the children as a merry-go-round. There was a wheel you turned and the whole platform swung slowly round. Hanna and Rolf and Traudl played on it for hours, taking it in turns to wind each other round.

Helene enjoyed being with Christa. It was such a relief to talk to a girl her own age, especially with all those boys always around. And she knew there was no ulterior motive for their friendship. It was an unspoken rule of theirs that they never discussed food. Helene understood Christa had a soldier boyfriend, an officer from Kiev called Ilya, who had fought all the way from Stalingrad to

Berlin. 'Ilya says his faith protected him,' said Christa with a shrug.

Helene was burning with curiosity to know more about him, though. 'I thought the commies were all atheists,' she said, trying to sound blasé.

'Not this one,' said Christa with a shrug. 'He keeps quiet about it, though, when the political officers are about. He told me a lot of his men prayed before they went into battle.'

Ilya was a good man, she told Helene. Kind to her, and to Rolf and Traudl, happy to bring them as much food as he could. 'He tells me he has two children their age back home,' said Christa, 'but he doesn't know if they are still alive, though he had heard his wife was killed fighting with the partisans.'

Helene had heard about the partisans – the Russians who carried on fighting behind the German lines. Nazi propaganda always called them 'terrorists'. They sounded as if they had been sent by the devil himself and she knew they were shown no mercy if they were ever captured.

Helene wanted to ask Christa how she could be close to someone from a country that hated the Germans so much. But she answered that question herself. 'Ilya doesn't hate the German people, but he does hate what the Nazis did in Ostland,' she whispered. 'They would destroy whole villages – all the women and children, too. Herd them into a church and burn it down. And they would bleed children dry to get blood for injured German soldiers.'

Helene had scoffed when Christa told her that. 'They never did,' she said. 'We're not vampires.'

Christa looked hurt. 'Ilya told me he had seen that with his own eyes. Children bled white. He said he sometimes feared they had done it to his own two. They treated ordinary Russians worse than farm animals. It makes me feel ashamed to be a *Volksdeutsche*.'

It was uncomfortable hearing those Nazi phrases still. The newsreels always called the conquered Eastern Territories 'Ostland'. And '*Volksdeutsche*' – pure-blooded Germans – was a phrase they had heard a lot at school in 'Racial Hygiene' lessons.

'I'm amazed they fed us when they arrived here. Ilya says when we invaded Russia we just took all the farm food we could and let the people starve. Millions of ordinary Russians died. But then they realised people were joining the partisans because they promised to feed them, so they relented a little. But the cruelty of it . . . to deliberately let whole populations starve to death . . .'

Helene had been appalled when she first heard Christa talk like that, thinking her disloyal. She didn't even believe her, and even now she was still not sure what to think. Recently they had all read about the Nazi death camps for the Jews in the newspapers the Russians printed, and seen the hideous photographs that accompanied the articles, and she began to realise that if even half of what Ilya said was true . . . well, she would never forgive the Russians for the way they had raped and murdered their way through

Berlin, but she was slowly coming to understand what had made them behave like that.

Christa was easy company. Sometimes they talked, but sometimes they just sat and said nothing and Helene's thoughts could wander, happy in companionable silence. Today she found herself thinking about Otto. Sometimes she would look over to him as he lay on his bed and admire his sharp features and that shock of curly black hair. Sometimes she would wonder what would happen if she ran her hands through that curly hair. She'd often noticed him watching her and had smiled to herself when he quickly looked away. She liked him too. More than she let herself admit. But the world they lived in was so strange, and she relied on their friendship so much. What if they fell out, and everything was ruined? What would the others think of her?

She had spoken to Christa about it once before, when they had sat with the younger ones watching them play. Christa had laughed gently. 'Helene, he's your age, isn't he? Aren't girls supposed to go out with boys who are older?'

Now Helene was feeling wistful. 'Wouldn't it be good to have everything back to normal?' she said to Christa. 'When, if you liked a boy, you would put on your best frock and hope he asked you out to a dance?' She plucked at her ragged shirt. 'Now I just feel like a tramp the entire time. I'd give anything for a nice long bath and a beautiful new dress.'

She stopped abruptly when she noticed Otto and Ulrich coming out of the hospital and walking towards them.

'No giggling,' said Christa as they approached, but neither of them could help smirking.

Otto seemed flustered by their smiles. 'We're off now, to Sophienstrasse,' he said, and Helene could see he was blushing a little. Ulrich just looked stuck-up. As usual.

'See you later,' she said to Otto.

They watched the boys walk away. 'I like Otto too,' said Christa. 'He's much nicer than his horrible brother. Though Ulrich *is* better-looking.' She giggled at the last admission.

Otto and Ulrich both turned round to look at them.

When they were further away, Helene muttered, 'I don't think he's better-looking.' She surprised herself, feeling quite defensive about Otto.

Christa shrugged. Then she put a hand on Helene's wrist. 'I think Otto would make a nice boyfriend. He's kind and he's thoughtful and he *is* nice-looking.'

Helene shook her head. They could barely feed and wash themselves. There wasn't the time to think of anything more. She was just lucky to have found Otto again.

As Otto and Ulrich walked into central Berlin together, Ulrich said, 'I do not understand girls. The Führer was right when he said they should be obedient and faithful, but above all silent. He said, "Talkativeness shows a need for attention, whereas modesty is silent." Helene and Christa, they both talk too much. And giggle.'

Otto sighed. 'Ulrich, you quote the Führer like a pastor quotes from the Bible. Hitler is dead. Do you not believe that?'

Ulrich looked straight ahead, that familiar expression of stubborn contempt on his face. 'The Führer will still be an inspiration to the German people two thousand years into the future,' he stated. Otto could not be bothered to reply and they walked on without speaking.

Otto was puzzled by the girls' behaviour, too. He had never really thought much about Helene Schuster when she and her mother had moved in. Otto had found her a little aloof. Frau Schuster was an educated woman – you could tell by the way she spoke – and so was her daughter. Now Otto found it difficult to take his eyes off Helene. Knowing she would be there when he returned to the hospital made him calm, even after a day when he had found no food. Sleeping shoulder to shoulder, sharing tiny morsels of food, even going on dangerous raids together, it all filled him with quiet joy. He could never tell her that, of course.

As the boys left Oranienstrasse and headed into the centre of the city Otto shared the last of the bread and cheese with his brother. Everywhere they looked there were notices on walls and lamp posts announcing the arrival of the Americans and the British. One notice had a map showing how the city was to be divided. The Russians remained in control of the whole eastern area, and the British and Americans each had a section of the west of the city.

'Good. We are going to be in the American sector,' said Otto, pointing. 'We're just there, close to the border between them and the Russkis.'

'That will be where the next war will break out,' said Ulrich sullenly.

'Ulrich – a cheerful quip for every occasion,' said Otto. 'You are a ray of sunshine.'

'You won't be laughing when it happens,' said Ulrich with a cold smile.

After they passed through the Brandenburg Gate and into the Tiergarten they saw at once that the park had been practically stripped bare of its trees and shrubs – no doubt by desperate Berliners searching for fuel.

They were also immediately confronted with a great milling crowd of people – like a swarm of insects. The noise and bustle was overwhelming. Civilians, soldiers, all bartering madly, swapping goods for food and cigarettes. All the soldiers were Russians; there were none from the Western nations yet. In a way, Otto thought, it was reassuring to see this ancient human exchange in action. In the first few days after the invasion, the Russians had plundered at will. Valuables had been taken at gunpoint, bicycles snatched away from old ladies . . . There was no bartering. But there was now. Perhaps basic human decency was returning.

They left the lakes and depleted greenery of the Tiergarten and walked through the once affluent streets of their former district. Otto had hoped the damage here would not be as catastrophic as the east of the city. But now he could see that heavy fighting had also taken place in the very streets where he had played as a child. The destruction was almost total, but here and there were houses with their elaborate plaster-and-brickwork facades intact, and some even had glass left in the windows.

'Maybe our house has been spared and Helene is wrong,' Otto said to Ulrich.

His brother nodded but did not reply. Otto was surprised to see he was looking flushed and almost tearful. The usual arrogant scowl was absent.

Most of the streets west of the park were lined with big apartment blocks but there were side streets with individual houses too, and it was in one of these that the Roths had made their home. Doktor Friedrich Roth had purchased a beautiful town house in Sophienstrasse not long before Otto was born.

The street was full of such houses and as they turned the familiar corner the utter devastation that greeted them was almost impossible to take in. Before the Russians came, Sophienstrasse had survived the day and night bombings of the Western allies almost intact, although one of the houses at the far end of the street had been demolished by a bomb one night. Otto could still remember the violence of the explosion in the spring of 1944, and how it had sucked the air out of their lungs as they sheltered in their basement. The Roths barely knew the people who had lived in the house that had been destroyed. They were an ambitious Nazi couple – he in his SS *Hauptsturmführer* uniform, she with her blonde plaited hair, fashionable floral dresses and five children, each a year apart. All seven of them, and their live-in Polish maid, wiped out in a flash.

On the night after that raid the Roths came out of their basement shelter at first light, and Otto could now remember that more clearly than the awful blur of the fighting he had just lived through. It had been a beautiful spring morning, blue sky hazy with the first heat of the day, but with a thin film of dust hanging in the air and covering everything around them. What had really shocked him were the bare trees. That previous evening they had been covered in luminous cherry blossom, now blown off in a single brutal moment.

That was the last night they spent in the house once the sirens had sounded. From then on the whole family all hurried to the nearby bomb shelter. That didn't save his Mutti though. She had been killed in a day raid, when an American bomb had hit her office in Mohrenstrasse one lunchtime in September 1944. On hearing the news, Ulrich had not cried but coldly promised Otto that he would kill the first American he met to avenge her. Otto often remembered the look on his brother's face that day and hoped he'd forgotten those words, though he too had moments of pure, hot anger when he remembered she wasn't here any more.

Now their old home stood before them. Not everything Helene had said was true. She said it had been destroyed, but it was still standing. There were still walls and a roof;

but not a single window remained, and a fire had caught in the bay window of the living room and half the house was gutted. The open door revealed a chaotic interior of fallen beams and charred furniture.

'I don't even want to go inside,' said Ulrich, and Otto could see his point. Anything of value would have been looted by now, and anything else would have been destroyed by the rain. Otto wanted his memory of their family home to remain as it had been. Now the house looked like it had been picked up by a giant and shaken violently.

'But there might be a message from Papa,' said Otto. He wanted to sob his heart out, but he did not want to appear soft in front of his brother. He willed himself to remain calm. 'We've come this far, we might as well have a look.'

'There won't be a message,' said Ulrich, almost defiantly.

'Come on, we have to have a little hope,' said Otto. He wondered how his brother could be so sure.

Otto steeled himself to enter, plaster and broken glass crackling underfoot as he came into the hall. The smell was indescribable – equal parts excrement, ash and dust. That was something the Ivans made a habit of doing when they had first arrived. Whenever they could they defecated in people's houses – usually on the living-room carpet. Ulrich said they were like animals marking their territory. Otto peered through the gloom, but could find no note pinned or even scrawled on the wall. There was nothing here to suggest his Papa had survived the battle. He pulled his mother's scarf up around his nose but the gagging stench deterred further exploration. The scarf triggered a painful memory, of the birthday when she had given it to him, and the hug she had given him when he blew out the candles on his cake. He could vividly remember her warmth and the soft scent of her perfume. He had felt so safe at that moment. And so convinced that nothing could ever go wrong in his world.

Otto emerged from the ruins shaking his head. The two of them walked down Sophienstrasse and turned east towards the Tiergarten. It was only when they reached the Brandenburg Gate that either of them spoke.

'We should have left a note,' said Otto. 'Just in case.'

Ulrich disagreed. 'What's the point? Papa is dead.'

'How can you be so sure, Ulrich?' Otto asked.

Ulrich said nothing. He stared straight ahead.

They walked the rest of the way home in silence. It wasn't one of those sulking silences neither of them wanted to be the first to break, more a sense of deep shock that their previous life had been so comprehensively eradicated and they would never be able to go back home. Occasionally their shoulders bumped against each other as they walked, and Ulrich thought Otto might put his arm around him, as he had done when they were very young, but he didn't.

The trip back to Sophienstrasse had shaken up Ulrich more than he liked to admit. For sure, the house had many bad memories, mostly revolving around the shouting matches he had had with Otto, and his parents' flinty-eyed, silent disapproval of his zeal for the Hitler Youth. But there were happier memories too. As he stood in the devastated living room he had vividly recalled those times they had sat around the dining table and Papa had carved the kind of roast pork dinner he would kill to eat now. And standing in front of the house he had also remembered how, when he was small, Mutti would read them both bedtime stories as they snuggled in the warmth of their eiderdowns in the room they had shared.

But there was something else choking up his thoughts. Something far more immediate and far more terrible. The scene played out in his mind, transporting him away from the eerily quiet, rubble-strewn streets to the final days of the battle for Berlin. He remembered with absolute clarity how he had spoken to the *Sturmscharführer* of his *Volkssturm* squad about his father. Dr Roth, he reported, had been behaving like a traitor and deserved the severest punishment. The man had listened with great solemnity, thanked him for doing his duty, and had gone off with a rope and an execution squad to take matters further.

They had been attacked by the Russians shortly after that and hastily retreated towards the centre of the city. Ulrich had never seen the man again, nor the rest of his squad, and his nights were often filled with remorseful thoughts. His father was almost certainly dead. He would never tell Otto this, of course. He didn't approve of his brother: he was too weak, and had never had the true fire and will required of a proper political soldier. But he was still his brother. And apart from Otto, Ulrich thought he had no other friends in the world.

That evening, over another meagre meal of bread and cheese, Ulrich sensed that Otto was going to tell Helene about their trip. He leapt in first. 'Our house has not been destroyed,' he said resentfully. 'It's still very much standing.'

Helene gave him a contemptuous look, daring him to say more.

Otto stepped in before an argument developed. 'It's completely uninhabitable, that's true. But I was expecting a pile of bricks.'

Helene grimaced as she chewed her bread. 'What are they putting in this?' she said, pulling out a scrap from her mouth and holding it up to the light.

'Looks like sawdust,' said Otto.

'Sorry. What were you saying?' Helene looked distracted.

There was no more to say, and an awkward silence descended.

'We need to find food,' Helene said. 'Look at us. The Russians are barely giving me anything now. You both must be starving if you walked all the way to Sophienstrasse from here. What was it? Three, four hours there and back?'

It was. They had checked the time on the wristwatch. They had walked for four hours today. Enough to work up a titanic appetite. Ulrich felt completely hollow inside. He'd have eaten paper if he thought it would stop him feeling hungry.

'There's a market in the Tiergarten now,' said Otto. 'There were thousands of people milling round there.'

'Ha! Getting ready for the capitalists to arrive,' smirked Klaus. 'The Russkis just steal things. The Yanks and Tommys will have a bit more decency.'

'And money!' said Erich.

'I don't see anything decent in bombing entire cities to rubble,' said Ulrich coldly.

Otto sighed. Ulrich knew what was coming next. He could almost predict what his brother was going to say.

'We did exactly the same to them.' Otto's voice came out harsh. 'And we did it first. London, Rotterdam, Warsaw. We all watched the newsreels gloating at the destruction of those cities. And what about those "Vengeance Weapons" we all heard about in the last year of the war. What were V-1s and V-2s for, other than to destroy the homes of Londoners . . .'

Ulrich looked back at his brother with scorn. 'Of course the Führer had to bomb those cities. How else was he going to convince the subject peoples to recognise the superiority of the Master Race? I don't care about the Poles, they are *Untermenschen*, but the Dutch and the British could have joined with us in our crusade. It was their choice not to, and they were justly punished for it.'

Otto shook his head. Helene was looking over at him too, contempt etched upon her face. 'It's like talking to a robot,' Otto said to her.

Ulrich would not take the bait. He was feeling light-headed with hunger and had no stomach for another exhausting row with his tiresome brother. He turned away. Let them have each other.

Otto pointedly changed the subject. 'And we saw a map, showing that Skalitzer Hospital will be just inside the American zone,' he said.

'Well that's a relief,' said Helene. 'I'm glad we're not in the Russian zone. They're the most dangerous ones.'

The table erupted in denials.

'I've heard they're all just as bad as the Russkis . . .' said Erich.

'That I find difficult to believe,' scoffed Helene.

Erich shrugged. 'Just watch yourself with all of them,' he said to her. 'Especially now your hair's growing back. I heard the French are coming too,' he continued. 'We'll all need to be particularly careful with them, seeing as how we took over their country, too.'

Ulrich couldn't help but flash a wicked grin at that. Oh, that had been a glorious day! He remembered the news flash announcing the fall of France as if it was yesterday. Six weeks it had taken them. That day he believed the German army would be able to conquer the world.

Helene shook her head and tapped Otto on the arm. 'We ought to go to the market, you and me. See what's going on. See what we might have to sell.' She looked pointedly at the wristwatch his father had given him.

'Oh no,' said Otto. 'I managed to make sure the Russkis didn't get that watch and they're not getting it now.'

Ulrich turned to Helene. 'You should not even ask,' he said angrily. It was bad enough that Otto had this gift from his father, but to *sell* it? That would be even worse.

'Russkis love a watch,' said Erich, keen to defuse the tension in the room. 'That's why they robbed so many. They're such a primitive bunch, only the very rich have watches.'

Klaus laughed. 'Isn't everyone the same in Russia? I thought they were supposed to be communists.'

Erich batted his twin brother over the head. 'Don't be stupid. Ivan gets a watch from one of us, sends it back to Kharkov, or some other dump, and his wife can swap it for a cow. That's why you always saw them wearing three or four watches on each wrist when they first got here. Peasants.'

Helene sighed at the boys' stubbornness. 'We need to eat. I've got a ring,' she said pointedly. 'That should feed us for a few days.'

Hanna shrugged. She had nothing, obviously. No one else offered anything of value.

'C'mon, Ulrich,' jeered Erich. 'Bet you've still got your "Blood and Honour" Hitler Youth dagger! I bet any of that lot will pay good money for that!'

Ulrich stared straight ahead, refusing to even acknowledge the question. Instead, he took a deep, deep breath and held it. He would not rise to this persecution. Just the other day, as he waited at a water pump, he had heard two boys talking about the Werewolf resistance. They were only eight or nine years old, but he could tell by their enthusiasm they had been keen members of the *Pimpfe* – the junior

80

branch of the Hitler Youth. He wanted to question them about this but the boys were with their mother and she loudly scolded them for believing in such nonsense. One day he would find and join these Werewolves and he would need to use the dagger. Then this group of pathetic traitors wouldn't be laughing.

CHAPTER 8

July the 4th

'There is a big parade today,' announced Helene. 'It's to mark the arrival of the Yanks.'

No one could muster much interest.

'We should go,' she continued. 'Take a look at our new conquerors.'

Otto smiled at her.

Ulrich scowled. 'I'll only go if I can find a loaded weapon,' he said. Otto shuddered when he remembered the promise Ulrich had made after their mother died.

'You'll do no such thing,' snapped Helene. 'You'll get us all arrested.'

Ulrich stared into space, his face a carefully composed mask of blank-eyed insolence. But he did go with the rest of them when they left later that morning.

They watched the parade from Oranienstrasse, the long road that led into the city centre. Although the crowd was five deep, most watched in silence, almost bemusement, although a few cheered. There was no booing, which surprised Otto, as these were the people who had bombed the crap out of his city. He wondered if the British, currently

82

occupying the north-west of Berlin, were being booed or cheered.

Ulrich flinched when he heard cheers for the Americans. 'That mongrel race', he had called them that morning, 'that cesspit of a nation', parroting the phrases of Joseph Goebbels. Otto had rolled his eyes and ignored him. Surely he would stop thinking like this soon.

The American troops marched along, and their gleaming, freshly painted tanks and jeeps seemed strangely out of place. It was like peering through a screen to another world of cleanliness and plenty. And the soldiers looked nothing like the *Untermenschen* – subhumans – of Nazi propaganda. They were well fed, well groomed, and looked approachable after all those weeks with the scowling Russians as occupiers. Otto could not imagine one of these amiable young men cuffing him to the ground if he went over to stroke one of their animals – not that the Yanks had pack animals. There were lorries here as far as the eye could see.

'I hope they are carrying some food for us,' said Helene, holding Hanna's hand. The younger girl looked bewildered at the spectacle, but she was always happiest when she was with Helene.

'Look at those tanks!' said Klaus. He and Erich had instantly spotted the firepower of the Yanks, and were openly admiring it.

Ulrich scowled.

The parade took a good fifteen minutes to pass. As the last of the troop-laden lorries trundled by, a tall dark-haired soldier threw a handful of sweets into the crowd. It was a catastrophic move. Everyone surged forward. Otto grabbed Hanna's hand as it was ripped out of Helene's. Klaus and Erich scrabbled on the ground. Even Ulrich lost his arrogance and was pushing others aside to try to get to a sweet. Fist fights quickly broke out among the ragged children who scrambled for them, and Otto dragged Hanna and Helene to the edge of the crowd. Hanna was so disappointed not to get a sweet that tears ran down her face.

The soldier stood aghast, seeing what his act of kindness had done. But his comrades with him in the lorry laughed and pointed. Ulrich noted that seeing German children fight for sweets had entertained them.

After the parade they went their separate ways: Otto and Helene to check out the market, Ulrich, Klaus, Erich and Hanna to scour the wastelands and gardens for wild fruit and vegetables. Otto liked having Helene all to himself. As they walked into the centre of Berlin they could talk freely. He loved it when she confided in him. It made him feel he was as special to her as she was to him.

'What was that about, yesterday,' she said, 'when I teased you about selling your watch? Ulrich looked really put out about that.'

'Ulrich is a source of many-splendoured bewilderment,' said Otto grandly.

She bashed him on the arm. 'Otto, stop talking nonsense.'

He grinned. 'But he is. I am constantly puzzled by him, and so are you. Especially all that Nazi nonsense he won't let go of.'

She sighed. 'Never mind that, though. Why was he so bothered by the watch?'

'Ulrich always resented me having it. It belonged to my grandfather and Papa made a big show of passing it on to the eldest son.'

'I remember,' said Helene thoughtfully. 'That was round about the time you and Ulrich really started to fight and fall out.' She paused, then said, 'I'll tell you what I think, Otto . . . Now, it's just a theory so don't be annoyed with me. I could see how your Papa found Ulrich's Nazi rantings tiresome – they liked you better because you weren't so die-hard about the Hitler Youth. Do you think that could have maybe made him jealous?'

Otto shrugged and they walked on in silence. *Was* Ulrich jealous of him? He always seemed so sure of himself. He wished his parents were there. It was hard having to feel responsible for Ulrich all the time.

Then Helene put her hand on his shoulder. 'Listen to that,' she said.

They could hear the Tiergarten market before they could see it – a strange clamour, almost something you could see in the air, like a mist. As they grew nearer, a densely packed crowd of soldiers and civilians milled around before them. Everybody here was selling or buying. Everybody had brought something with them in a bag or knapsack.

The soldiers were a mixture. Otto recognised Russian, American and British uniforms. The civilians were every variety of surviving Berliner – young and old, male and female; anyone who had not been rounded up by the Russians. The only thing the Germans had in common was that pinched, undernourished look and the fact that very few of them had managed to wash their clothes for several weeks.

Otto could see that most of the bartering was done by hand signals.

A fallen log lay across their path and a line of young women sat together, shoulders touching, like birds on a telegraph wire. They had made an effort to make themselves attractive and looked like they were wearing their best frocks. Several soldiers were talking to them. Everyone seemed terribly friendly.

'OK, so where do you think is a good spot to sell from, when we come back?' asked Helene.

Otto shrugged. He had deliberately left his watch at home. He didn't want to even think about the possibility of selling it. 'Let's go that way,' he said.

In parts of the Tiergarten you could walk through the crowd, but in other places you had to shove. Here and there were burned-out vehicles, the smell of engine oil and charred metal mingling with the stale-dishcloth whiff of the civilians and the sweat and polish of the soldiers.

Otto was afraid to look at the Russians. These were the monsters whom he had been fighting, who had been trying to kill him, barely six weeks before. And now, when he saw them in the street, they were often in patrols, angry and violent, or drunk at the end of the evening, when you just knew they could do anything and get away with it.

But when he did look at them here, he couldn't help but like them. They had open, friendly faces, and several of them were young women, dressed in the same uniforms as the men. One soldier particularly caught his attention. A fresh-faced boy around his own age, still too young to shave, standing next to an older Russian, talking to an elderly German man. The boy was so polite and pleasant to the old man, almost as if he were his own grandfather. Otto could almost imagine him as a friend and felt a momentary stab of pity. He didn't think he had killed anyone in the fighting – he had always closed his eyes when he fired his gun – and, seeing this boy, he suddenly hoped he hadn't.

As they carried on pushing through the crowd, they didn't notice a tall, blond teenager watching them. Konrad Zeigler thought they looked like an easy target. That dark-haired boy was just about old enough to have fought in the *Volkssturm*, but he didn't look too strong, and the short-haired girl with him would be no trouble at all. An experienced Hitler Youth squad leader like Konrad, who had evaded death, injury and capture while fighting in the final weeks of the war, would have no problem relieving them of anything they'd bought or brought along to barter.

Konrad had a new gang now, all desperate, hungry boys, and they followed him like wolves as he slipped into the flow of people behind the two teenagers. At times like this, he felt something approaching excitement. How quickly the world turned, he thought. As a child he had been promised an estate out in Ostland with Russian or Polish peasants as his serfs, and now that future had been denied to him. So he would pick up the pieces and make his fortune here in this ruined capital instead. The arrival of the Yanks and the Tommies would make life even more exciting. But making money from them required him to take from weaker elements. That didn't bother him. It was nature's iron law. They had taught them this in the Hitler Youth. Not that he still believed in most of that Nazi crap. Hitler had lost. Hitler had let him down.

Now the dark-haired boy and the girl had stopped to look around. She was pretty, he noticed, with a twinge of interest. 'We'll get them on the way out,' said Konrad to his gang. It would be easy enough. They probably wouldn't even have to threaten them with violence. Konrad felt a twinge of disappointment. Ever since kindergarten he had realised violence had thrilled him, especially if the odds were in his favour.

'What *isn't* for sale?' Helene marvelled. Everywhere you looked, the most bewildering variety of goods was changing hands. Varied though they were, the goods went strictly one way. Jewellery, china plates, watches, cameras, in fact anything of value that you couldn't eat or smoke, went to the invaders. Food and cigarettes went to the Germans.

'This is wrong,' said Otto under his breath. 'Here we are, selling our valuables just to stay alive.'

88

Helene took his hand. 'Oh Otto, my friend, this is progress. Look, there's no threat of violence, there's no stealing. Four weeks ago, a Russki saw something he wanted, he just took it. Now here we are, bartering, exchanging goods like civilised human beings . . .'

She was interrupted by raised voices. Two Americans were arguing angrily over by the women sitting on the tree trunk. Helene grabbed his arm. 'We're going,' she said. 'There's a brawl brewing.'

As they left the Tiergarten a gang of older teenagers stood right in front of them, blocking their path. There were six of them and they all looked hungry and desperate. Otto placed himself between them and Helene. He sensed the situation could turn violent in an instant.

'We haven't got anything,' said Helene defiantly. She held her hands up, making it clear there was nothing valuable hidden about her.

The tallest youth approached her, a lazy swagger to his walk. He looked her up and down, his gaze lingering on her face. 'All right,' he said. 'I believe you.'

Otto's hands were clenched by his side. He tried to keep calm.

'And what about you?' said one of the other boys to Otto.

Otto shook his head, so angry he wanted to shout at them. But the worry of what they might do to Helene made him hold his tongue. He too held his hands up, opening his coat to show there was nothing worth stealing.

The tallest one spat in frustration and then batted him round the head, a contemptuous gesture to send them on their way.

As they walked off, Otto burned with shame. He looked over to Helene, almost expecting to see contempt in her eyes. But she gave him a sweet smile and said, 'Otto, you did well to stay calm.' He could sense her sympathy and that made him feel better. 'Boys like this,' she went on, 'they wouldn't go out robbing without a weapon or two. That could have been a lot nastier. Anyway, just look around. Someone else will probably rob them by the time the day is out.'

It was true. All around the fringes of the market were gangs of toughs, just hanging round, fidgeting, eyes darting, not even trying to look like they were casually loitering.

'They're like lions around a herd of wildebeest, waiting to pick off the weakest,' said Helene, and gripped Otto's arm tightly.

As they walked home along Unter den Linden they saw scores of other Berliners hurrying to and from the Tiergarten. Some were carrying beautiful ornaments, even dragging pieces of furniture. Others, hastening away, clutched tightly to bread and tins of meat.

'Otto, this is the future. We've got to find things to sell or we're going to starve.'

'I know. You're right,' Otto said. He still didn't want to sell his watch though.

* * *

Back in the Tiergarten Konrad's gang had encountered a serious problem. A Russian officer was asking for identity papers, wanting to know why these teenage boys were not prisoners of war. They all looked old enough to have fought in the *Volkssturm*, in fact some of them looked old enough to have been in the regular army. Konrad knew exactly what to do. He had pulled this trick at least three times over the last few weeks. He sauntered up to the officer, gave him a friendly smile, and pulled out his identity papers. The Russian spoke a little German and was quickly satisfied with the story he heard. He patted Konrad on the back and sent him and his boys on their way.

As they walked back to the ruined house they shared in Wilmersdorf, just south of the Tiergarten, Konrad looked at the identity papers and reflected on his good fortune. As the fighting ended, he had retreated to a well-stocked cellar he'd had the foresight to prepare for the occasion. Venturing out only at night he had quickly discovered from the women and children huddled in the ruins that all men were being rounded up by the Russians. He was just seventeen but he looked much older. In the street next to his cellar there was a group of slave workers from occupied Denmark – Nordic boys not much older than him. Konrad had been taught the Scandinavian nations were Aryan brothers to the Germans but these ones had been sent to Berlin as punishment by the Gestapo – maybe they had been hiding Jews or defying the regime in another way. Now they were waiting for the Russians to send them home. He had known exactly what to do.

He smirked when he thought of the boy whose identity he had stolen. That boy had been tall and blond, just like him, and Konrad could use his identity papers without a second glance. He looked at the boy's photograph and pictured him thinking the war was over, and that he had survived.

The Danish boy had been easy enough to dispose of. Konrad just followed him out one day when he went foraging on his own, and slipped a knife between his ribs when he turned into a dark side street. Sure enough, the boy had carried his identity papers in his jacket pocket. The Ivans would not be able to tell a Dane from a German and he could be sure any sort of Russian demanding to see his papers would not be able to check if he spoke Danish. Perfect.

From that moment on, he had never gone hungry. He had a knack for buying and selling things on the black market and stealing was easy if you picked the right victims. And now here he was with his own little wolf pack, which he ran with the same firm hand he had applied to his Hitler Youth squad. None of the other boys had the right identity papers but now, whenever they were stopped, he simply showed the soldiers his papers, assuring them, in the little Russian he spoke, that all his boys were slave labourers waiting to go home. It worked every time. Last week, some Ivans had even given them a generous portion of their rations. Konrad smiled at their stupidity. He wondered how they had ever managed to win the war.

CHAPTER 9

As Otto and Helene neared home they heard the strange thunder of a collapsing building – like a brick avalanche. A great cloud of dust drifting from a side street showed exactly where the building had fallen. Otto held on to Helene's arm. 'Let's go to look,' he said.

There were few people about – it was now eight weeks since the fighting ended and something like this no longer attracted a crowd of curious onlookers. The front of a four-storey apartment block had fallen off.

'Imagine living in that and not realising it was so unsafe,' said Helene with a shudder.

'When will the rest of it come down?' wondered Otto.

Helene shrugged. 'No one living here, by the look of it,' she said. 'Hope no one was walking past when it happened.'

It was a surreal sight. Like a massive doll's house where you could see directly into the separate rooms and floors. Each one had different wallpaper or painted walls, different light shades, different pictures on the wall. Several of the apartments still had their obligatory portrait of the

Führer. Along one side of the building, four floors up, a bath hung halfway over the void.

'Good thing there's no water in the pipes,' said Otto. 'Or there'd be a pretty little waterfall here now.'

Helene laughed.

In one of the apartments, two floors up, they could see a smartly laid-out dining room, with a big oak table and a lace tablecloth.

'I *bet* they've got something worth nicking for the market,' said Helene. 'Let's go and have a look.'

Otto didn't need telling twice. They ran into the stairwell and began climbing the sturdy stone stairs.

'This feels solid enough at least,' said Otto.

Two floors up they stopped on the landing, guessing which door led to the apartment they wanted.

The door was locked.

'How are we going to get in?' said Helene.

Otto launched himself against the door. He bounced off and fell on the floor. Plaster fell from the ceiling.

She helped him up. 'Together,' she said.

They did, winding themselves while the door barely registered their assault.

Then Helene noticed something under the window in the stairwell. A fire extinguisher covered in dust and debris. It was a heavy brass one, with a ring handle at the top. The perfect battering ram.

They both grabbed it and rammed it hard into the door, right by the lock. After a couple of blows the door splintered and flew open, and they tumbled in. Even in the dim light from the landing they could see that the hall seemed untouched by the fighting of the previous few months and the collapse of the outer wall. A Persian rug lay on a parquet floor, and the faint smell of polish tickled their senses. Everything here was so clean. At once Otto felt really filthy: like an urchin in a palace. It seemed unreal being somewhere so neat and tidy, as if they had fallen into another dimension.

'It's a lottery, isn't it, this whole world we live in,' said Helene, looking round. 'No fighting here and no one has broken in to loot. There's got to be plenty here for us to sell.'

Otto was still standing in the hall, unwilling to tread on the rug. 'But what if someone is still living here? What if we're stealing from someone who's going to starve if they don't have anything to sell for themselves?' He felt like a burglar, trespassing in someone's home.

Helene smiled at him. 'Come on, Otto. No one's been here since before the Russians arrived. Fortune favours the brave! Let's see what we can grab and get out of here before anyone else comes.'

They began to cautiously open doors off the main corridor.

'Hey, look at this!' said Helene.

Light spilled in from the open door of the bathroom. White fluffy towels sat plump on a bathroom chest. On another shelf were piles of soap, wrapped in packaging. There was a mirrored vanity unit too, with a bottle of Chanel perfume.

'What I'd give to run a hot bath,' she said wistfully.

On reflex, she turned the tap and a little water dribbled out. Clearly, no one had been here since the water supply had been cut off at the very end of the fighting.

'And look!' she shouted excitedly. 'Edelweiss toilet paper!'

Otto looked over her shoulder. There were six rolls, five still wrapped in the distinctive floral packaging of the brand. 'Straight into the bag with those!' he said.

They noticed a pair of highly polished boots in the hall. The sort SS officers wore. 'They'll fetch a good price at the market,' said Helene.

'Let's go,' said Helene. She went to the bathroom to grab the soap and perfume.

'No. Let's see what's in that dining room,' he said.

They opened another door on the other side of the corridor and this one led out to the big room they had seen from the street. It was bizarre standing in the doorway looking out over a room with no far wall. Halfway across was a table stacked with fine crockery, and a pair of silver candlesticks. Two half-drunk glasses of wine, two half-eaten plates of food, still there on the table. There were flies in here too, and the smell of the rotten food made them both feel sick.

In the far corner of the room an upright Bechstein piano stood pushed against the wall, its ivory keys gritty with dust and debris. A book of Chopin's Nocturnes rested on the stand, the last music the apartment's occupiers ever played. Otto thought of the officer who had been shot the other night.

Otto stepped into the room, but the floorboards sagged under his weight.

'Come on, this is too dangerous,' said Helene.

'I can do it. I've got a plan. Stand by the door. That feels solid enough,' he said. 'And hold on to me in case the floor collapses.'

He reached out to the table, gingerly testing the floor as he edged forward. Helene leaned forward, one hand gripping the door frame tightly, the other holding on to Otto.

'Careful!' she said.

As the floorboards creaked under his feet he grabbed a silver candlestick and carefully placed it on the floor by her feet. Then he fetched the other one.

'So far so good,' he said with a grin. 'What else can we see?'

'Look over on the mantelpiece,' whispered Helene. 'That ornamental clock.'

It was extraordinary. Gold, marble, in the shape of an elephant, it looked hundreds of years old.

'I'll be careful –'

His words were cut off by the sound of a crack, and a piece of plaster fell from the ceiling, landing on the other side of the room. They both began to cough violently.

'Otto. It's not worth it. You'll be killed if the room collapses.'

But Otto was not listening. He let go of her hand and in a nimble few steps around the edge of the room had skipped over to the mantelpiece and snatched the clock. As he returned to the door, the whole of the plaster ceiling collapsed in front of them.

Acting on pure instinct, Otto and Helene ran out of the apartment and hurled themselves down the stairs three at a time. As they emerged from the main entrance a cascade of plaster and brick slid down, missing them by a metre. Then, as they hurried away, the sound of falling objects filled their ears. The floor in the apartment they had just been in had collapsed to forty-five degrees, spilling the contents of the room in a steady stream – heavy leather armchairs, a cabinet full of china, the table and all its crockery. Then the piano slid slowly off the edge of the floor before tumbling to the ground with an almighty crash, sending keys, levers and hammers flying in all directions.

They ran up the street, breathless and scarcely believing what they had just done. Back on the main road Helene hugged him tight, over the heavy clock he was still carrying.

'This will stop us getting hungry for weeks,' she said, her eyes gleaming brightly.

Otto felt a surge of pride. He'd done it. And that stupid gang of boys had nothing. They had forgotten the boots, but they had got away with their lives.

Back at Skalitzer Hospital that evening they proudly placed the candlesticks and clock on one of the empty shelves. The little clock Otto had risked his life so foolhardily to steal was a thing of beauty. It was in the shape of an elephant, and carved from white marble. The clock itself sat inside the body of the beast, and an ivory and gold-plated Indian girl sat on its back, with a great parasol to protect her from the tropical sun.

'Isn't it exquisite?' Helene said. 'This is something from a world I want to live in. Somewhere safe . . . somewhere full of lovely things. I only want to sell this if we're really starving to death.' Everyone, without exception, agreed with her. 'And if anyone steals it, I shall catch them and beat them senseless,' she said.

Hanna had a coughing fit laughing at that, so Helene gave her a hug.

Klaus and Erich were particularly keen to hear about the flat and what had fallen out of it. Otto related, with particular relish, how an entire glass cabinet of ornaments and crockery had fallen two floors on to the pavement. Best of all was the upright piano.

Erich began to fantasise about what he would most like to push out of a high apartment.

'A big kitchen cabinet full of plates and glasses . . .'

'A wardrobe!'

'A great glass chandelier . . .'

'And never mind an upright, I want to see a concert grand piano!' announced Klaus with a flourish of his hand. 'Imagine the mess that would make of the pavement . . .'

Hanna watched the older kids with total fascination, her eyes getting bigger with every outlandish suggestion before suddenly blurting out, 'A great big tram, full of pots and pans and . . . and . . . and *pianos!*' she announced, falling into hysterical laughter along with the others.

CHAPTER 10

When Ulrich awoke the next morning, Helene and Otto had already eaten their share of stale bread and the remains of a tin of spam. That was the last of the food.

'We're off to the market today. I think the rest of you should stay inside, and keep still,' Otto said.

'Read, rest, wash those cuts, Erich,' said Helene sternly. He had cut up his hand foraging for blackberries. 'Hanna, have a drink when you're coughing. Today we're going to try to sell the candlesticks we found in the apartment.'

'Tonight,' Otto promised, 'we will be back with a feast!'

'I'm coming with you,' announced Ulrich, putting his boots on. The market sounded interesting. And he really didn't want to be stuck there with the others all day.

'No, no, you stay here,' Otto said.

'You wouldn't let me before,' said Ulrich. 'It's not fair.'

'Ulrich, I don't want you scowling at everyone, telling them they're race traitors and all that,' said Otto.

Helene raised her eyes to the ceiling. 'Not another row, please, boys,' she said. 'I'm too hungry for a row.'

Ulrich stopped frowning at his brother and tried to

arrange his face into a reasonable expression. 'Otto. Listen. We have to find food. We are all hungry. I want to help.'

Helene intervened. 'Otto, remember those toughs we saw hanging around the fringe of the crowd? We need somebody mean to come along with us, to warn them off.' She reached over and ruffled Ulrich's hair when she said it, and gave him a wolfish grin. Ulrich tried to look stern, like this was inappropriate behaviour, but he couldn't help the little smile that passed over his face. She had never touched him like that before.

Otto sighed. 'OK, but one quip about *Untermenschen* and I'll batter you with a brick.'

'Me too,' said Helene.

Ulrich allowed himself a grin. 'No need for ugly threats.'

It was difficult walking all that way into the centre of Berlin with no food in his stomach, and Ulrich had to pretend he didn't feel light-headed. But he prided himself on his ability to withstand the everyday discomforts of soldiery. They had spent their entire childhoods being told they needed to be 'as hard as Krupp's steel', and every day was a challenge to live up to this.

They reached the market by nine, and already the sun was hot on their faces. Ulrich had never seen such a disorderly mixture of people. There were soldiers and civilians, refugees, prisoners of war . . . and already soldiers were chatting up the *Hausfrauen* lined up on a fallen tree. His face wrinkled in distaste, but he remembered Otto's warning to him, and decided he would play the game and keep his feelings hidden. He also noticed the gangs of teenage boys circling around and sizing up who they could rob. He was glad he had his dagger with him hidden under his shirt.

There was a lot going on. Ulrich felt invigorated by the buzz of activity. He was fascinated by the trading. He listened carefully to the bartering and noted what was for sale. He saw one exchange for food where a seller swapped a single cigarette for a loaf. Two minutes later he saw some hapless fool give away ten cigarettes for a single tin of soup. They obviously didn't know the worth of what they were swapping. I could do this, he thought to himself. Then he tensed as he saw one German woman exchanging an Iron Cross for a book of food coupons. He couldn't believe that it had come to this. That woman should be ashamed. He clenched his fists, but made himself relax when he caught Otto looking at him.

'OK, let's see what we can get,' said Helene, looking around. 'Let's start with him.'

They walked up to a genial-looking Soviet captain. Helene showed him one of the silver candlesticks and he raised an eyebrow. He offered them a tin of corned beef – American, by the look of the packaging. This was the sort of thing they routinely risked their lives to steal.

Otto stepped forward and held up ten fingers. The Russian laughed and shook his head, then walked away. It wasn't a contemptuous gesture. More an amiable 'You must be joking.'

'Maybe they're worth less than we thought,' whispered Helene to Otto.

A British sergeant swaggered up to them. 'What you sell?' he asked in poorly spoken German.

Helene, who spoke a bit of English, told him they had a couple of silver candlesticks. She carefully got them out of her bag and held them up. He tried to look unimpressed but there was a momentary spark in his eyes that told them all he was interested.

'You wait here, *Fräulein*,' he said.

Otto and Helene exchanged hopeful glances. Ulrich edged closer. They needed to get a good price for this. He thought of the food they would be able to buy and his stomach began to gurgle.

The British soldier returned moments later with a young officer – a flinty-eyed fellow with a little moustache. Ulrich thought he looked like a ferret or a weasel. 'So, what have we got?' he asked in a clipped tone. His German was excellent.

Ulrich didn't trust this fellow. Otto seemed to be thinking the same, because he placed a hand on Helene's shoulder.

She took out one of the candlesticks.

The officer nodded. 'Worth more as a pair,' he said, and began to walk away.

She called out. 'We have two.'

Now he was smiling. He took the one from her hand and for a horrible moment it looked like he might never give it back.

Holding it up to the sunshine he squinted and spoke with enthusiasm to his sergeant.

Helene smiled and nodded, although Ulrich guessed she didn't understand what he had said.

The officer said, 'I'll give you bacon, butter, cheese and a packet of Chesterfields.'

The sergeant brought out a large block of cheese, a small pack of butter and a fist-size pack of bacon wrapped in greaseproof paper. And he plonked down a packet of Chesterfield cigarettes. Then he gestured at both candlesticks.

Otto and Helene looked at each other. Ulrich could see how surprised they were at being offered so much. He made an effort to keep his expression as neutral as possible.

He could see Helene was prevaricating. 'Should we ask for more food instead of cigarettes?' she said to Otto.

Ulrich's patience snapped. He stepped forward. '*Zehn Pakete,*' he said decisively – ten packets – holding up ten fingers to make his meaning clear.

Otto turned around, eyes blazing. He thought Ulrich had messed up the sale.

But the officer brought out an entire carton, unopened. He nodded and said, 'Yes, but no more.'

Helene handed over the candlesticks, clearly wondering what she was giving away that had led them to be so generous.

As the British soldiers walked off in search of other booty, they stuffed the food into their own knapsack and placed the cigarettes on top.

Otto turned on Ulrich. 'Clever move with the cigarettes,' said Otto with a hint of sarcasm, 'but not one of us smokes.'

Helene put an arm around Ulrich and gave him a squeeze. 'Thank you, thank you,' she said.

Ulrich shrugged nonchalantly, trying not to smile. Helene understood. But why were they so surprised? He knew how the world worked. He was happy to get as much as he could from those Tommies.

Otto smiled tightly at him. 'But we can't eat cigarettes,' he said pointedly. He still didn't get it.

'Watch this,' said Ulrich. He pulled out a packet, and tipped out the twenty cigarettes into his jacket pocket. Then he stood away from them and held up a single cigarette. 'Last one. Five Reichsmark,' he called out. 'Genuine Chesterfield.'

Within seconds a crowd gathered round – Russians, German civilians, all clamouring to buy. A Russian produced a loaf and Ulrich held up two fingers. Two loaves appeared. He handed over the cigarette.

'Ulrich, where did you learn about that?' said Otto.

Helene's mouth was open and she was staring at Ulrich.

And there were still nineteen cigarettes left in the opened pack, and another nine packs in the carton.

'I keep my ears and eyes open.' Ulrich's mouth quirked up with a smile. He was feeling pleased with himself. And he was enjoying this bartering. He was a natural. 'I watch people haggle. See what's worth what. Cigarettes are the best currency now. These will keep us fed for a month.'

Otto looked at his younger brother with admiration. Ulrich couldn't remember the last time he'd looked at him like that. It made him feel warm, but also uncomfortable.

They sat down in the shade of one of the few remaining trees and devoured half of one of the loaves. It was a point of honour between them that all those who lived in the hospital on Skalitzer Strasse shared fairly, and even Ulrich understood this. But that didn't mean they couldn't eat their share sooner rather than later.

They left the market in high spirits – almost skipping back through the Brandenburg Gate, laughing among themselves.

'D'you know, I'm not even going to think about what those candlesticks were really worth,' said Helene happily. 'Those British soldiers could have given us just the bacon and I'd have handed them over. Thank goodness you were there, Ulrich. Besides, they weren't ours anyway, and we're going to have a lovely dinner tonight.'

But as they walked along Unter den Linden they began to suspect they were being followed. A group of four or five youths were tailing them, stopping and loitering whenever they looked around. 'Otto, don't look now but it's those boys again,' said Helene. 'The ones who gave us some trouble when we were here before.'

Ulrich's heart started to race.

'What are we going to do?' asked Helene. 'It's not as if we can call the police.'

'We've both fought the Russians,' said Otto, clearly doing his best to sound brave. 'They can't be as bad as that.'

Ulrich stuck out his chin. 'We have to show them we're more trouble than we're worth,' he said.

'How about we split the haul and then run off in different directions?' said Helene.

'No,' said Otto decisively. 'With the three of us, we can fight together.'

The gang were getting closer.

'We're going to have to run,' said Ulrich.

'In here,' said Helene, as they passed the bombed-out shell of a grand department store.

As they broke into a run the boys following them did too. They dashed through the rubble of the shop floor, where everything of any value had been looted. Running to the right they came to a great arcade – Ulrich recognised it as the Linden Passage – where a massive conservatory dome had shattered into a million pieces. One of the boys following them tripped and fell and screamed in agony as he slid along the slivers of glass. As they emerged through the other side and out into a narrow passage, one of the boys shouted, 'We're going to kill you when we catch you.' His angry voice echoed eerily in the empty building.

'Keep going,' panted Ulrich.

The passage led back to the main strip of Unter den Linden and they hurriedly crossed over, keeping to the side, peeping behind to see if they were being followed.

'Up here?' asked Otto, leading them up another bombed-out side street, with rubble piled high either side of gutted buildings. The middle of the street was completely clear, though, and they ran down it as fast as they could.

'I've got to stop,' said Helene, her hands clutching her sides.

'Let's hide in here, while we get our breath back,' said Ulrich. He dodged past a burned-out lorry and into the doorway of an apartment block.

They walked up a stairway that seemed solid enough, then sat on the landing by a window that gave a clear view down the street.

Helene gasped in great lungfuls of air and crouched down. She looked pale and frightened. Otto was trying to look tough but Ulrich thought he looked frightened too.

'Here's two things we can do,' Otto said. 'Hide here and wait a bit for them to go away, or make a break for it now, and hope we're lucky.'

They all looked at the sky. It was black over to the west and a strong wind was picking up. Ulrich thought through the options. 'If we wait there'll be fewer people about,' he said. 'So we'll be easier to spot. And if they do catch us it'll be less likely anyone will come to help.'

'Who's going to help us?' said Otto ruefully.

'Then let's go now,' said Helene quickly, 'before the rain drives everyone off the streets. Sometime soon there's going to be a deluge.'

Ulrich held his hand up. 'But if it rains, those boys might go home too. It would be better for us to get wet than lose our booty.'

Then they heard voices in the building, somewhere above them. Loud, swaggering teenage voices. 'That can't be them, surely?' said Helene.

Ulrich shook his head. 'It's another bunch. Those boys were definitely behind us when we came here.'

Otto swallowed hard. 'I say we go. I don't want to wait any longer.'

Helene and Ulrich nodded.

'This lot up there might be even nastier . . .' said Helene, her hands shaking as she stood and brushed dust from her trousers.

Leaving the safety of their hiding place they began to carefully weave their way through the side streets that led to Friedrichstrasse and then Oranienstrasse – the main streets on their route home.

As they passed the churned-up wasteland of the park at Prinzessinnengarten, Ulrich began to think they were going to make it safely home. Then three figures came into view before them, staring with unguarded hostility.

They stopped. The boys kept staring. They weren't really boys. They were seventeen or eighteen. Young men lucky enough not to be regarded as soldiers and sent to a prisoner-of-war camp.

'Hand it over, you little shits, and we won't beat you to a pulp,' declared one of the boys – a tall, blond *Übermensch*.

He was exactly the kind of older boy Ulrich had hero-worshipped in the Hitler Youth.

Only a few weeks previously, Ulrich might have respected his strength. But now he was threatening the food they'd worked so hard to get. Ulrich pulled out his 'Blood and Honour' ceremonial dagger. He advanced ahead of Otto and Helene, waving the sharp blade before him.

'Watch him, Konrad,' hissed one of the gang. They all backed away.

Otto and Helene edged forward, to be level with Ulrich. 'You wouldn't dare . . .' said the one they were calling Konrad. He was obviously the leader. Konrad drew a long bayonet from his own belt and held it out towards Ulrich.

Ulrich heard a gasp, then from the corner of his eye saw his brother being dragged backwards in a stranglehold by another boy. He concentrated on the leader of the gang. This was up to him now.

Suddenly Helene snatched the carton of cigarettes from her bag and threw it to the other side of the street. The packets sailed in an arc as if in slow motion, scattering here and there across the street. Konrad let out a yell and ran past Ulrich to grab them. And Otto was pushed roughly aside as the gang scurried to pick up the precious haul.

The three of them ran away as fast as their legs would carry them. When they stopped to look around, the gang were nowhere to be seen. They were nearly home.

'I think we did rather well,' said Helene.

No one mentioned the cigarettes.

'You saved our lives there, Helene. Thank you,' said Otto.

She ruffled his hair. 'Well, maybe. I don't think they were going to kill us.' She put a hand on Otto and Ulrich's shoulders, dragging them together. 'Who knows? But we were lucky to keep what we did. And Ulrich,' she added, 'you were a great help to us. Thank you for coming.'

Ulrich allowed himself a smile. For the first time he felt some sense of comradeship with these two.

'I can't wait to show the others,' Helene said.

That night they ate like royalty. Bacon fried in butter with hot melted cheese sandwiched between fluffy slices of soft white bread. It was the best meal any of them had tasted for a very long time.

CHAPTER 11

It had been three days now since their successful Tiergarten market trip and there was very little food left for breakfast. They all slept late in the hospital, no one stirring until at least nine.

Otto and Helene set out with two buckets each to fetch water. It was a good opportunity to talk in confidence.

'I'm worried about Hanna,' said Helene. 'She rarely sleeps on her own mattress now. Every night she begs to curl up with me.'

Otto had noticed.

'I don't mind, in a way,' Helene continued. 'You know, it's nice having this little girl to cuddle, it reminds me of sleeping with our little dog when I was a girl. But she's such a restless sleeper. She wakes me up with her nightmares, then she's asleep again almost at once.' She laughed, to show she meant no ill feeling. 'But I just lie awake staring into the darkness, trying not to think about my mum, and wondering when Hanna will disturb me again.'

Otto could sympathise. 'She's not eating either,' he said. 'Even when the rest of us are ravenously hungry and we get lucky with provisions, Hanna just plays with her portions.'

'It's no wonder she's so low, Otto. She's having to come to terms with losing her mum and dad.'

'But aren't we all,' said Otto.

'I know,' she said. 'But the rest of us, we're just getting on, trying to survive. Hanna's not coping.'

'Maybe we need to encourage her to be more independent,' said Otto. 'You know, she almost never leaves the room. That would get anyone down.'

'She's eight,' Helene chided.

'Yes but we're all wrapped up in keeping alive and making sure there's enough food. She just waits for us to look after her. Maybe if she had something to do it might take her mind off things.'

'I don't want her to feel she's a useless eater,' said Helene quietly. Otto flinched at the familiar Nazi phrase and the world of cruelty it suggested.

He put an arm around her. 'If this was the real, ordinary world, then I wouldn't think twice about doing everything for an eight-year-old. But we don't live in the real world. This is like some horrible nightmare.'

She tapped his arm thoughtfully to show she understood. 'But what could she do?'

'Let's take her out foraging. Let's take her to the market. Try to get her to sell things too? Who could resist those big blue eyes?' At this, Otto bent down and looked up at Helene in such perfect imitation of Hanna that they both fell about laughing.

When they got back, they all sat round the table, sharing out the last of a stale loaf.

'Hanna,' Helene said casually, 'how would you like to come out with us today? Maybe we could all go to the market together. You could even try to sell something. Wouldn't that be exciting?'

Hanna managed a weak smile. 'OK,' she said.

'Will the Yanks and the Tommies let us work for them?' asked Klaus. 'Or will we still have to worry about being arrested?'

'We must wait and see,' said Erich. 'Helene, when you next go out to work with the *Trümmerfrauen*, see if there are any boys like us on the work gangs. If there are, then we can go and do it.'

'That would be a real help,' said Helene wearily, 'but I see a lot more men out with the *Trümmerfrauen*, now the Americans are looking after our section. You boys are facing stiff competition.'

No one was getting by on the meagre rations from their ration books. The message was clear: if you didn't want to starve, you had to work or barter. Helene still occasionally volunteered for the *Trümmerfrauen* work. But it was heavy labour clearing away rubble and now she was rewarded with barely enough to keep her alive, and certainly not enough to share with the others. The chances of finding fruit or vegetables growing wild, with so many other people starving, were also increasingly slim. Their best chance was the market.

Helene clapped her hands together and declared she was leaving for the Tiergarten market shortly. Only Otto volunteered to come with her. There was a pair of children's shoes in their Winter Relief hoard, one that would suit a five-year-old, he said. No use to anyone here. Perhaps they could trade those for something with another German – certainly none of the soldiers would be interested. Then they would see if they could trade that for food.

'Come on, Hanna, are you coming with us?' said Otto, shrugging on his coat.

'Yes, come on, *Mausi*,' said Helene. 'It will do you good to get out of the basement.'

'OK,' she said, and rose wearily to her feet.

'We'll go foraging,' said Ulrich to Klaus and Erich. They both nodded. They would be a good team, those three, thought Otto.

On the walk up to the centre, the city was starting to show more signs of life. The sun was out and people in their sector seemed more relaxed now the American soldiers were on the streets rather than the Russians. Around the water pumps, cheerful *Hausfrauen*, their heads wrapped in colourful scarfs, stood hunched over big oval buckets, hands kneading and pummelling their washing. There was no detergent, but the water alone was enough to rinse out dust and the more pungent smells. Behind one of the pumps was a small artillery piece lying on its side, blackened and buckled in the explosion that had destroyed it. Every day there were fewer of these relics of the fighting.

Somewhere nearby, an American tractor was pulling one of them away, tortured metal scraping agonisingly along the cobblestones.

Otto felt pleased about the change he sensed in the street. There was a lightness in him he hadn't felt for months. Their world was somehow safer. Helene could sense it too. He noticed she had even worn a light cotton dress to go out in.

Enterprising Berliners now set up stalls, selling scraps of food – pieces of turnips or carrots – but you needed something to trade for that, usually some other kind of food. No one was interested in their shoes. And everywhere you looked there were these great human chains of *Trümmerfrauen* passing bricks down the line, clearing away the derelict buildings and streets. As Helene had said, there were very few teenagers or children helping – it was mainly women but, noticeably, young men were among them, now.

It was still a bizarre world, especially when you saw families, invariably without a father, sitting in a pile of blankets and mattresses, right there out on the street. They were waiting – for what, Helene could only guess. Hanna looked up briefly every time they passed someone, but mostly she trudged on with her head down.

She tugged on Otto's sleeve. 'Will you carry me?' she begged.

Otto picked her up, but could only go for a street's length before he had to put her down again. None of them had the energy to carry even a light eight-year-old.

'Helene, it's so far,' whined Hanna. 'I can't walk any more.'

Helene sighed, and scooped her up for a while. And when they got to the Tiergarten, Hanna was not the asset they hoped she would be. She sat and sulked, and here, too, no one was interested in an old pair of shoes.

By mid-afternoon they were all tired and their spirits were low.

'Let's go, before we don't have the energy to walk home,' said Helene, stroking Hanna's hand.

Hanna looked distraught, on the verge of tears.

'Don't you worry,' said Otto. 'Someone will buy our shoes and we'll get something to eat on the way home.'

She smiled bravely but they all knew she didn't believe him.

Walking down Oranienstrasse, on the way back to Skalitzer Hospital, they came across a side street almost destroyed in the fighting. There were individual houses here, not just big apartment blocks. Perhaps there would be a garden with something to eat. Three houses down, in a row of grand mansions in the turn-of-the-century style, was a house with a white stucco facade. The building itself had collapsed inward with all four of its outer walls still standing. The roof was somewhere down in the crater of rubble.

'That's got to be worth a look,' said Helene.

They peered through glassless windows, trying to ignore the horrible smells that emanated from the debris. There was a garden at the back of the house. A narrow passage led to the rear on the right hand side. Rubble was piled high all along its length and a wrought-iron door at the front had been blown off its hinges.

'Hanna, this might be dangerous,' said Helene. 'I want you to promise you will wait here for us. Keep an eye out for anyone who comes along – especially if they are a policeman, or soldiers.'

Hanna clung tightly to Helene. 'No. I want to come with you.'

Helene did not have the energy to argue. 'OK. But be very careful.'

They looked around instinctively, to check no one was watching them trespass, and began to pick their way carefully along the side passage. Otto slipped, causing a small landslide of bricks and mortar, and Helene cursed his clumsiness. Hanna, on the other hand, being light and nimble, easily negotiated the debris.

Beyond the peak of the rubble, the pile sloped down to a patch of grass, now at least half a metre high, and beyond that was an overgrown rear garden.

'There's got to be something here for us,' whispered Otto.

'Why are you whispering?' said Hanna with a smile. Being allowed to come with them into the garden had cheered her up.

Otto shook his head. 'I know it's odd, *Mausi*, but it feels like we shouldn't be here.'

Helene looked at Otto fondly and smiled. She liked how

he had started to call Hanna that, too. Her Mutti had called her '*Mausi*' – Little Mouse – when she was younger.

A shadow passed over them. They looked up to see a couple of circling crows – great, black birds with vicious-looking beaks.

'This place gives me the creeps,' Otto said.

The crows fluttered down to perch on a shallow brick wall that had been built between the path and the garden lawn. It was a metre or so high and Otto guessed it had been put there to grow climbing plants against it, then left unfinished. Maybe they had run out of bricks? They were difficult to get hold of once the bombers had started arriving in force in 1943.

Hanna pointed towards the undergrowth. Something was moving and the grass was parting. She clung tightly to Otto, who lifted her off the ground, and all of them peered cautiously over the wall. There was a glimpse of a bushy tail. 'A foxy,' she whispered, eyes wide with curiosity and a little trepidation.

'Big one, too,' said Otto. 'Are they worth eating?'

'God knows,' said Helene. 'But why not? Have you ever caught a fox? I wouldn't have the first idea how to do it.'

The fox moved nearer and they could see its russet, pointed face. It froze as it sensed their presence, then turned to run. They watched, peering over the wall. A sudden upward movement caught their eye, and Otto pushed Helene and Hanna down below the wall. There was a loud explosion and shrapnel peppered the whole garden, thudding into the house and the wall they were sheltering behind. The two crows fell dead at their side.

'What the hell was that?' said Helene, eyes wide with alarm.

Hanna looked confused and began to cry.

Otto's heart sank. 'S-mine. *Springmine*, they call them. The fox must have set it off. They told us about them in the Hitler Youth. We've had a lucky escape.'

'Poor old foxy,' wailed Hanna, unaware how very lucky their escape had been.

'But we're all fine, *mein Schatz*,' said Helene to Hanna, ruffling her hair. 'At least none of us was hurt.'

Helene breathed deeply, shaking a little. Otto hugged her and she leaned into him.

'Jesus, that was close,' he said.

'Is it safe to stand up now?' Helene asked.

He nodded.

She looked over the wall. 'Grass is still there. It hasn't made a crater.' Fortunately, the fox was nowhere to be seen. It was almost certainly dead in the long grass.

'They shoot into the air, a metre or so, and then they explode, throwing shrapnel all around,' explained Otto. 'Horrible weapons, aren't they? Our boys must have mined this place in the days before the surrender.'

Helene cursed. 'Just our wretched luck,' she muttered. 'This garden is probably full of stuff we can eat, but getting to it might kill us.'

Hanna tugged on her sleeve. 'Come on, let's go away,' she said.

Helene shook her head. 'I'm not giving up yet, *Mausi*.'

Propped against the garden wall behind them was a long broad plank – probably a replacement floorboard. 'We're in luck,' said Helene. 'We could use this to make a passage through to the far wall.'

Otto nodded cautiously.

'So, we bang it down,' she continued, 'and then run behind the wall, in case it sets a mine off.'

They dragged the floorboard out, careful to keep it vertical, walking it along the paved area by the wall.

'Just here,' said Helene. 'Drop it so it reaches the far wall.'

'On three,' said Otto. 'One . . . two . . . three!'

They let go, dashing behind the wall as quickly as they could.

Nothing happened. Hanna giggled.

They breathed again.

'Hanna, you stay here. Crouch down into a little ball behind the wall,' said Otto. 'OK, Helene, let's grab some bricks and throw them around the plank. Make sure there's nothing there that could go off.'

They threw several bricks, dashing for shelter as soon as they left their hands. The bricks produced no explosions either.

'I'll go first,' said Otto, standing up.

'No, you're too clumsy,' Helene teased, and was walking along the plank before he could stop her.

'Let me go!' said Hanna.

Otto grabbed her to stop her following. 'No. This is a job for a grown-up.'

Helene ventured out cautiously, arms out like a tightrope walker, sweat spreading through her dress in dark patches. Sometimes she wobbled and Otto called out for her to be careful.

'Look, I can see potatoes there by the wall,' she called, pointing at some tell-tale green shoots.

'Helene, look out for tripwires. Be careful where you put your hands!' Otto called.

She gathered her courage and delved warily into the soil until she pulled up a potato as large as a fist. 'What a beauty,' she cried. She carried on digging until a small pile lay at her feet.

'We'll come back here for more, I'm sure,' she said as she pulled up her skirt to her waist to make a pouch for her haul. 'No peeking,' she called out as she began to walk cautiously along the plank back to safety.

Otto blushed and dutifully shielded his eyes until she returned, revelling in her triumph. She looked at the crows lying still on the paving stones. 'Can you eat crows?' she asked.

'Euurrghh,' said Hanna.

'Not sure,' said Otto. 'It's worth a try. If they're inedible then we won't cook them again.'

They clambered back over the debris with their haul. If they could get home safely they would have something solid to eat tonight.

'It's been quite an adventure,' said Helene. She bent down and picked Hanna up. 'I'll carry you, and Otto can carry the potatoes and the crows.'

As they walked along, with Hanna scampering in front of them, Otto grasped Helene's hand and drew her close to him.

'You were amazing in the garden,' he said softly. 'You're so brave.'

She smiled stiffly, trying not to be unfriendly. He sensed at once that he was making her feel uncomfortable. She gently disentangled her hand from his and adjusted the back of her hair with it, before giving his arm a friendly squeeze. Friendly but not too close.

'You too, Otto,' she said. 'We are lucky to have you.'

Otto felt a blush spread across his face. He had over-stepped the mark.

There was an awkward pause but Helene filled it. 'I can't wait to see their faces when we show them our haul.'

He smiled at her kindness. Trying not to make him feel awkward. He loved that about her.

But when they arrived home they were surprised to see a stranger leaning against the sink casually smoking a cigarette. He was of medium height, with a shock of dark hair, spectacles, fairly stocky. Erich and Klaus, and Christa, Rolf and Traudl were sitting against the far wall, watching in uneasy silence. Ulrich was sitting apart, at the table. He had his 'tough' face on and his eyes were boring into the stranger.

The man stood straight as they entered, greeting them with a genial smile and a warm handshake. 'You must be Otto and Helene.'

Several things about the stranger made Otto feel uneasy. He was clean shaven and well dressed – in a light summer suit and clean shirt. And he smelled of . . . nothing. These days in Berlin everyone stank, whether it was grime or sweat, or the low haze of clothes that never dried without getting that dank mouldy smell. He'd got so used to it he almost never noticed. But this man was clearly living in another world.

The stranger had put them off guard with his amiable welcome. Otto guessed he was someone who spent a lot of time putting people at ease, like a doctor or a dentist. He felt almost pleased with himself when the man said, 'My name is Doktor Holzman. I live nearby.'

'He wouldn't go,' burst out Traudl, clearly emboldened by their return. 'We kept asking him to go, but he said he wanted to meet the older children and he would wait here, if we didn't mind. Well, we *did* mind, but he still stayed.'

Holzman smiled. He held out his hands, palms open to them all. 'I have seen you coming in and out of the ruins. I have a place just across the road, right at the top of the apartments there, which has mostly escaped the devastation by some miracle. No water or electricity, of course, but it's comfortable enough. I mean you no harm and, look, I've got a little food you can have.' He held up a small loaf. 'I came here today to see if there's anything I can do to help you.'

'What sort of doctor are you?' asked Helene, her tone neutral. All of them, over the last few months, had become wary of offers of help. There were almost always strings attached.

'I was in general practice, then the casualty wards. So I do all sorts,' said Holzman.

'Can you get us medicines?' asked Otto, thinking of Hanna's cough. And the boys were always scraping themselves on rubble. And Helene's hands had cuts that had never properly healed.

Holzman shrugged. 'It depends on what you want. Iodine for cuts, no problem. Penicillin for a bad wound or a chest infection, far more difficult. Almost impossible, in fact.'

Helene put an end to that conversation. Otto could tell she was wary of the stranger. 'Well, we're all right here, just about,' she said with a genial smile. 'Apart from never having enough to eat.'

'Have you been lucky today?' asked Holzman, eyeing their knapsacks.

An awkward silence descended. Was he after their food? Holzman detected their unease and laughed.

'Don't worry. I work with the Russians in the clinic on Rungestrasse. They give me rations. If anything, I can help you, if you need extra food.'

Helene gave an embarrassed laugh and fetched two sorry bundles of feathers from her bag. 'We found these crows. We were wondering if they were safe to eat?'

Holzman nodded. 'Yes. Crows are good. A lot of people don't like to eat them because they're carrion. They think they'll pick up all sorts of germs from the disgusting things the crows eat, but they have strong digestive systems, like vultures, so you should have no fear. The meat is not delicious, but it is not inedible either. I see you have a little stove to cook with. I have a little butter you can have. You can fry those crows like chicken.'

'How do you know about that?' said Otto with a smile.

'I was in the army during the war. You pick up these useful culinary tips living in the field.'

Ulrich looked up at that, Otto noticed. He was still idolising men who'd seen action, he thought sadly.

Holzman got up to leave. 'Look, I just wanted to say hello to you, and to let you know who I am, and that I am available if you need me. I'll get a little butter for you. I'm pleased you have a stove and pans. That's good. You are doing well for yourselves.'

When the door closed behind him, the children erupted in excited conversation. Helene gave Otto a twisted smile. 'I don't know what to make of him,' she said.

Otto shrugged.

'He's a slimy creep,' said Ulrich. 'And he looks Jewish.'

'He's nice,' said Hanna petulantly.

Erich and Klaus chimed in. 'He's all right.'

'Well, you seemed a bit frightened of him earlier,' said Helene.

Christa said, 'We just dropped in to ask about the market

126

and in he came, bold as anything. I'm not sure of him at all.'

'Let's see if he comes back with that butter,' said Otto.

Christa, Rolf and Traudl left, and as soon as they were out the door, Helene said, 'Look at this, kids!' and held up the potatoes they had found. 'We're going to have a proper feast this evening!' She felt bad not offering to share with their friends, but they couldn't feed another three mouths. Besides, Christa's relationship with her young Russian soldier meant she usually managed to get enough food for herself and her two little friends.

Helene sent Klaus and Erich to gather a couple of buckets of water from the pump, and they began to peel the potatoes with an army bayonet. Holzman returned, knocking politely on the door before he came in. In his hand was a small portion of butter. 'Only the finest,' he said with a smile.

As he was leaving, his eye alighted on the carriage clock on the shelf above the sink. 'My, what is this?' he said.

The children exchanged glances.

'We found it in a derelict apartment,' said Otto, swiftly moving between the doctor and the clock. Ulrich moved to stand next to him.

'It's very unusual,' said Holzman. 'May I have a look?'

Helene looked at Otto and nodded. Otto reached up to bring it down.

'Lovely weight to it. Marble, obviously,' said Holzman. 'And look at the detail in the figure. This is a valuable piece.' He looked at the bottom and the back to see if there were any hallmarks. 'Late eighteenth century, Black Forest, I'd guess. Probably manufactured in Furtwangen. Rivals to the Dutch in their time.' He placed it back on the shelf. 'If you ever decide to sell, I know people who are keen on buying antiques and they will pay a good price for a museum piece like this. I may even want to buy myself. Still, that is for you to think about. I'm not trying to make you part with it.'

'Do you know a lot about antiques?' asked Helene.

'A fair amount, but paintings, drawings, that's more my thing. Before the war it was a hobby. Something to take my mind off medicine.' Holzman gave them all a warm smile and then he was gone.

'I'm not selling,' said Helene when they all looked at her. 'We'd have to be starving to death before I sold that.'

No one was going to argue.

CHAPTER 12

Early August

A few weeks later, one hot early morning, when Otto went out to look at the sky it was pure blue. On an ordinary day, before the war, a morning like this would fill him with joy. Swimming in the lake at Wannsee, a trip out to Grunewald, he could still taste the ice creams Mutti and Papa would buy them on the journey home. He thought longingly of something luxurious and sweet to eat – a fruit salad with double cream, *Schwarzwälder Kirschtorte*, *Stollen* – and realised food like that had not passed his lips since at least last Christmas. Even then it had been a barely imaginable treat. 'Fancy an ice cream?' he called back to Helene as he left their basement refuge.

'Don't,' she scowled.

The day he tasted ice cream again would be the day Berlin was getting back on its feet. No one makes ice cream when you don't know where your next meal is coming from.

But things were getting better. Earlier in the summer they had all dreaded the scorching hot days. With no water in most homes, and rubble everywhere, a hot day in Berlin was a torment. The choking smell of sewage hung heavy in

129

the air, and a terrible decay that was part burned-out homes and vehicles, with an ominous undertow that they now all recognised as dead bodies. On days like those it was best to stay indoors and only venture out in the brief hours between early evening and curfew. In hot weather the thick clouds of bluebottles that were an everyday part of life now, were even worse. Otto remembered as a child how he had seen a necklace of little golden flies in the Ägyptisches Museum und Papyrussammlung, and how they had been given by the pharaoh to a general who had been victorious in battle. At the time he had thought it quaint. Now he realised its true significance, it turned his stomach.

Today, though, even in the rising heat, the city did not smell as bad as it had done. Brick by brick, Berlin and the basic requirements of civilisation were being rebuilt. There was still a tinge of effluent and brick dust hanging in the air, but nothing to make you cough or retch. Today, thought Otto, we shall go to the market and tonight we shall feast on black bread and bacon.

Ulrich, Erich and Klaus had left early to go foraging in the Brandenburg countryside – 'hamster trips' they called them. In another sign of returning normality the U-Bahn and S-Bahn had begun to run a restricted service. So hopefully the boys would be back by evening and not too exhausted by their journey. Otto was happy to see them go as a trio. They all had that cock-of-the-walk strut that let other foragers know they would be tricky to take on in a fight for their precious food.

When he returned from the water pump with a couple of overflowing buckets, there was only Helene and Hanna left. 'What would you like to do today?' he asked Hanna.

She smiled and shrugged. 'Don't know. What can I do?'

'Here's a little job for you, Hanna,' said Helene. 'Take one of those empty buckets and fill it up at the pump. We'll use up the water Otto brought back soon enough.'

'Want me to come with you?' asked Otto.

Hanna shook her head. She had taken well to their encouragement to do more on her own. 'I like going out to do a job,' she said brightly. 'Like a big girl.'

'She'll be fine,' said Helene. 'Off you go, Hanna, and when you get back we'll have a wash and you can come with us to the market to sell the vase I found in that house the other day.'

It was nice just sitting there together, just the two of them round the dining table. No stroppy Ulrich, no nonsense about blowing things up from Klaus and Erich. Coffee and bagels would be good, but stale bread and water was better than nothing.

Otto looked at Helene as she stared up at the shadows that passed the X-ray plates that still served as glass in the high windows. He felt an impulse to reach for her hand and was rattled by it. She was more like a sister than anything else, he had told himself again and again. But there was a certain flash in her eyes when she found something to sell, or to eat, that he found mesmerising. And when she confided her worries in him it made him feel warm, even though he had the same concerns. And all of a sudden, especially now her hair was growing back, he thought she was so beautiful. She looked back at him and he hurriedly averted his gaze. 'I'll go and meet Hanna,' he said. 'Give her a hand with her bucket.'

She put a hand on his shoulder. 'No, leave it a while. She likes to feel she's doing something to help, and it takes her mind off her Mutti and Papa. She'll still be a while in the queue, anyway.'

So Otto lay down on his bunk and tried to read a novel he had found in one of the derelict hospital wards. It failed to hold his attention – not least because he could see Helene right at the edge of his field of vision, washing in the corner and dressing for the day. Most of the time, this lack of privacy didn't seem to bother any of them – when you were starving or facing the prospect of a violent death there were more important things to worry about.

The sun moved round the room, coming down at a sharper angle as it rose in the sky.

'Hanna's been a while,' said Helene. 'I think I'll go and see if she's having trouble with that bucket.'

'I'll come too,' said Otto, and sprang to his feet.

The water pump was three blocks away on Muskauer Strasse and there was always a queue. They could see about twenty people there that morning, with their buckets and little tin baby baths and cans. Hanna was not among them.

'Excuse me,' announced Helene to anyone who would

listen. 'Has anyone seen a little girl, about so high, eight years old, wavy blonde hair?'

Most people ignored her, although a few shrugged.

'She's wearing a little flowery blouse and a blue cotton dress.'

'She was here a while ago,' said an older woman at the front of the queue. 'Left with her parents, heading back towards Oranienstrasse.'

Otto felt the blood drain from his face. Helene was looking pale. 'What did they look like?' she asked.

The woman gave an exaggerated shrug. 'Oh, top hat and tails for the man. Very dashing he was. Ballgown for the woman . . . What do you *think* they looked like?'

A few people sniggered unkindly. Otto could tell Helene was getting angry.

Another woman was more helpful. 'Young couple, around thirty, though it's difficult to tell these days. Both dark hair. Dusty ragged clothes. Looked half-starved . . .'

'Let's go,' said Otto and they headed off towards Oranienstrasse – the main road into the centre of Berlin. Hanna could be anywhere by now but they both knew they had to look for her.

The streets were busy, everyone was going somewhere, carrying something, though there were still few cars about. A jeep or two drove down the centre of the thoroughfare at reckless speed, but the trams were still not running in this part of town. They hurried up Oranienstrasse all the way to the crossroads at Moritzplatz and scanned

133

the crowd in panic. There was no sign of a couple with a small girl.

'Hanna!' Otto yelled.

'Hanna, it's us! Come back!' Helene cried.

No one answered.

'They could have gone anywhere from here,' said Helene. She sounded frantic. 'What are we going to do? How can we find her?'

Otto was feeling a rising sense of dread and all of a sudden he also felt terribly tired. They were both out of breath so they stopped to slake their thirst at a street water pump, then sat on the crumbling remains of a wall, wondering what to do.

'She could be anywhere in this mess,' said Otto.

The whole of the area was devastated – every building a pile of rubble.

'Both of them had dark hair,' said Helene. 'Can't say they sound like her parents. She told us her parents were quite old, and that her friends at school had asked if they were her granny and grandad.'

'Helene, I don't think we can do any more for now. Let's go back home in case she's gone back to look for us.'

Helene looked miserable, but she had to agree.

They walked home, calling out for Hanna all the way. Everywhere they looked they saw malnourished people, hungry eyes staring from pinched faces. Otto kept thinking about the rumours he'd been hearing ever since the collapse of the Third Reich, of children being killed and eaten.

People talked about it at the water pumps and food queues, so much so that you sometimes wondered if some of them were fishing for customers. The more he thought about it, the more realistic the threat felt.

Hanna was not at the hospital. Helene collapsed on her mattress in tears. They spent a slow afternoon, wrapped in anguish and guilt. Helene could not stop crying and Otto held her as she sobbed. 'It's not your fault, Helene,' he told her over and over. 'We both thought Hanna would be happier if she was busier and a bit more independent from us. And sending her round the corner for a bucket of water was a simple enough thing to ask her to do.'

She gripped his hand and nodded. 'You're right, Otto. It's not like we asked her to come on one of those night-time depot raids . . . Let's hope the people who took her are looking after her.'

She sat up and kissed him on the side of the head. 'Thank you for being so kind.'

The sun came and went through the high windows and by late afternoon both of them had started to doze. They woke with a start when they heard a commotion at the door. But it was Ulrich, Erich and Klaus who swaggered in, full of the excitement of the chase. They all put bags of blackcurrants and nettles on the table. 'Some thugs tried to snatch them off us,' declared Klaus, 'but Ulrich frightened them off with his knife.'

Ulrich looked very pleased with himself. 'So why the long faces?' he asked. 'What's been going on here?'

'Hanna has gone missing,' said Otto. Erich and Klaus looked shocked and immediately went over to console Helene.

Ulrich also looked shocked, and then uncertain. 'Run off to leech off someone else, has she?' he said, tentatively. Then his expression became bolder. 'Well. Good. That's a mouth we no longer have to feed.'

'Ulrich!' Otto said.

Helene looked horrified. 'Did the Hitler Youth really make you that heartless?' she snapped. 'Do you honestly have no concern for our poor little girl?'

Ulrich was clearly startled by her reaction. And everyone else in the room was looking daggers at him too.

'There's something Semitic about her, I've always thought,' he said, his voice dripping with resentment. 'Maybe she's one of the "chosen people" who slipped through the net. She's certainly been a parasite on our backs.'

Erich stepped forward and swung a punch that hit Ulrich hard on the side of his head. He fell to the floor, too stunned to get up and retaliate. 'You utter turd,' said Erich. 'I don't care how good you are with a knife. She's a little girl.'

Ulrich slowly got to his feet. 'You have made an enemy, Erich,' he said quietly. Then he looked around the room, his eyes blazing with anger. 'You can all go to hell,' he said. He grabbed his coat and rucksack and stormed out.

Otto laughed with scorn. 'He'll be back.' Then he turned to Erich, who was nursing his hand and looking rather shaken. 'And if he starts any trouble, then you'll have me and Klaus to help you out.'

As Ulrich stomped out of the hospital, he told himself that he would kill Erich when he had the chance. He had killed plenty of Russians in the battle for the city, he reasoned, and killing a little traitor like Erich would be no different.

He headed for Görlitzer Park – a big open space, where he would think about what to do. For several weeks now he had thought he would be better off away from that gang of political criminals. He had shown them how much money you could make from cigarettes, he had protected them when other boys had tried to steal their pitiful belongings, he had made perfectly good suggestions which were totally ignored, such as objecting to the assimilation into their group of the girl Hanna. The more he thought about it, the more he was convinced she was Jewish. She had many of the characteristics.

He was surprised to find himself feeling hurt and almost tearful. That was inappropriate for a political soldier. So he forced a scornful laugh and told himself they needed him far more than he needed them. In school they had often been taught about the survival of the fittest. He would show them all and leave them to starve. He stopped at the water pump on the corner of the park and filled his canteen, then sat on a hillock to think what he would do. He would find somewhere to live, even if it was a derelict apartment.

And he would use his wits to survive, trading on the black market. He had no worries for his future.

And besides, now he was away from his mithering brother and that girl, he was now free to make contact with the Werewolf resistance. They must be out there somewhere. He would keep his eyes peeled and pick up clues. Once he had found them, he knew they would take in a boy like him.

Sitting a couple of metres away from him was a lean, sharp-featured young man in civilian clothing – an unusual sight in Berlin in August 1945, when most German men his age had been rounded up for a prison camp, or sent east. He wore a plain white shirt, filthy now but obviously of good quality, and black trousers, and smoked an American cigarette. A Chesterfield, Ulrich's nose told him. Clearly this was someone with connections.

A couple of women, dressed in their Sunday best, strolled by, arm in arm with two Russian colonels. For one brief instant, the young man's eyes narrowed in disapproval, but he carefully rearranged his face into a blank expression as they passed by. Ulrich was not so cautious. He stared hard and hostile, but they did not even notice him, so wrapped up were they in flirtatious conversation.

'Hey, comrade, have a cigarette,' said the man, approaching Ulrich once the women and their partners had gone by, offering an open packet with one Chesterfield extended.

Ulrich was startled by his boldness. He did not smoke himself (like the Führer, he thought it a filthy habit), but he still took the cigarette. He would exchange it for food at the market. 'Thank you, comrade, I'll save it for later, if you don't mind,' he said.

The man smiled. He knew exactly what Ulrich was doing. 'You're a clever boy. I can see it in your face.' Ulrich continued to look at him, holding his gaze and unabashed by his flattery. The man spoke again. 'And I can see you are still a National Socialist.'

'Race traitors are a cancer in our national community,' said Ulrich, referring to the women who had just walked by. He sensed at once that he and the stranger were on the same page.

'And how quickly the people acquiesce,' said the man. His words hung in the air.

Ulrich's heart was beating faster. He liked the look of this fellow. He had the blond hair and blue eyes of a model *Übermensch* – exactly the sort of SS officer you would see at the head of a great parade. The sort of man Ulrich would follow into battle without hesitation. He had a steely quality – Ulrich could see it in his eyes – the kind of ruthlessness and determination that they had all been told they needed to make the Eastern Territories a great colony for the German people. In that moment the losses of the war struck Ulrich all over again: the *Übermenschen* had been cheated out of their birthright as leaders of the world by a mongrel group of Jews, Soviets and the race traitors of the Western alliance. And yet, here was such an *Übermensch*, dashing and brave, right here before him.

Perhaps the Nazi cause was not lost yet. Perhaps there was hope.

'You look like you could do with a good meal inside you,' said the man.

Ulrich, much to his embarrassment, felt his stomach lurch and gurgle at the thought of food.

'I don't have much but you are welcome to share it,' said the man. 'Wait here and I will return shortly.'

Five minutes later he returned with a couple of pretzels and some cheese. 'It's not very exciting, but it will keep you going.'

They sat together and both ate in a companionable silence. It reminded Ulrich of his Hitler Youth picnics with his comrades and he felt a strange mixture of pride and sadness. He longed for those days, a time when he felt he really belonged. There were no doubters. All of them staunch National Socialists with a common purpose and a glorious future.

Ulrich had so many questions, but he was too embarrassed to ask – 'Where did you get the bread?' – 'How come you're not in a camp?' – 'What did you do in the war?' Maybe he would ask, if he got to know this fellow better.

'You look like a political soldier,' said the man.

Ulrich flushed with pride. The whole of his life he had been brought up to serve the Führer and the National Community. Since the surrender in May his faith had wavered. Now he saw the opportunity to relight the flame. At that moment this man could have asked him to do anything and he would have done it. He had felt like that when he'd heard the Führer speak on the radio or the cinema newsreels, and on the two magical occasions he had seen the German leader at a rally.

Ulrich thought he ought to say something important. 'I was born to die for Germany,' he declared, reciting a phrase they had been taught to say in the Hitler Youth.

The man seemed taken aback by his zeal. 'And what is your name, young fellow?'

'Section Leader Roth,' said Ulrich, trotting out his Hitler Youth rank automatically. He almost stood to attention to deliver a Nazi salute but caught himself – even he realised that Sieg Heiling in the open, with all these Russians around, was not a sensible thing to do.

The man put out his hand to shake. 'You may call me Ernst,' he said.

Ulrich was flattered and a little embarrassed to be allowed to call this gentleman by his first name. 'And I am Ulrich,' he said, feeling a little shy.

'Well, today I have tasks to perform,' said Ernst. 'But tomorrow, we shall meet here again. I look forward to talking to you.'

Ulrich sensed destiny calling. Tomorrow would be the start of his own crusade against the Jewish-Bolshevik horde, and he intended to wreak a terrible revenge.

CHAPTER 13

Ulrich made good use of the Chesterfield cigarette Ernst had given him, but the ham and black bread it bought in the Tiergarten market was not enough to stop him feeling hungry by the evening. And he was surprised how difficult it was to find somewhere safe to spend the night. Buildings that looked watertight and empty were full of ragged people who shooed him away like a stray dog or a scurrying rat.

It was getting dark by the time he did settle on somewhere to stay – a bombed-out apartment with rubble strewn all over the floor. It stank of damp and human waste, but if you kept away from its broken windows you would be dry at least. As Ulrich rested his back against a hard plasterboard wall he began to think longingly of his mattress and blankets back at the hospital, and the washing they had constantly drying in the sunny spots of the room. He had taken Skalitzer Hospital for granted a little, he realised, but now he was beginning to see it had been an oasis of normality.

He thought of Otto with bubbling contempt. He wanted an elder brother he could look up to, someone, he realised, like Ernst. Otto lacked the spirit of a true political soldier.

Ulrich had always thought Otto soft, and was puzzled and hurt that his parents often seemed to prefer him. The Hitler Youth had taught them that kindness would not win them an empire. Otto had not absorbed that lesson. Ulrich thought too of Helene and wondered if she had feelings for his elder brother. He felt a twinge of jealousy at the friendship and closeness those two had. Burrowing deeper into his thin jacket, Ulrich smothered any feelings he had towards Helene. He told himself she was too skinny to be a proper German girl. She lacked the broad 'childbearing hips' the Eugenics lessons had stressed were so essential to efficient procreation.

He thought of the times Helene had scolded him and how his defiance had made her even angrier. It was not a woman's place to rebuke a section leader in the Hitler Youth. The only women deserving of respect, they had been taught, were mothers who produced four children or more for the National Community. But . . . he liked it when she was kind to him. Sometimes she reminded him of his Mutti, and with that, thoughts of how he had often spoken to his mother came unbidden. Especially that time he had been complaining about a teacher at school who was never first to offer the Hitler salute to her colleagues or pupils. Ulrich had said he was going to denounce her. His Mutti had told him he would do no such thing and Ulrich had told her she ought to watch her step or he would denounce her too. He remembered, with a sharp twinge of regret, how she had fled the house in tears. That was the day she had been killed in the air raid. Remembering his mother made him think of his father, too, and a churning black ball seemed to settle in his guts. He shut off that line of thought by recalling the stories he had read in *Der Pimpf* magazine of heroic resistance and comradeship during the siege of Stalingrad. Finally he drifted off to sleep.

In the early hours of the night he was woken by dreadful shouting and screams coming from a room a floor down from where he was hiding. He couldn't make out whether someone was being attacked down there or whether it was just one madman making that noise. It didn't sound like there was anyone else there. All at once he felt very small and vulnerable, even though he had his dagger in his hand, and hoped that whoever it was would not come up and find him.

After ten minutes the noise stopped abruptly and he tried to settle himself to sleep again by plotting out the practicalities of the day. Tomorrow he would have to steal something to sell. But Berlin was full of such opportunities and he wasn't overly concerned. In his head he heard the voice of the Hitler Youth banner leader: 'That will be no problem for a resourceful boy like you.'

But as he began to slip into sleep another thought, which he had long ago pushed down and tried to forget, rose up like a black tide without warning. The moment he had told the SS officer his father was behaving like a traitor. Ulrich recalled the pride he had felt when the officer had patted him on the shoulder and thanked him for doing his duty. But now the memory made him shudder. If he had been right to do that, why did he feel so guilty thinking about it now? Hitler himself had said the youth of the country had to instruct their elders in the creed of National Socialism. Ulrich had spent his childhood doing that with his teachers and his parents. Had he been wrong to believe in that? No, he told himself angrily, men like his father had let the Führer down. Had let him down.

Ulrich woke at first light, his bones aching from the hard floor he had slept on. He crept gingerly down the staircase, hoping that whoever had been doing the shouting and screaming in the night was no longer there. As he passed the rubble-strewn landing a hand snaked out from what looked like a pile of stinking rags and grabbed his leg. Panic surging through him, Ulrich kicked the hand hard with his other leg, and the grip loosened. He kicked again and then ran in terror down the apartment stairwell, pursued only by deranged drunken howls.

Only when he approached Görlitzer Park did he realise he had been hurt in the attack. Somehow, the man had slashed his leg with a thin blade, maybe even a razor. It was a neat, deep cut into the flesh of his calf. It bled a bit, trickling down his leg, but he was determined to ignore it.

After wrapping a grimy handkerchief around his leg to staunch the wound, he waited two hours in the park, eventually curling up in the grass to sleep when the hot summer sun began to beat down. He woke some hours later to Ernst shaking his shoulder gently.

'Hello, my friend,' Ernst said kindly. 'I have brought breakfast.' To Ulrich's astonishment he poured coffee from a Thermos flask, and produced some more pretzels with cheese and pickled cucumber. Ulrich didn't feel it was his place to ask where such rare delights could be found.

'I hope you slept well?' asked Ernst. Then, before Ulrich could answer, he said, 'You have injured yourself, my friend.'

Ulrich poured out his tale.

'Is that where you usually stay?' asked Ernst.

'No, but I've left the group I was living with,' Ulrich said. 'They are traitors and unworthy of my company.'

Ernst listened carefully, his face giving nothing away. Then he said, 'I like you, Ulrich, and so I will tell you now what you must do. You must return to these traitors. You are too important to risk your health and your life, sleeping in such dangerous conditions. If needs be, you must apologise for your behaviour. I know a good German boy should not lie, but when dealing with enemies you must be cunning as a fox. You do not have to mean it. But we live in difficult times, Ulrich. It is your duty to maintain your strength for the coming hour of retribution.'

Ulrich had hoped Ernst would offer to let him stay with him, but he didn't, although he did go and fetch a small tube of antiseptic ointment, which he smeared on Ulrich's injury. Ulrich prided himself on not flinching when the ointment smarted.

'OK, I will see you here again tomorrow. Perhaps we will

146

talk again of how we might resist our conquerors,' Ernst said with a smile.

Ulrich nodded eagerly, but as he limped off he felt so sorry for himself he almost began to cry. He reminded himself that such feelings were unbecoming in a member of the Master Race. He would stay out another night, at least. To punish them. He was sure they would be worried sick about him.

Back at the hospital the next morning, Otto and Helene were indeed beginning to feel very concerned.

'What can we do?' asked Helene. 'I didn't sleep at all last night. Every time I heard a noise outside, I thought it was her coming home.'

'We must go and report her missing,' said Otto. 'And what about Ulrich? He's a tough little *Arschloch* but he still shouldn't be out on his own.'

Helene shrugged. 'Otto, I'm sorry about him too,' she said, not entirely convincingly. 'But he can take better care of himself.'

'I know you're right,' said Otto. 'But there's just us left of our family now. Even if I don't like him, he'll always be my brother. And you have to admit, he has been pretty useful to us recently.' Otto dragged a hand through his hair and sighed. 'Let's wait until noon, and see if either of them comes back. Have one last look around the streets. We can all go. Then we can go to the police. They ought to be interested in Hanna, at least.'

'We'll help,' said Klaus, from across the room.

Erich nodded. 'I miss her little face,' he said sadly.

They all searched, but in vain, and that afternoon Otto and Helene went to a makeshift police station on Lausitzer Platz. It had a temporary sign above a broken doorway, like all the police stations now. Even from twenty metres away they could tell that inside was bedlam.

In a courtyard through the doorway there was a desk where sat an extremely harassed-looking man with thinning hair and spectacles. Maybe he was in his late fifties. Standing either side of him were two other middle-aged men in the green uniform of the German police. Surrounding them was a mob of people, pushing, shoving, a whisker away from exchanging blows. Their troubles were legion. Stolen goods from shops, burglaries, physical assaults of all descriptions . . .

'How do we make ourselves heard in this?' said Otto, trying not to despair.

'We shall wait,' said Helene, with a determination that told Otto this was something she was not going to discuss.

It was late afternoon when the crowd had thinned and eventually Otto and Helene were able to speak to the old man behind the desk.

'We are living with a little girl called Hanna,' said Helene. 'And we heard she went off with some people yesterday. We think they might have kidnapped her.'

'Kidnapped?' said the man incredulously. 'Who would kidnap a child? Who in their right mind would take on another mouth to feed?'

'One of yours, is she?' said one of the policemen standing beside him. 'They start young these days,' he said out of the corner of his mouth. His companions smirked along with him.

Otto tried to be polite. 'Please, can you help us? We have been looking after her. Her parents have vanished.'

'Well, that was them,' said the man at the desk in a bored voice. 'They've taken her back. Problem solved.'

'Won't you at least take a description?' asked Helene. 'Even a name?'

The man meshed his hands and rested his chin on them, leaning over the desk to look down at Helene. 'Young lady. Do you know we have about a hundred reports a week of missing children – maybe even two hundred?' He sounded terribly weary, like a parent speaking to a selfish child. 'If we had a telephone that worked, if we had a car, if we had a newspaper or radio station where we could announce such things, if we had a printing press to put up leaflets . . . well, you get the picture I'm sure.'

Helene was all but speechless. 'So there's nothing you can do?'

'Put up your own notes,' said the man. 'You must have seen the walls all over Berlin for people who are looking for other people.' He looked over her shoulder and called out, 'Who's next?'

Otto and Helene walked back to the hospital in silence, seething with indignation. Of course they had seen the walls covered with missing-person appeals and how easily they blurred in the rain. Halfway home, Helene sat down in a doorway and began to cry. 'What if the people who took her are going to hurt her, Otto? Do you think those stories about children being murdered for meat could be true?'

Otto put an arm around her shoulder and she wept into his chest. He stroked her head, feeling awkward and wondering if this was the right thing to do. But she didn't mind. She just hugged him harder. 'People say all sorts of nonsense,' he said. 'I don't believe it. Can you imagine anyone knowingly eating a child? We are good people, aren't we? Even in defeat.'

She said nothing but seemed to recover her composure. She stayed where she was, though, wrapped around him. 'Look at us, Otto. We're sixteen and we're acting like parents. Worrying about our little ones. Wouldn't it be good to go back to being in school, hoping you were going to be picked for the swimming team?'

Otto stroked her head again and sighed. 'Helene, at least we are alive . . .' His voice trailed away. Thinking of the desperation he saw every day, he had a horrible feeling that the cannibalism stories were all too true. The thought of it made him feel sick.

The twins had set out that afternoon determined to find something for them all to eat. Back gardens and communal patches of grass in the courtyards of apartment blocks were always good spots for wild fruit and vegetables. But everyone in Berlin knew this now. So it paid to look in the more obscure and dangerous corners for that patch of blueberries or wild potatoes.

The house on Muskauer Strasse looked like the scene of a terrible battle. All the usual signs – blackened outer walls, bullet-scarred walls, especially around the doors and windows, and that awful charred smell of burning wood, plaster and brick that lingered still, so many weeks after the fighting had ended. They both knew it was worth a try, even if it meant they discovered a body. They had seen things like this often enough.

There were stairs leading down to a basement, and beyond they could see a patch of overgrown courtyard. 'Look out for booby traps,' Erich called out, as Klaus boldly entered the basement.

'Good point,' said his brother. 'I wonder if this is one of the places we put one down.' He laughed, looking up and squinting. 'That would be an irony, wouldn't it? If we were caught by our own booby trap.'

There were no tell-tale wires, which was a relief. But the garden held no fruit or vegetables either – just coarse grass and weeds.

'We'll be eating grass next,' said Erich. 'Unfortunately the Third Reich did not manage to breed members of the Master Race with four stomachs.'

Klaus mooed.

They turned back into the basement, peering into the gloom to see if there was anything worth taking down there.

'Hang on, what's this?' said Klaus. In one of the basement rooms, barely lit by a broken fanlight, they could see a pile of wooden boxes. Most were empty, but among them was one they recognised from their *Volkssturm* training.

Erich's eyes lit up. He placed a hand at the base of a rectangular box and pushed against it to test for its weight. 'Think of the mess we can make with these!' he said.

'Shall we open it?' said Erich. 'Might be booby-trapped?'

'Worth a try,' said Klaus.

They cleared away the other boxes around it. Then Erich pulled open the lid a couple of millimetres. 'Strike a match,' he demanded.

Klaus held a burning match along the side of the lid. 'Can't see any wires inside that.'

They pulled back the wooden lid, and inside, with that unmistakable smell of metal and grease, were four unused *Panzerfaust* anti-tank missiles.

When the twins had returned from their foraging, Otto and Helene agonised about what they could do to find Hanna.

'I can draw a picture of her,' said Erich. 'We can show it to people.'

'No!' laughed Otto. 'You can draw?'

Klaus leapt to his defence. 'Hey, he's really good. Erich can draw people from memory.'

'So you can too, right?' said Helene.

Klaus shook his head. 'Everyone thinks twins are exactly the same. Well, we're not. Erich's good at drawing but I'm good at acting. I can't draw to save my life; he can't act. It's like this in school, too. In science, he likes animals. I like plants. Funny old world!'

'So where are we going to get you some paper and a pen?' asked Otto.

'There's some in one of the upstairs rooms,' said Klaus. 'I noticed the other day when I was nosing around.' He disappeared, then returned a few minutes later holding a medical writing board, with sheaves of paper and a sharpened pencil still miraculously attached by a clip to the top.

It took Erich three attempts before he captured a good likeness, but Otto was amazed at his ability to conjure a human face from his imagination.

'That's her all right,' said Helene looking at the third sketch. 'I can almost hear her laughing,' she said sadly.

'Hey, Erich, do us all,' said Klaus.

And he did. That late afternoon he sketched them all, and the portraits were pinned to the wall. Later that night they ate well – a dinner of sausages and black bread Helene had traded for a pair of shoes in the market, along with some crisp apples Klaus and Erich had found. It felt good to go to sleep on a full stomach, and Otto whispered to Helene, as they settled down for the night, 'Tomorrow we will go and see if anyone recognises our Hanna.'

She gave him a warm hug and he drifted off, feeling that a bit of good luck was definitely going to come their way. But Otto woke with a start in the early hours of the morning, feeling guilty. Shouldn't he be worrying about Ulrich too?

They trudged through the streets the next morning and rapidly discovered no one wanted to look at a picture of a little girl, especially if you tried to approach them first. It was as if they thought you were going to ask them for food or, even worse, to try to rob them.

Eventually, by trial and error, they learned the best technique was to get Helene to approach people at the water pumps. She would stand a couple of metres away and announce that she had a picture of a lost little girl, and would anyone be kind enough to look at it in case they recognised her. Most people responded to that. But although a few people thought they knew her, no one said anything useful.

Hours later in the late afternoon they were tired and dispirited. 'It's as if she's vanished into thin air,' said Otto.

By now, dark clouds were gathering. 'I want to get home before the rain comes,' said Helene. 'I don't want Erich's picture destroyed.'

There was a queue for the water pump near the hospital. 'Let's just try these people,' said Otto, 'now that we're nearly home.'

Helene made her announcement as Otto stood well back. If anyone thought they were pickpockets, and he her accomplice, they might become uneasy.

There were a couple of dark-haired children in the queue, the sort Otto had regularly seen in the Racial

Hygiene books shown in school before the war, who were chosen to represent Jews – they both had pale skin and large dark eyes. While they spoke to Helene, Otto wondered how they had survived the war. Finally they said they could not help but would keep an eye out for the girl. Helene smiled her thanks at them.

'I haven't seen Jews in Berlin in several years,' said Helene, as they walked home together. 'Perhaps they've been hiding somewhere?' She had not talked to him about the conversations she had had with Christa, the pictures she had seen in the Soviet newspapers. It was too hard to put into words. 'Mutti would whisper to me that they had transferred all the Jews to the east . . . and killed them. And I've heard and read other terrible stories too. But it all sounds too much, even for our Nazis. Surely, they could not have been so wicked?'

Otto felt numb. He had heard those rumours too. He remembered that the boys at school had even made jokes about it. He hadn't believed it then, either. It had seemed too monstrous. He couldn't have ever imagined his own people doing something like that.

But since the fall of the Nazis, when he had seen how they had forced people to fight until their own beautiful capital city was destroyed, in a war that was obviously lost, he had begun to believe they were capable of anything.

As Helene spoke to the queue there was a distant explosion over to the east. People shifted uneasily. 'It's the Werewolves,' said a young woman. 'They're up to no good

155

again.' Other people alongside her murmured in agreement. 'Hitler's taunting us from the grave,' said an old man next to her. 'He's sowed dragon's teeth with those young fanatics.' No one was interested in their drawing of Hanna.

'Werewolves!' said Helene as they walked home. 'People will believe any old rubbish, won't they? I'll bet that was just an unexploded bomb or a shell. Or a couple of scamps like Erich and Klaus.'

Otto smiled, then something dark occurred to him. 'I don't really believe in them either,' he said. 'But if they are getting themselves organised, that's just the sort of thing our Ulrich would love to get mixed up in.'

CHAPTER 14

Ulrich thought hard about how he could return to the hospital. He knew that they would still be angry with him, so he decided he would have to do something to placate them. And the best way to do that was with a gift.

Yesterday he had found a gold ring in the basement of a bombed-out house where he had spent the night and pocketed it with a smirk. This was a clear sign, he thought, that the gods were on his side. He was no expert in these things but he would sell it at the market as his mother's wedding ring – it could be, after all. But on the way back home he was grabbed by a gang of teenage boys who pinned him to a wall and went through his pockets. They took the ring without a word and left him bewildered and shaken at this sudden reversal of fortune. It had happened so quickly he had barely had time to even think about toughing it out. But he was too tired to fight and there were too many of them, anyway.

Moments later, he passed a small house facing on to the street. A middle-aged woman was sitting on the porch with a paper bag at her feet. She looked drawn and haggard, as if she hadn't slept for a week, and when another woman arrived with a key to their home, she could barely lift herself up. The two women went inside their house and she absent-mindedly left the bag on the step. In an instant Ulrich scooped it up, realising at once it held a loaf of bread, and hurried away. Thirty seconds later he heard a grief-stricken wail and fought every instinct to look round. Ulrich was sure it was the woman, discovering her bread had gone.

Ulrich's jaw tightened into what he hoped was that look of steely determination he had seen on young soldiers in the propaganda films, and he suppressed a twinge of pity that caught him by surprise. Now he could go straight back to the hospital. He had his gift.

They were all there when he arrived; he could hear them talking. Otto and Helene were arguing with Erich and Klaus about what was left to eat. Very little, from what he overheard. A gleeful smile passed his lips. This was a good moment to make an entrance. He composed himself, tried to look contrite, and entered the room.

At first they all fell silent and stared at him, clearly wondering what he was going to do or say. No one looked especially pleased to see him, although he thought he caught a flash of relief from Otto. Mainly, though, he had to try hard to mask the pleasure he felt seeing Erich refuse to catch his eye. He was obviously uneasy to see him.

'I am sorry I behaved badly,' he said. They continued to stare at him blankly. He felt under pressure to say more.

'My behaviour was not up to the standard of . . .' He struggled, trying to think of a suitable expression that did not have Nazi overtones. 'A member of our community,' was the best he could manage.

'We are pleased you are safe, Ulrich,' said Otto carefully. 'But if you are going to live here with us you're going to have to learn to respect us.'

Ulrich felt a rising indignation in his chest. He wanted to point at Erich and blurt out, 'Well, he started it,' but realised even as the thought formed in his head that this would make him sound like a kindergarten whinger.

'I am sorry I made you all angry,' he replied. He reached into his knapsack and pulled out the bread. 'I have brought you something to eat.'

The gesture had the desired result. Helene smiled. The expressions of the others softened. They sat round the table and divided up the bread with the remains of a small block of hard cheese.

But as Ulrich ate he found the bread tasted heavy in his mouth. He remembered the desperate cry of the woman he had stolen it from, and was reminded of the time when he was a child and had upset his mother by stealing sweets in the KaDeWe department store. The guilt he had felt, disgracing her like that, still made him shudder and he thought sadly of how much he had distressed her.

Late afternoon, back at the basement, Ulrich, Erich and Klaus found themselves alone together. Ulrich had noticed

159

how Erich seemed more relaxed around him, and he was pleased about that. Maybe he would make an ally after all. As they shared a small pile of strawberries they had picked on the way home, Klaus told Ulrich about their latest discovery.

'We found a box of *Panzerfäuste* on Muskauer Strasse,' he said.

Ulrich's eyes flickered with interest despite himself. 'What will you do with them?'

'Something spectacular,' said Erich. 'But we need to plan this carefully. An opportunity like this won't come up every day. I think we should set them off in a church – one that's half falling to bits already.'

'We are not barbarians, after all,' said Klaus with mock pomposity.

'There's a semi-derelict church in Wrangelstrasse. That could be perfect,' Erich said. 'It's only a block away from where they're hidden. So it would be easy to smuggle them over. Then we can take them to the top of the spire, and build a bonfire there to set them off.'

'I reckon all four of them together would make enough of an explosion to bring the whole central tower crashing down,' Klaus said. 'It would certainly make the most spectacular explosion.'

'And best of all, if we do it right, we can be back at Skalitzer Hospital, and up on the roof of the west wing, to watch it all, and no danger of being caught in the act!' Erich beamed.

'It will be our greatest adventure yet,' said Ulrich. He was playing along with them, of course. He certainly wasn't going to tell them he had far more grand and ambitious ideas for those rockets.

Over the next few days Ulrich made a special effort to fit in with the Skalitzer Hospital gang, even apologising for being so unkind about Hanna. As another day passed without her return he pretended to be genuinely sad she was no longer there. Erich even drew his picture to place with the others on the wall. To begin with, Otto and Helene had eyed this friendly, open behaviour warily, but after a few days they let that go. At night, as they settled down to sleep, Ulrich curled up in his mattress and tried to guess what everyone might be thinking about. Otto and Helene would be worrying about Hanna, about the future, and how they could survive the coming winter. Klaus and Erich would be dreaming of blowing things up, or pushing grand pianos from half-abandoned apartment buildings.

But Ulrich thought of the stock of *Panzerfaust* anti-tank weapons Klaus and Erich had told him about, in a basement in Muskauer Strasse. He would tell Ernst about these weapons as soon as he had the chance. He hadn't seen him for a few days. Erich, keen to mend their friendship, had even told him exactly where they were hidden.

He wondered what he would do with such a weapon. There was a woman close to their hospital who regularly had a whole gang of Ivans around for Sunday lunch. He had seen them turning up with a joint of beef or lamb, and vegetables and bottles of wine, and she would entertain them all for the rest of the day. Sometimes he would hear laughter late into the night. It was the very sound of treachery itself. But the more he thought, the more he realised that with a weapon this powerful he had the opportunity to do something far more ambitious. There was talk of a big victory parade happening soon – one with famous generals on a podium, saluting their troops. Could he launch a *Panzerfaust* at them? What a message that would send out to the world! The German resistance was not dead. Maybe, he thought dreamily, it would trigger an uprising. And if he was killed in the action, so be it. In the future, German boys and girls would sing songs about him, as they had done with Horst Wessel, the brave Hitler Youth leader killed by communists before Hitler came to power. That night, as the rest of them snored and grunted in their sleep, Ulrich tried to contain his excitement, and the pride he would feel when he told Ernst of his discovery.

The next day Ulrich sat in the park on the usual hillock, waiting for Ernst. The morning came and went, and, stiff and chilled from his vigil, Ulrich was just stretching himself ready to go when Ernst arrived. 'Heil Hitler,' he said under his breath and Ulrich had to suppress his instinct to spring to attention and deliver a Nazi salute. Instead, he grinned stupidly, and they fell into rapid conversation.

Ernst told him in a whisper that he had come into ownership of a large carton of Lucky Strike cigarettes. He would like Ulrich to go to the market to sell them for him. He was prepared to go fifty-fifty on the profits.

'But Ernst, why do you not go yourself?' asked Ulrich, reasonably. 'Then you would have a hundred per cent of your takings.'

Ernst looked into the distance, as if weighing up whether to disclose a secret. 'I prefer to remain close to the park during the day,' he said quietly. 'And it is only at night that I feel safe enough to forage.'

Ulrich was strangely thrilled by this information. 'Look, you can ask me to help you any time,' he said. He could easily imagine Ernst was a wanted man, hunted by the Soviets for acts of heroic resistance.

'I know I can trust you, Ulrich,' said Ernst, putting a brotherly arm around the boy's shoulder. He kept it there until Ulrich began to feel uncomfortable and shrugged Ernst off with a grin.

Ernst either did not notice Ulrich's awkwardness, or didn't care. 'Here's what I suggest. I'll give you two packs of cigarettes, but you must sell them individually – that is the way to the greatest profit. When you have done so, for whatever price you can get, then you must return here and give me half your takings. I will trust you implicitly, Ulrich. I can see you have a strong sense of duty. And when you have sold the cigarettes, then I will give you more.'

'Didn't you have to barter to buy them?' asked Ulrich.

Ernst gave a cruel laugh. 'I bought them with the point of my dagger,' he said.

Ulrich was thrilled to know that he was handling goods that had been procured through the threat of murder, or even murder itself. Ernst really was an outlaw. Ulrich tried not to think about how it had felt when he had been robbed of the ring he had found.

As Ernst got up to go he said, 'Meet me back here tomorrow afternoon. Around four o'clock. If you do well, I have other work for you.' Then, as an afterthought, he added, 'Oh, and one more thing. See if there are any enemy officers who are particularly interested in antiques – particularly paintings, sketches, that sort of thing. See if you can get a feel for the prices paid for them.'

'I will, Ernst,' said Ulrich. But he was puzzled. 'I haven't seen anything like that being sold in the market. Do you have a painting to sell?'

'A good soldier does not question his orders,' Ernst said briskly.

Ulrich was startled by this response. Was this man his commanding officer or a new friend?

Ernst nodded and patted him on the back by way of farewell.

Ulrich sat there for a while, watching him disappear into the trees. As he wandered back to the hospital he felt disappointed. He had not even managed to mention the *Panzerfaust* weapons and his plan to attack the parade. He had imagined they would talk of armed insurrection and the elimination of traitorous elements, but maybe that was to come. And he would be ready.

CHAPTER 15

The following morning Ulrich took himself off to Alexanderplatz, in the Russian zone, where he had heard there was also a thriving black market. His instincts told him that he had met someone genuinely dangerous in Ernst, and that it would be best not to let the others know about him. Otto, Helene and the rest usually went to the Tiergarten, so it was less likely he'd bump into them in Alexanderplatz.

It felt a little claustrophobic there, as tall buildings surrounded the crowd on every side. Alexanderplatz had been terribly damaged in the bombing and fighting and he did wonder if one of the huge office blocks or department stores would be likely to crash down on them. He certainly wouldn't want to be there in the winter, with a howling gale winding around these skeletons of buildings. But no one else there seemed to mind. He pushed through the dense crowd. It was like the end of a football match, when everyone got up and left at once, only here they had something to sell.

The market was smaller, without a doubt, but they were the same people you saw at the Tiergarten – the conquerors in their different uniforms, the hungry-eyed locals, pinched men in oily rags, and the odd woman in her Sunday best, trying to catch a soldier's eye. Ulrich tried to hide his revulsion. Four months ago, any German having relations with a Slav who worked in the city as a slave labourer could expect a trip to the guillotine.

Brushing aside his annoyance, Ulrich began to call for buyers. He sold his cigarettes one at a time – hiding them in his jacket pocket and hoping any likely buyer would imagine this was the last one in the pack. Within an hour he had sold all twenty of his first pack, to Russians and Germans alike. He never sold for less than five Reichsmark a cigarette and now he had a hundred and twenty-three Reichsmark in his pocket.

He traded his last cigarette for bread and cheese and sat in the sun to eat. A nagging doubt began to worm its way into his consciousness. What if Ernst was not an ally in the uprising he imagined coming? What if he was merely using him as a seller while he laid low himself? He dismissed the thought with the last mouthful of stale bread, and began selling the second pack of Lucky Strikes.

The afternoon trade was slower than the morning, and it was getting on for four when he sold his last cigarette. And there were no paintings or drawings for sale – just the odd ornament, as far as he could tell. Weary from his haggling, he sat on a low wall, placing another handful of Occupation Mark in his bag. But as he stared listlessly into the milling crowd he saw a face he thought he recognised. A tall figure swirled in and out of sight in a great sea of people. Ulrich caught another glimpse and immediately stood up to see better. The distant figure was too gaunt to be his father and his dark hair was too lank. It couldn't be him. It couldn't be. Ulrich of all people should know that. But he had to be sure. He began to run, pushing through the crowd to catch up before the figure disappeared altogether.

He felt himself grabbed from behind. Ulrich turned to see two American military policemen. One held each arm and they spoke to him angrily. Ulrich prided himself on his ability to speak only German. He was certainly not going to stoop to learning the language of the conquerors. He looked blank and replied as calmly as he could, indicating with a shrug that he did not understand.

Another American came to the rescue – a sergeant by the look of the stripes on his arms. 'Hey, kid,' he said in passable German. 'They want to know where you got those cigarettes.'

Ulrich was a quick thinker. 'I bought them at the Tiergarten market yesterday,' he lied. 'I exchanged them for a pair of leather shoes.'

The military policemen looked at him warily. The sergeant said, 'They want to show you something. I'll come along too, and translate.'

Ulrich wanted to protest and was immediately worried that they would take away his money. One of the policemen grabbed his arm tighter. The crowd parted and people stared. It was most uncomfortable.

They took Ulrich to a jeep parked at the edge of the crowd and sat either side of him on the back seat. The sergeant leaned in behind them, translating as the policemen spoke. 'They're going to show you some photographs. If you recognise the man who sold you these cigarettes you must tell them.'

One of the policemen pulled out a cardboard file and withdrew several black-and-white photographs. They flicked through. Most of the shots were of hard, mean-looking men, criminals in any society, but one made Ulrich blink. The lean, handsome face of Ernst stared out at him.

'Did *he* sell you the cigarettes?' translated the sergeant.

Ulrich feigned denial. 'I do not recognise this man,' he said.

The police began to argue between themselves. 'They want to take you in,' said the sergeant. 'Accessory to murder.'

At that moment Soviet soldiers arrived and spoke sharply to the police. This was a Russian zone, one of them said in broken English. It was not an appropriate area for American policemen. The three Americans got out of the jeep and stood before the Russians, ready to argue with them. Ulrich chose his moment to slide out and vanish into the crowd.

Running the long way home, he thought uneasily of what had just happened. Once again he wondered if Ernst really was at the vanguard of the resistance or, more likely, just a squalid criminal, like those other men in the police photographs. Only much later did he realise he had broken the promise he had made to kill the very first American he met. He wondered if he ought to feel shame, but consoled himself with the thought that he would have plenty of opportunity to do that at the Allied victory parade they had been talking about.

As he waited for Ernst later that afternoon, Ulrich began to feel increasingly uneasy about the money he carried in his bag. As he sat in the park he watched every gang of youths pass with trepidation. Ernst arrived an hour after he said he would, and Ulrich had begun to feel quite chilled as the late summer sun disappeared behind a thick grey cloud.

'Success, I expect,' said Ernst. 'How much did you make?'

'Two hundred and twenty-four marks,' said Ulrich. His suspicion and annoyance had vanished as soon as Ernst had sauntered over to him.

Ernst's eyes sparkled. 'You are an excellent comrade, Ulrich. And now, let us retire and divide the spoils. Come. You have proved yourself trustworthy to me, now I will trust you. I will show you where I am living.'

They walked towards the edge of the park and to a patch of woodland, where Ernst told Ulrich to wait. Here he began to worry. Was this the moment the man enticed him into his lair and killed him for meat? Ulrich believed those stories and had even started to worry about Hanna. How could you not believe it happened? So many people thought so. He felt a momentary stab of shame over the way he had behaved when he heard she had gone missing.

Now Ernst was moving leaves and branches inside the trees and shrubs. By the side of a large tree with splayed roots there was a covering of green tarpaulin, which he pulled back to reveal an entrance. Ernst looked around to make sure no one was watching them, and then beckoned Ulrich to follow. Heart in his mouth, he ran up to the hole and peered inside.

'Keep your head down for a moment, and I will light a candle or two,' said Ernst.

Inside was almost comfortable. Ulrich's eyes darted around in the gloom. Wood panels, scavenged from bomb sites and battlegrounds, lined the side of the dugout. Planking formed the floor. Along from the narrow entrance, Ernst had hollowed out a space large enough for a bed and a chest of drawers. It was a remarkably sophisticated abode for a hole in the ground.

'I learned to make such a dwelling in Ostland,' said Ernst.

Ulrich was impressed with Ernst's soldiering skills. He sensed he was someone who would be able to make himself comfortable in the most spartan surroundings. Ulrich had fantasised about leading a soldier's life for all his child-hood, in the *Pimpfe* and in the Hitler Youth, and now here was a man who had put into practice all the things they had learned about in their evening meetings.

But he also felt uneasy. He felt he had been enticed into a dragon's lair. It was like something from a fairy tale. In the flickering flame of the candles he caught a glimpse of

Ernst as he really was: a sinister figure who had done terrible things and was now hiding from vengeance, and – the thought lurked in the back of Ulrich's mind – even justice. He dismissed it. This was weakness. They had all been taught to monitor their thoughts for weakness. He had been having a lot of trouble with that recently. He suspected it was too much association with the Skalitzer Hospital gang. Their kindness was weakening his resolve. Kindness was not a good quality in a political soldier. It said 'Blood and Honour' on his Hitler Youth dagger. That was what had taken the German army to the banks of the Volga and the shores of the Arctic Ocean. There was no room for kindness in 'Blood and Honour'. The hawk would show no kindness to the mouse in the field. It was nature's way.

'You are lost in thought, my young friend,' said Ernst.

'I was thinking of our great successes in the field of battle and how they were undone,' said Ulrich. 'I do not understand how it happened.'

'We were stabbed in the back by Jews, my friend. It is an eternal story, played out again and again in human history. And this is why we must rise up again and ensure the flame of National Socialism continues to burn in the hearts of the Master Race.'

'So what can we do?' asked Ulrich.

'We have to wait for now. Marshal our strength. Find comrades who will support us. I sense the Russians and the Western countries will soon begin to squabble. We had hoped, as I'm sure you realise, that this would happen before the end of the war. But it did not. But time is on our side, and very soon armed struggle will commence between our conquerors. It is inevitable. And the Jews on both sides will see that it happens. There is profit in war. And they will warm their hands on the flames of battle.'

Ulrich was taken aback by this speech. It was the sort of thing Reich Minister Goebbels said to them on the radio in the closing months of the war. But it was good to hear such stirring words again, and good to know that some Berliners still had a steely sense of purpose in their hearts.

'Let us divide the spoils. Let me count your takings, young Ulrich.'

While Ernst tallied up the money, Ulrich continued to look around this cluttered lair. A field-glasses case hung from a nail on the wall. The name 'STANDARTEN-FÜHRER ERNST BARTH' was stencilled neatly on to the khaki material. Ulrich's heart quickened. Was this the Ernst he was talking to now? Instinct told him not to ask. He had never spoken to someone of such high rank before. But looking at him, and the way he carried himself, Ulrich could believe it.

There were 224 marks, and Ernst was scrupulous in his division of the money. When he had divided the pile of notes he gave Ulrich an extra twenty marks from his pile.

'You have done well, young comrade,' he said. 'Now, we shall drink a toast to our partnership.' He took out a bottle of schnapps from a canvas bag and filled two shot glasses.

'To our final victory,' he said. Ulrich knocked his glass back, feeling very grown up. The fiery liquid made him cough a little but it settled in his stomach with a warm glow, and immediately he began to feel very proud of himself.

'You must return to your friends,' said Ernst. 'But here are two more packets of cigarettes. Come to see me tomorrow. And look, here is a loaf of bread –' he reached into another bag '– which I picked up this morning. Keep yourself strong, Ulrich.'

The house on Muskauer Strasse was barely ten minutes from the hospital, and when Ulrich returned from his rendezvous with Ernst he decided to see the *Panzerfaust* rockets Klaus and Erich had told him about for himself. The building was exactly how the twins had described it. Clearly it had been hard fought over and was now a sinister wreck. Good German soldiers had died here fighting for the Fatherland, thought Ulrich, so it was only right that the house should provide him with the opportunity to avenge their deaths. He picked his way through debris and tried to ignore the hideous stench of decay and human waste that invariably filled a house like this. The basement staircase was at the back of the house, and sure enough, in the gloom of the late afternoon, he could see a wooden *Panzerfaust* box lying flat on the floor among a pile of other boxes.

Ulrich's instincts told him he should not disturb this scene unless he really had to. But just to be sure the twins' claim was not just foolish boasting, he lifted the lid a little. That familiar smell of wood, steel and oil seeped out. The silver head of a projectile glowed in the dim light. All four of them were there. What fantastic luck.

As he walked home he turned his mind to transporting one of these missiles through the streets of Berlin. They were too big to hide under a coat and carrying one in the open would invite instant arrest or even execution.

While crossing Waldemarstrasse he heard the mournful sound of a cello drifting from an upper window. He stopped to listen, ears straining. Was this Jewish music? He had been caught once listening to a Felix Mendelssohn violin concerto on the school gramophone player. He had found the record in the back of a cupboard and he put it on out of random curiosity and was transfixed by the haunting melody. His teacher, a stern but beautiful woman who supervised the League of German Maidens cohort at his school, had come in and asked him what he thought. Ulrich was not a great lover of music, but afraid of looking ignorant, he said it was very moving. The teacher looked on him with scorn and announced that Mendelssohn was an infamous Jew, and what did he think he was doing listening to this Yiddish tripe. Ulrich burned with shame at the memory. It was not just the fact that he had been caught listening; he knew in his heart he had enjoyed it.

Then he realised in an instant how he was going to get that *Panzerfaust* away from the house. He needed a musical instrument case – one for a cello would be exactly right.

There was a music conservatoire over in Kottbusser Damm. It was a derelict shambles of course, but perhaps there would be some instrument cases there, still intact. It was the perfect solution.

Ulrich was lucky, although he was surprised to discover how heavy a padded wooden cello case actually was. He returned to Muskauer Strasse with it a week later to pick up one of the rockets. It was a tense business removing it from the case. Like all *Volkssturm* veterans he knew a box like this was likely to be a booby trap. But he had taken some matches and lit them one after the other, carefully studying the rockets for wires before he gingerly lifted his one out of the box and into the cello case.

Then he waited and sneaked back to the hospital when he knew the others would be out. Somewhere at the back of the basement, there was a courtyard where a battered old cello case would not be noticed among the general debris. He would be ready for that parade.

CHAPTER 16

Otto returned footsore and thirsty from the market, with a small loaf of bread, all he had managed to exchange for a pair of shoes. He thought sadly of the time he and Helene had taken Hanna there and how tired she had been. He missed her more than he ever expected. Every morning when he woke up, she was the first person he thought of. Was she still alive? Every street he walked down he hoped to see her. But it had been over a week now and she had still not returned.

The day had started bright but now it was humid and heavy. There was a small queue at the water pump at the top of Oranienstrasse and Otto thought it best to refill his water bottle there. That was how to get by with the minimum amount of effort, he thought to himself. Take every opportunity you can.

As he sat on a wall overlooking a bomb site, eyeing approaching thunderclouds and wondering too if there was anything edible growing in the vegetation that was sprouting through the rubble, an arm snaked around his neck and he was pulled roughly to the ground.

'You again,' said an angry voice. A swift kick to his body winded him and as he gathered his senses he recognised the thugs who were attacking him. It was Konrad and his gang.

Before he could wriggle free, he was dragged by the neck inside a derelict apartment block, his legs kicking wildly to take the pressure off his throat. As one of the youths held him tightly Konrad held a Hitler Youth dagger right next to his throat. He saw it glint in the light and understood at once it had been sharpened to a lethal edge.

Otto could feel his heart beating hard in his chest. He tried with all his strength to break free but he was held in an iron grip.

'Shall we kill him?' said the boy holding him from behind.

'Yeah, why not,' sneered the blond boy, his eyes glinting maliciously.

Otto felt the blade slice his neck, and cried out in pain. But it was only a flesh wound, no deeper than a paper cut.

'Ha, you pissed your pants,' said the youth in front of him. Two other boys, who stood watching, sniggered.

But Otto had done no such thing. The boy was just tormenting him like a classroom bully.

'You bled on my shirt,' said the boy behind him. 'Look, Konrad,' he said in a horrible sing-song whiney voice. 'Look what this little turd has done to my shirt.'

Konrad held the knife point on Otto's windpipe. 'Take your shirt off,' he said.

Otto undid the buttons carefully, his eyes not leaving the knife. When he had done so, Konrad said, 'And the rest.' Otto's hands were slick with sweat. Were these boys really going to kill him?

He took his shoes off and then his trousers, and when the knife pressed harder into his throat, he took off his underpants. This was like one of those dreams he had had as a child, where he had stood naked in a school assembly, burning with embarrassment.

'Look, he's got a watch,' scoffed Konrad, when he took his shirt and found it in the top pocket. The other boys whooped with glee.

'You bastards,' snarled Otto. He could not suppress his anger. Then he pleaded. 'Please don't take my watch. My father gave it to me.'

In response, the boy behind cuffed him hard across the top of the head, then let go. The gang ran off with his clothes, his water bottle, his watch, and his little loaf of bread.

Otto lay for a moment behind the wall, stunned by this sudden turn of events. His watch was his most treasured possession. It was a direct link to his father. It was irreplaceable. In that moment he had never felt more miserable in his life.

The sun went in as the thunderclouds rolled across it. He realised he was covered with anxious sweat and the drop in temperature made him shiver. Maybe he was shaking too from fear.

What on earth was he going to do? He was at least two kilometres from home and stark naked. He lay there trying to choke back the sobs that rose from inside his chest. He would have to be bold and just brazen it out.

He stood up from behind the wall, in view of everyone else out on the street. A woman shrieked in shock and two children pointed and sniggered. A deep hot blush rose in him and his face felt as if it were burning. Otto took a deep breath. This was the most embarrassing thing that had ever happened to him. 'I have had my clothes stolen,' he shouted angrily at anyone who looked at him. Even in Berlin a naked boy wandering the street was something you didn't see every day.

As he gingerly picked his way home he was grateful the streets at least had been cleared of rubble and although the ground was painful on his bare feet, it could have been much worse. At Moritzplatz crossroad a policeman saw him and hurried over.

'What do you think you're doing?' he demanded.

Otto covered himself as best he could. 'My clothes have been stolen. This gang . . .'

'Well you can't just walk around naked,' the policeman spluttered.

Otto was speechless. *What else am I supposed to do?* he was bursting to say, but he sensed this would not help.

Help, though, did come from another quarter.

'Excuse me, *Herr Wachtmeister*,' said a familiar voice, addressing the policeman with studied formality. 'I know this young man and I can help him.'

The policeman stepped back and nodded his head. He had recognised an authoritative voice and responded to it. The new arrival was Dr Holzman. He was wearing a light linen suit, which was now rather grubby, and a panama hat. He looked like a man who had not slept for three days. Otto felt his blush returning.

'I've been robbed, *Herr Doktor*,' he said. 'They took everything.'

'Evidently,' said Holzman, a smile playing around his lips. '*Herr Wachtmeister*, I have a suggestion. This young man can have my trousers for his journey home. I will still be decently clothed although I will look a little ridiculous. But at least Otto here will retain some of his dignity.'

The policeman nodded, thanked the doctor for his kindness and went on his way.

As soon as the policeman was out of sight, Otto's gratefulness bubbled over. 'You are very generous, *Herr Doktor*,' he said. 'I really don't know what I would have done if you hadn't arrived.'

Holzman smiled. 'Well, we both look a little absurd now but no matter. You are lucky our paths crossed on my day off.'

They walked along in awkward silence. People stared, of course. But they no longer shrieked or pointed.

'The whole world is absurd at the moment,' Holzman mused. 'Do you know what I heard just last week? Two of my colleagues at the clinic, where as you can imagine we are ludicrously busy, were removed to work with the

Trümmerfrauen. The Americans discovered they were former SS doctors and wanted to punish them. So now they have taken them off their highly skilled work helping the sick and they toil alongside the women carrying away our rubble. The stupidity is extraordinary. But here's a thing – d'you know, the two doctors don't care. The clinic is hell on earth. Exhausting. We work twelve, fourteen hours non-stop. Many times a day you are called upon to make decisions which could be a matter of life or death. Now they are out in the sunshine, they are fed a decent ration, and best of all they can sneak away with firewood at the end of the day. But having them gone makes life more difficult for the rest of us, as I'm sure you can imagine.'

Otto felt embarrassed – he hadn't spoken to an adult in a long time and this talk of colleagues and work seemed so remote and unimportant. He didn't know what to say.

'But no matter,' said Holzman, filling in the conversation with practised ease. 'How is your charming friend Helene, and lovely Hanna?'

Otto was amazed to see how Holzman had remembered their names, and told him Hanna had disappeared. The doctor's concern was clear. 'You have heard the rumours, of course,' he said sadly. Otto nodded. 'Well, we must hope they are not true,' he said. 'So what else did they take from you?'

'My watch.' Otto felt tears well in his eyes. He stopped for a moment. 'My water bottle and a loaf I had. It's all we have to eat tonight.'

'Well, don't worry. I have a loaf you can have. You must not go hungry.'

Otto had disliked him instinctively when they had first met, but now he was moved by the doctor's generosity. 'Thank you so much.'

When they reached the hospital, Holzman said he would come with him and reclaim his trousers. They walked in to incredulous looks from Helene and the twins. Ulrich laughed but showed concern as soon as he noticed the cut on Otto's throat. Helene went to their Winter Relief store and returned with a pair of trousers and a rough workman's shirt.

Otto dressed quickly and said, 'I'm sorry. It was that gang again. They took everything I had.' Their faces fell.

Holzman put his trousers back on and smiled. 'I will be back shortly with something for you.' With that, he turned and left, inclining his panama hat toward Helene as he did.

'Otto, those *Arschlöcher* have it in for us,' said Helene, wringing her hands together. 'Maybe we need to avoid them for a while – keep out of their territory.'

They looked shocked. It was not like Helene to use such language.

'Ulrich – those boys are older and stronger than you,' said Otto. 'You can swagger all you like, but I don't want them to kill you. And don't think they won't.'

Helene came over to Otto and put an arm around his shoulder to show her support. 'Otto is right. I don't want you getting killed trying to prove how tough you are.'

Ulrich was seething. 'You have no fighting spirit,' he spat.

'Ulrich, when will you drop this Nazi nonsense?' said Helene. She was getting angry too. 'Look around our ruined city. Millions of us living in holes in the ground. That's where your fighting spirit got us.'

Holzman's return brought an end to their angry exchange. He left a soft brown loaf and a small Emmentaler cheese wrapped in wax paper – which was gone almost before they could thank him.

'I think we have been wrong about the doctor,' said Helene as he left again. 'I think he is a good man trying to do the right thing. Thank heavens there are still good people in the world.'

CHAPTER 17

Mid August

When Ulrich had sold his final pack of cigarettes Ernst had invited him once more into his underground hideout. 'We shall do something special tonight,' said Ernst. He brought out a bottle of Bärenjäger – a honey liqueur – which Ulrich found delicious, and they drank a toast. 'Now, the Russians have provided us with tonight's banquet,' said Ernst, and unwrapped a loaf of black bread and a jar of caviar. There was also a small bottle of vodka to go with it.

Ulrich didn't really enjoy the salty taste of the little eggs on the bread but he was so hungry he wolfed them down. The vodka helped mask the flavour. He didn't like its sharp taste either, and the way it burned his throat, but the more he drank the more he liked the way it made him feel. After they'd eaten, what he really wanted to do was sing the Hitler Youth songs they had always sung at the end of the evening: 'When Jewish blood spurts from the knife, things go twice as well', 'The Horst Wessel Song', and especially 'Germany Awake'.

He started to hum them, hoping Ernst would join in. Instead, he put a hand on Ulrich's shoulder and said,

'We must be careful, young friend. I do not want people to hear us.'

Ulrich stared into the blank wooden walls of the bunker and wondered when he would ever be able to sing these heart-stirring songs again.

He had never seen Ernst drink so much. He seemed keen to talk and began to tell Ulrich about his time on the Eastern Front. 'What a war that was. To begin with we had victory after victory. Some days from dawn to dusk we would advance a hundred kilometres. I rose from *Leutnant* to *Standartenführer* in the first two years of the campaign. But survival in war, young man, is a matter of sheer luck. I firmly believe if you have a shell or a bullet with your name on it, then there is nothing you can do. I never did. But I have been in trenches where the man next to me was shot by a sniper. Why did the Ivan choose him and not me? I left a command bunker once and thirty seconds later a shell landed right on top of it. Right on top. Everyone inside was killed. Those things happened all the time in Ostland.'

An hour of such reminiscences passed, during which Ulrich listened in wide-eyed admiration. Ernst took another slug of vodka straight from the bottle, and let out a sigh. 'It is good to talk of these things, young comrade,' he said. 'But tell me about you and your friends back at the hospital.'

Ulrich told him everything. About Otto and his girl-friend, Helene, and how they were weak and showed kindness to useless eaters, and about Erich and Klaus, and how they liked to blow up discarded munitions. Ulrich expected Ernst to disapprove, but he laughed indulgently. 'I expect I would be doing that if I was fourteen years old,' he said. And he mentioned Dr Holzman, who had befriended them all. Ulrich didn't trust him. Ernst suggested that perhaps he had an eye on Helene. But upon hearing that Holzman worked for the Russians, in a hospital, and seemed very well connected, Ernst pressed Ulrich for details. Ulrich racked his brains. What else could he tell the *Standartenführer*? Holzman was interested in art and antiques, he remembered, and paintings. He knew people among the enemy who would pay great sums of money for art treasures.

Ernst was listening very intently. He seemed to light up inside at this piece of intelligence. 'I have something the good *Doktor* might find of interest,' he said. 'Perhaps you could arrange for us to meet?'

'I don't know where he lives,' said Ulrich. 'But I will find out. What do you have? He will want to know, I'm sure.'

Ernst's eyes darted from left to right. 'Tell him . . . tell him I have some drawings by a famous artist. From the Renaissance. German, of course. That should be enough.'

Ulrich tried to look impressed, but the word 'Renaissance' meant little to him. 'Yes, I'll tell him,' he said.

Ernst was staring at him hard, looking right into him. He could tell, of course, that Ulrich was not impressed with this revelation. He wiped his mouth from his latest vodka mouthful. Then he nodded to himself and did something that astonished Ulrich. 'Look, I will show you,' he said quietly.

He pulled up a floorboard and then began digging down with a small trenching tool. Perhaps twenty centimetres down he pulled on a canvas strap and a cylindrical metal gas-mask container emerged. In the candlelight he brushed off the soil and carefully undid the clasps that held the lid in place. Carefully shaking off any remaining soil from his hands, he slowly pulled a tightly coiled roll of parchment from within.

Ulrich stared into the gloom. The drawings were beautiful – a stork, an owl and a parrot – each one rendered in exquisite detail. Even he could see they were made by someone who was a master of his craft.

'These, my friend, are very valuable,' said Ernst.

'And how old are they?' said Ulrich.

'They are by Albrecht Dürer. Around 1500, I think. They are over four hundred years old. Imagine that. You have heard of Albrecht Dürer, of course.'

Not wanting to appear foolish, Ulrich nodded, though for all he knew Dürer played for FC Nürnberg.

Ernst chuckled to himself. 'And here they are, wrapped in a tube, buried beneath the park. It's a strange world, isn't it?'

Then his genial air vanished in an instant. He looked very stern. 'But if you betray me about this I will know and I will kill you.'

Ulrich didn't doubt it. That warm, floating feeling he had vanished in an instant. He went hot and cold, and all of a sudden everything fell into sharp focus. Then he felt a little sick.

Ernst smiled and said, 'But I do not want to kill you, Ulrich. So don't make me.' He sounded sad, almost remorseful. Then he continued, as if he had not said anything out of the ordinary: 'I came across them in Prague Castle, when I worked with Reich Minister Reinhard Heydrich. I always knew they would come in handy one of these days. And I am right. They are worth many millions of Reichsmark, for the right buyer. Or perhaps I should now be thinking of dollars. I do not know who will introduce me to such people. I am only a humble soldier. But your Doktor Holzman might be able to help?'

Ulrich felt rather speechless to be presented with such a request, especially one that came with a death threat. 'I shall make enquiries,' he said eventually, trying to sound as adult and serious as possible. All of a sudden the vodka and the caviar seemed to well up inside him. He was desperate for fresh air.

Ernst closed his eyes and remained silent. This was Ulrich's cue to leave.

He dashed through the park in the encroaching twilight, wondering if he had missed the curfew. Perhaps it was too late to be out. Hugging the shadows he reached the hospital, to be greeted by people he despised, who were pleased to see he was safe.

Ulrich woke the next day wishing he had been sick on the way home. Now he had a raging thirst and his head felt mushy. Something had happened last night, he remembered through the fug, and it had made him deeply uncomfortable. He had always been proud to be a bully – he revelled in it. His Youth leaders had called it 'fighting spirit', and throughout his childhood the urge to dominate and intimidate had been cultivated in him. Only his parents had encouraged him to moderate his behaviour. But something that Ernst had said to him last night had turned his guts to ice: he had threatened to kill him. And the way he had looked him in the eye and said it very calmly had made the threat even more chilling. This was no schoolyard taunt. This was a plain statement of intent by someone who was no stranger to murder. Ulrich thought of all the weaklings he'd bullied at school, those bespectacled boys whose lives he'd made a misery, and he began to feel uneasy. He did not like this feeling. Thoughts of his father rose again to the surface before he could stop them. What if he had been wrong to report his father for lack of fighting spirit during the battle for Berlin? Then that voice, the voice of Nazi ideology, came through loud and clear. Ulrich was just being weak. And weakness does not deserve to conquer the world.

Ulrich did not like Dr Holzman. He doubted his motives and was convinced he was Jewish. Everything about him pointed to it – he was shifty, he was smarmy, and even his name sounded suspicious. And after his conversation with Ernst he was sure he had his eye on Helene. But today, when the doctor turned up at the hospital late that morning to ask if there was any news about Hanna, Ulrich was surprised to find he was pleased to see him.

Holzman responded to Ulrich's smile with kindness. 'Hello, young man,' he said.

Ulrich decided he would have to be bold, and followed him out into the corridor so they could speak alone. '*Herr Doktor*, may I ask your advice?'

Holzman gave him an open smile.

Ulrich felt uneasy. He was way out of his depth and felt unusually tongue-tied. Staring at the ground, he began to speak: 'I have a friend –' his stomach tightened '– someone who has something –' he could sense Holzman shifting, getting restless '– something of great value.' He took a deep breath and it all came out: 'I know you have an interest in antiques. I am asking if you would know what it might be worth. And especially, I am asking if you know anyone who might want to buy it?'

Holzman's interest had returned. Ulrich could sense it in his posture. But he was trying hard to present a poker face. Ulrich had expected him to look surprised, but he didn't. Instead, he stared blankly. 'And what is this object?' he asked.

'Not "object", several drawings. I think they are by Albert Dürer,' stuttered Ulrich. He found himself blushing.

Holzman couldn't help but raise an eyebrow. 'Dürer?' Then he laughed. 'If they are by Albert Dürer I'm not interested. Are you sure that's the right name?'

In a flash it came to Ulrich. 'Albrecht,' he spat, before the name could escape him again.

Holzman had his serious face on. He was looking at

Ulrich with a quiet intensity. 'If you would like to tell me more, or indeed introduce me to your friend, then I might be able to help you further,' he said carefully.

'I will talk to him about it,' Ulrich said. He smiled to himself. How fortuitous that he knew someone who could be helpful to Ernst. Perhaps once Ernst had sold the drawings they could use the money to help the Werewolf resistance, if he was ever lucky enough to make contact with them.

When Ulrich returned to the park that afternoon he was full of excitement. Ernst was there waiting on the usual grassy bank. Ulrich imagined he would be happy to see him after their comradely meal together, but Ernst was looking stern. He leaned in close enough for Ulrich to recoil from his harsh breath and spoke in a threatening whisper. 'Last night I was foolish,' he said. 'I showed you something I should not have showed you. Do you understand?'

Ernst was holding his arm in a vice-like grip. Ulrich nodded. His throat had gone terribly dry.

'If you tell anyone, anyone at all, about this, I will kill you. There are only two people in Berlin who know I have these drawings. You and me. I want to keep it like that. I will make my own enquiries. I will not need you to help me. Is that clear?'

Ulrich felt his stomach turn over. He began to tremble. 'You are hurting my arm,' he managed to say.

Ernst's eyes glittered with malice. 'Good. And I will hurt you a great deal more if you tell anyone.'

They sat there in silence, Ulrich's heart beating hard in his chest. He had not been so frightened since the battle for Berlin back in May.

'Now, come back tomorrow and I will send you to the market with more goods to trade. You may go.'

Ulrich didn't know if he would be able to stand up, but he surprised himself and managed to walk off. His mind was in turmoil. There would certainly be no more cosy chats in the hideaway. And what was he going to say to Dr Holzman?

CHAPTER 18

'We're going to the parade,' announced Otto over their meagre breakfast a few days later.

'Who's coming?'

The British and Americans had announced a victory parade to celebrate the end of the war. In the Far East, Germany's ally Japan had surrendered. The world war was finally over.

Erich and Klaus looked undecided. 'The Japs weren't much use to us,' said Klaus.

'Better than the Italians,' said Erich. 'At least they didn't change sides.'

'The Italians weren't stupid enough to fight to the end like we did,' said Otto. 'I'll bet Rome is still in one piece.'

'Come on,' said Helene. 'Let's take another look at our new overlords. It's not as if there's anything else we can do for entertainment.'

'OK,' said the twins.

Otto looked at Ulrich with a sceptical expression, and Ulrich suppressed the rant that was forming in his head about the Americans. He kept his council and said,

'I am not coming. I have no intention of honouring our conquerors with my presence.'

'Good,' said Otto. 'I'd be worried you'd start a fight or get us all arrested.'

Helene put a hand on Otto's arm. 'No quarrelling, boys,' she said wearily. As they left, Ulrich gave them all a sly smile. He looked especially at his brother and wondered if he would ever see him again. Ulrich could never imagine Otto appearing in a history book. He was too fragile. The next time Otto heard *his* name, he would be a hero of the new German resistance. He liked the idea of that.

Ten minutes after they left he went at once to pick up his cello case from the back of the hospital. It was a back-breaking combination, the wooden case and the *Panzerfaust*. He was quite surprised. He'd always thought the boys who played musical instruments at school were soft – unless it was trumpets and drums in the Hitler Youth, and even those ones seemed a little soft. But you had to be pretty strong to cart a cello case around, it seemed.

Ulrich marched up Oranienstrasse into the centre of Berlin, pausing every few hundred metres to rest when the canvas straps on his case began to really dig into his shoulders. At first he was disappointed to see how many fellow Berliners were going into town. He thought they ought to have stayed at home and ignored the Americans. But then he realised that the more Berliners there were, the greater his audience. He thought little of what he was about to do – keeping his mind carefully blank. Did German soldiers worry about being killed before they went into battle? No – they thought only of their duty and the glory they would bring to the Reich. Ulrich had been taught the slogan 'We were born to die for Germany' since he was a little boy and he was quite prepared to do it. Still, as he rested at the edge of a bombed-out square, drenched with sweat in what was turning into a hot summer day, he found himself tormented by regretful thoughts that buzzed around him like flies. If he managed to fire his rocket and then melt into the crowd then he would be able to fight another day. That was the ideal outcome. But if he was killed in this action he would never again feel the sensation of the hot sun on his face, or the cool relief of a swim in a lake. He would never enjoy a succulent roast and he would never know what it was like to kiss a girl . . . he shooed those thoughts away like he would an irritating cat pestering him for attention.

'Going to a music lesson are you, mummy's boy?' said a sneering voice.

It was Konrad and three of his gang.

Ulrich jutted out his chin and stared them out, cursing the fact he had not brought his Hitler Youth dagger with him.

'He's a tough one, for a mummy's boy,' said one of them.

Konrad grabbed Ulrich by the chin and looked him straight in the eye. 'Who the hell is teaching someone to play a cello in this hellhole?' he said. 'And why would you even be thinking of learning?'

He let go and the others began to push and prod him. 'Play us a little tune, mummy's boy,' they said. Ulrich wriggled out of the canvas straps and crouched ready to spring as the boys continued to circle him at a careful distance.

'You are a brave boy,' said Konrad. 'You should join us. Leave those little mice we usually see you with.'

'Only if you are prepared to carry on fighting for the Fatherland,' said Ulrich.

Their reaction surprised him. They all began to laugh – genuine, incredulous laugher. 'You still believe in all that crap?' said Konrad. 'Forget it, you're too stupid for us. Go on, run away.' He waved his hands contemptuously. 'Go on, piss off back to your mummy . . .'

'Then let me take my cello,' said Ulrich.

Konrad was losing his patience. 'Make the most of this opportunity, little boy. We won't let you go so easily if we have to tell you again.'

Ulrich wasn't going to run, even though his heart was thumping hard in his chest. He put down the case and walked away from them, not even speeding up when a stone skidded past his feet. When he was a safe distance away he started to hear a splintering, thumping sound. The gang had started to hit the case with iron pipes. They had not even bothered to open it. As though in a daze, he realised he ought to go back and warn them in case the *Panzerfaust* detonated.

But he did not. Instead he turned to watch from a distance, standing out in the open so they could see him, but far enough away to outrun them if they decided to chase after him.

All at once, the banging stopped. The foulest language drifted over. The boys began to run towards him, clearly expecting the case to explode at any second. Ulrich took off and easily outran them, quickly losing himself in a maze of rubble and derelict buildings.

When he was sure they had given up trying to find him, he bided his time, slowly making his way back to the square where they had stopped him. The cello case was broken enough to see inside through splits in the wood, but it was still intact. He was too late for the parade now, so he would come back later that afternoon with an old coat to wrap around the case and hide its contents, and a leather belt to hold it all together. Then he could take it back to the hospital.

Ulrich was surprised at how he was feeling. He should be bitterly disappointed, having screwed up his courage to carry out his heroic act of resistance, and then been thwarted. But he wasn't. Instead, he kept grinning, thinking of the faces of those stupid boys, when they realised the cello case they were hitting had a *Panzerfaust* in it. He thought that was a story that would make Klaus and Erich howl with laughter – not that he could ever tell them. Today he was not going to die, and he told himself he was quite prepared to wait until another opportunity came his way.

As he returned to the hospital he felt the sun on the back of his neck. It was such a lovely feeling. Then he noticed a couple of pretty girls his age looking at him as he passed, whispering and giggling. He was confident enough to realise they were admiring him. He thought they were empty-headed, silly little things, just as the Führer had described, but a part of him also flushed with pride at the reaction he'd provoked. As he walked past Waldeckpark on the way home, he noticed how the sun danced on the different shades of green in the trees and his eye caught a red squirrel as it leapt from one branch to another. For a moment he stood transfixed by the simple beauty of the world, even in the terrible ruins of his shattered city. He had never thought like this before. But then, he had never been so certain he was going to die, even when he was fighting the Russians in the closing days of the war.

CHAPTER 19

Later that week Otto asked Ulrich to come with him to the Tiergarten market. He had found some china plates in a bombed-out house – pretty hand-painted porcelain – and just the thing a discerning Yank or Tommy might exchange for food or cigarettes. Ulrich's reluctance surprised him.

'I know we have made some enemies with the other boys,' Otto said. 'But Ulrich, we have to eat. I'm prepared to go on my own but I'd much rather have you with me to ward off the wolves.' Otto knew Ulrich well enough to know how he responded to flattery.

'Very well,' he said. 'I will come too.'

Sure enough, an American officer thought the plates worth a packet of Chesterfields, although Ulrich's insistence that they were worth five packets nearly lost them the sale. The boys split the packet in two to set about selling them individually. But before they could start they noticed some familiar faces fifteen or so metres ahead in the milling crowd.

'It's them, Ulrich,' said Otto, recognising the gang that had attacked him the other day. 'It's the boys who took all my clothes and stole my watch.'

'Go south through the park,' hissed Ulrich, 'and maybe they won't see us.'

Otto didn't dare look behind him but he began to hear catcalls. '*Scheisse*, they've spotted us,' he cried.

'Head for the Flak Tower,' said Ulrich. 'There will be people there. Less chance they will attack where there are people.'

Outside the market the park was thinly populated that late afternoon, and as Otto and Ulrich hurried south to the huge Flak Tower by Zoo Station they broke into a run. Otto was tired and light-headed after the exhausting walk into town but fear kept him going. The Flak Tower was a great grey concrete monolith, built earlier in the war as an air-raid shelter and platform for anti-aircraft guns. It had also been used as a last-ditch strongpoint when the Russians arrived and was now pockmarked by shell blasts. But it still looked as solid as the day it had been completed. There was a hospital here, on the second of six storeys, and Otto and Ulrich slipped in with a crowd of other shabbily dressed Berliners there to visit patients. Inside the hospital it was dank and smelled like a drain. The light from low-watt bulbs and small windows with metal shutters was as grim and grey as the exterior.

'Do you know this place?' asked Otto. 'I've never been here before.'

Ulrich nodded. 'Yes, I worked with a Flak squad a few times. Keep going up. There is a machine room on the fifth floor. That will be the best place to hide. They will never find us there.'

They hurried up the concrete stairwell to the second floor, where there were American soldiers standing guard. A long line of visitors stood patiently awaiting entry to the hospital wards.

'Let's go further up,' said Ulrich. Otto was happy to let his younger brother tell him what to do. He had the fighter instinct for survival, and this was no time to argue.

When they got to the fifth floor they were in for a shock. The cavernous machine room was almost empty.

'What's the point of coming here?' said Otto angrily, his voice echoing across the bare concrete walls.

Ulrich was looking around – astonished at the sight that confronted him.

'It was full of machinery last time I was here,' said Ulrich. 'Generators, water tanks, ventilation fans, electrical junction boxes . . .' He seemed as surprised as his brother. 'The Ivans must have stripped out the machinery, like they have with every factory in the city.'

All that was left was the remains of the tower's ventilation and heating system. The boiler was gone but the ventilation pipes – big metal ducts suspended from the ceiling and already starting to rust – were still in place.

Now there were multiple footsteps behind them, running up the stairs.

'The roof?' said Otto, turning round wildly.

'No, that's where they'll expect us to go,' said Ulrich.

'In these pipes, then?'

There was a duct hood about two metres above the floor, which quickly turned at a right angle along a shaft held in place with thin metal struts.

'Let me hop on your shoulders, Ulrich,' said Otto. 'I'll get up there and then I'll help you get inside.'

The footsteps on the stairs were getting nearer.

Ulrich lifted Otto up first, struggling with his weight. Otto scrambled inside the duct, and balanced himself on the rim that ran around the bottom. He bent down and caught Ulrich's outstretched arm. Otto realised how much weaker he was now, after months of barely enough to eat, but he just managed to haul him up. The piping creaked a little but it seemed sturdy enough to take their weight.

There was a strong metallic smell inside the shaft, as well as something musty and animal-like. Otto tried hard not to retch. Together they squeezed past the right angle and lay still, side by side, along the pipe. As Otto peered along its length he could see the odd shaft of light through empty screw holes and cracks. Otherwise it was an ominous black void. Up ahead there was a scratching noise.

'Someone else is in here,' Otto whispered.

Ulrich put a finger to his lips.

Moments later they heard footsteps, and loud voices echoed around the room.

'They can't be in here, Konrad,' said one. 'It's too obvious.'

'No, they will have gone to the roof,' said another.

'Let's throw them off.'

'See what they are carrying first.' They recognised that voice. It was Konrad.

'We'll throw that dark-haired one off, but let's keep the other. He could be one of us, you said so yourself.'

'Not after that stunt with the *Panzerfaust*,' said Konrad. 'That crazy little shit nearly killed us all.'

Otto didn't understand what he meant, but concentrated on keeping very still.

Then they heard a voice up close. It sounded like one of the boys was standing right under the vent and shouting into it like a megaphone.

'Are you up there, *Idioten*?'

The rest of them started to laugh hysterically.

Otto looked over in the dim light at Ulrich's face. He had his determined scowl, the one he put on when he was trying to be brave. But his eyes were darting to and fro, and Otto could sense his fear.

'Hey, Gunter, give me a leg up, in case they've gone up here,' they heard Konrad say.

'No, they wouldn't be so stupid. Come on. We're wasting our time.'

Something furry brushed against Otto's leg. He stiffened but managed to stop himself shouting out. Then he felt a sharp pain on the end of his outstretched finger and yelped.

The intruders shouted with glee. They gathered around the vent and howled and barked like a pack of dogs. One of them ran a broom handle along the length of the pipe.

'We're going to rip you to little pieces,' said one in a sing-song voice. A couple of others were using the foulest language to describe exactly what they would do to Otto and Ulrich when they winkled them out of the pipe.

There was a scrabbling and banging and Otto looked down the pipe, past his feet to the vent entrance. He was horrified to see a face peering at him with a look of malevolent glee. It was him, the blond boy Konrad. 'You amateurs,' he laughed. 'This is just too easy!'

Otto kicked out with all his strength, and Konrad fell back howling in pain.

'My nose! That little shit broke my nose.'

'We'll smoke them out,' said one. 'Set them on fire.'

'There's some sacking in the corner – that'll do. Gunter, give me your lighter.'

Was this how they were going to die? Set alight or choked to death by smoke from oily rags? Otto's fear was over-ridden by outrage. 'We should fight them, rather than let them do this.'

Ulrich nodded and tensed, ready to leap from the duct.

Then Otto and Ulrich heard another angry voice – this one belonging to an adult. 'You boys, get out of here. Get out before I have you all arrested.'

Otto put a hand on Ulrich's shoulder. 'Wait a minute,' he said.

There was someone else there too – an American soldier

probably. He seemed very angry too, although they couldn't understand what he was saying.

The boys stopped immediately. 'Yes, sir, we will go at once,' someone said.

Footsteps receded. Otto and Ulrich stayed still for another twenty minutes, covered in nervous sweat.

'Do you think they've gone?' said Ulrich.

'Let's go,' Otto said. 'We have to hope those *Arschlöcher* aren't hanging around outside.'

They crept cautiously out of the Flak Tower and kept to the roads to the south of the park, avoiding their usual route. Every time they saw a group of boys, they darted into a doorway. But none were from Konrad's gang. It looked like the soldiers had really scared them off.

Otto asked, 'What was that talk about a *Panzerfaust* all about?'

'I don't have the first idea what they were talking about,' Ulrich said firmly, not meeting his eye.

Otto didn't believe him. Hadn't he heard Klaus and Erich talking about finding some *Panzerfäuste* recently? But he was too tired to argue.

Konrad could tell that the American soldier and his German colleague were both wary. He guessed they could tell these boys were more than just casual delinquents, and tried to hide the smirk that played around his lips. The soldier was trying to act tough, determined to show the boys he meant business, and had attached a bayonet to the end of his rifle.

Konrad sensed being tough was something that did not come naturally to him. They would let them go as soon as he showed them his papers. Konrad was sure of that.

The older policeman began to berate them. 'I've had a bellyful of people like you,' he said. 'You Nazi thugs. I know your type. You've lost the war. You are no longer in charge of Germany.'

Konrad knew all they had to do was keep their traps shut. But Gunter rose to the bait. 'Piss off, you old git,' he said under his breath. The policeman bristled but he did not hit him. Konrad wondered if they should just make a run for it, while these two were afraid to push them too hard. But there was a rifle and a bayonet to contend with. 'Let's be sensible,' he said to Gunter quietly.

When the gang reached the exit to the Flak Tower the policeman demanded to see their identification papers. If they were going to run, this was the time to do it. But Konrad quickly realised why the policeman had chosen his moment. There were several other police and American soldiers there at the exit. He was going to have to bluff his way out.

Konrad swaggered to the front and presented his stolen Danish slave labourer's identification card. 'So, you're Danish,' said the policeman with a poker face. 'And the rest of you? You don't sound Danish.'

'They don't have cards,' said Konrad. 'Lost in the chaos of the occupation, but they are all comrades of mine.'

'*Du er dansk?*' said the American soldier, in Danish. It was similar enough to German for Konrad to understand what the man was asking. The soldier was grinning ear to ear, looking like he was quite prepared to forgive their loutish behaviour. He turned to the policeman and said, 'My family came over to the States from Denmark in 1904. We all speak Danish back home in Minnesota.'

Konrad felt light-headed. He sensed the bluster and cockiness of his gang evaporate around him.

The soldier turned to Konrad and put out his hand. '*Mit navn er Niels Mikkelsen!*' Then he started speaking very fast.

Konrad stared at him blankly, shaking his hand and feigning a casual arrogance. '*Ja, ja,*' he said.

'*Så hvor er du fra?*' said the soldier. He was looking confused now. He could tell something wasn't right.

'He's no more Danish than you are,' he said to the policeman in German. 'I want to take the whole lot down to the police station.'

'Good. I will come too,' said the policeman. 'Well, this is a good day's work.'

The soldier cocked his rifle and prodded Konrad with the tip of his bayonet. Not enough to draw blood, but enough to let them all know he'd kill them if there was any trouble.

Down at the police station Konrad was interviewed alone by two serious-looking German detectives and the American soldier who had arrested them. Niels Mikkelsen had met some Danish boys a couple of days earlier, he told the detectives. They were still waiting to go home and they had told him a terrible tale that had upset him greatly.

Their friend had been murdered soon after the Russians arrived. His identification card had been stolen. They suspected a tall, blond Hitler Youth boy who was hiding in their block but who vanished on the day of the murder.

Konrad could see a photograph of the boy he had killed there among the papers spread out on the desk they had sat him at. He could already feel the rough hemp of the hangman's noose around his neck.

CHAPTER 20

Back at Skalitzer Strasse, none of them had the courage to return to the Tiergarten after the incident at the Flak Tower. But the streets in the sector around them were really coming back to life now, and it was common to see people setting up stalls on the side of the road, trading family treasures and food. The bartering was slower than the hurly-burly of the Tiergarten but they still managed to trade goods for bread, cheese and sausage. But three days later, their food supplies were running low again. And now there was a more serious problem to contend with.

'Otto, what the hell has happened to your finger?' said Erich as they sat around the table at breakfast. 'You need to get something done about that.'

Otto flinched. The middle finger on his right hand had failed to heal after the rat bit it in the Flak Tower, and now the tip had swollen and turned an alarming shade of black and green. The nail seemed to be floating in a great blister of fluid and he had started to worry that he would lose it.

'I scrubbed it with soap and water. That usually does the trick,' he replied. 'I hope this will go in a few days if I can keep it clean.'

'You need antibiotics,' said Klaus. 'That'll sort your finger out.'

'Well thanks, Klaus,' said Otto. 'That's useful advice.' He might as well have suggested they airlifted him to New York for a specialist operation. The conquerors had their own priorities when it came to medical treatment and Berliners of any age were well down the list.

And antibiotics like penicillin, a new wonder drug they'd heard the British had invented during the war, were so rare in Berlin that the black market price was completely beyond their means.

'Rats, horrible things who never clean their teeth,' said Klaus. Otto managed a weak smile.

By midday Otto was beginning to feel really poorly. His finger throbbed with every beat of his heart and he was dizzy and feverish. Worst of all, that horrible black and green bruising around the wound seemed to be spreading. When Klaus and Erich announced they were going out to look for food Otto begged off, saying he felt too weak to leave the room.

They understood. 'We'll try and find you a nice bit of fresh fruit,' said Klaus. 'Get some vitamins inside you.'

None of them were ill-fed enough to be suffering from scurvy, but Otto worried that day would come soon enough.

An hour or so after the twins had left, Helene came back from her *Trümmerfrauen* work. Otto felt an almost childlike sense of relief to see her.

'Otto, my dear friend, what is wrong with you?' she said. He held up his finger. 'My God, is that gangrene?'

She held his hand tenderly and raised it to her nose. 'No, it's not that. I saw enough of it to know, when I worked on the wards. Gangrene has a very distinctive smell, and that isn't it.'

She ran out of the room, returning soon after with a nurse's cap, which she dipped in one of the buckets and began to mop his face. 'And look at you, you're covered in sweat. You have a fever.'

Otto looked up at her, framed in the late afternoon light, and thought she had never looked more beautiful.

'Lots of rest, that's what you need, young man,' she said in her officious voice, but then she leaned down and kissed him on the forehead. It was not something a nurse would do, and for a moment, Otto felt a flash of joy. He reached for her hand and fell asleep.

That night, when the others came home, they all spoke in whispers, although Otto still caught snippets of their conversation.

'Why can't we take him to a hospital?' asked Klaus.

'He's too weak to move,' said Helene. 'And it's not like we can just ring up for an ambulance.'

'We could get Holzman to look at him,' said Erich.

Helene nodded. 'Good idea, if we can find him. I'll try and track him down.'

Everyone looked back at Otto with tenderness, even Ulrich. Otto opened his eyes when Helene came over to feed him, spooning the thin soup she had made into his mouth and soaking stale bread to soften it.

Klaus came to sit on the mattress. 'You know, when penguins are looking after their chicks, they chew up food to soften it before they give it to them,' he said. 'Let's hope we don't have to do that for you!'

'Tomorrow I will be going to the market to see what I can get,' said Helene. 'There must be antiseptics that will sort out that bite. Meanwhile, I'm going to boil some water and then sponge it down with that.'

'Boiling water?' said Ulrich. 'That will cause the wound to blister even more, surely? And it will be agonising.'

Otto felt pleased his brother was concerned about him.

Helene batted him away. 'This isn't the Spanish Inquisition, Ulrich,' she said. 'We'll let it cool down and then wash the finger. Boiled water will be sterile – at least, we can hope it will be.'

And she did, tenderly bathing the wound, trying to rinse the gunk away that had formed around it. Klaus and Erich came to look and made disgusted noises.

'That's really not helping, boys,' said Helene.

'Yes it is, nurse,' said Klaus. 'The patient is smiling. That's got to be good for him.'

Otto was strangely happy. It felt good to be the one being looked after.

That night, as they settled down, Helene came and lay down beside him, holding his good hand. 'We will make you better, Otto, so don't worry,' she whispered. 'Tomorrow, I will go to the market and I won't come back until I have found something that will help you. We'll keep an eye out for Doktor Holzman too – see if he can help us.'

Then she mopped down his feverish body with a cup of cold water and kissed him goodnight.

The next morning Otto woke from his fever, feeling light-headed and feeble. His finger no longer throbbed and the pain had settled to a dull ache. He called out to Helene but no one answered. They had all gone out. He had the strength to sit up, and noticed a small jug of water and an apple next to his bed. There was also a note:

> *Gone to the market.*
> *Don't do any heavy lifting, running about or trench digging.*
> *See you later with something useful,*
> *Helene xxx*

He stumbled off to the lavatory at the end of the corridor and then came back and collapsed on his mattress, over-come with fatigue. As the room swum around him he felt drenched in sweat and desperate once again to sleep. A quick inspection of his finger was not reassuring. The green

213

and black bruising had spread down the finger. It was also beginning to smell really vile – like a dead animal.

Before he drifted off, his eyes peered lazily around the room. Today the X-ray plates in the broken windows were really bothering him. He could swear some of them were moving. And something was missing, too. It took him a while to remember what it was. There was a gap on the shelf above the sink. Helene had taken her beautiful elephant girl clock.

Ulrich banged on the door to the basement and called out. 'Otto, let me in. I don't have a key.'

No one came.

'Otto, shift your lazy arse and let me in,' Ulrich called impatiently. Why didn't Otto drag himself out of bed? It was only his finger that hurt.

'Otto, you useless piece of crap. Open the door, you *Arschloch.*'

Finally he heard the key turn in the lock and then a heavy thump. 'What the hell are you doing?' said Ulrich angrily. 'Let me in.' He pushed on the door but something was blocking it. 'Stop messing about,' he said, giving it a mighty shove. Slowly he pushed the door open enough to see his brother's unconscious body on the floor.

'Oh God, Otto, what's happened to you?'

He squeezed through the gap in the doorway and picked Otto up under the shoulders. He was too heavy to be carried so Ulrich gently pulled him over to his mattress. He fetched water and mopped his brow with a cloth, then tried to get him to drink from the jug by the bed. Otto seemed to be hovering on the brink of consciousness, his eyes up in their sockets. Ulrich had seen people in this state before, usually right before they died.

There was a smell about him too – like rotten meat. With a shudder, Ulrich remembered Helene's whispered conversation that morning. 'I changed my mind about the gangrene. I think he might have it after all,' she had said. 'And that could kill him. If that is the case, we'll have to amputate his finger. We must find Doktor Holzman. See if he can help us.'

Ulrich also remembered his last conversation with Holzman. He hoped he wasn't going to ask him about the Dürer sketches.

Otto groaned again.

'Otto, Otto!' Ulrich cried out, gently tapping his face. 'Don't die on me, my brother . . .' He swallowed hard to stop the tears that were brimming in his eyes. Why was he crying? He mustn't be so soft.

But no, this was Otto. The only one he had left.

Otto began to twitch and shake, and then the restlessness left his body suddenly and he seemed to relax and breathe more slowly. Ulrich carried on mopping his forehead. He even held his hand. Every now and then Otto would squeeze his hand back. It was as if he was in a deep, deep trance and Ulrich could not rouse him.

'Otto, don't die on me,' he said again, in a low voice. 'Don't leave me alone.'

Otto grew restless. It was as if he was having a bad dream. He began to murmur, 'Mutti, Mutti,' and occasionally his eyes would flicker open.

'Helene – Klaus – Erich – please, come home,' Ulrich cried out to himself.

Ulrich sat there watching the long, deep breaths that Otto struggled to take, and thought about the life they had shared together. He had never liked his elder brother, although everyone else seemed to. He had even suspected that Mutti and Papa liked Otto more than him, although they made efforts to try to hide it. But when Ulrich joined the *Pimpfe* – the junior Hitler Youth – his life had changed. He had been admired. He had won merit badges and been easily promoted. The leaders had thought he was the perfect young man. But the better he did in the *Pimpfe*, and then the Hitler Youth, the more his parents seemed distant from him. When he brought home his Racial Hygiene badge he had expected his father to be as proud as the squad leader had been, but instead of a beaming face he had been met with a tight, dead-eyed smile. Otto was half the political soldier that Ulrich was becoming, but his parents still seemed to love him more. So it had not been a difficult decision to make. He had chosen long ago to make the Nazi Party his family and to hell with the Roths.

But now? Ulrich had tried to be everything the Führer had asked him to be – 'slim and slender, swift as a greyhound, tough as leather and hard as steel'. Hitler had called upon him and all the other greyhounds of his generation

216

to fulfil what he had called 'the greatest task of our century'. Well, he had failed the Führer. And the Führer had failed him. His 'good Empire with happy people' had crumbled into this mess. Until then, Ulrich had really believed no power on earth could stop people like him and Ernst. And until the moment of surrender he had really believed something was going to happen to save the Nazi state. An SS division would sweep down from the north, or the High Command would employ some so far unknown wonder weapon – but of course that never happened, and now his city lay in ruins . . . He stared into space lost in thought.

It was then that what he had done hit him like a Tiger tank. He had betrayed his own father to the SS. He had seen the execution squad head off to find him, the officer carrying the rope they would hang him with, and the placard with the word 'Traitor' already written upon it.

If Ulrich gave up on the Nazi faith, if he lost trust in the Führer, then what would he do? If he no longer believed in his actions as a Hitler Youth, or when he was in the *Volkssturm*, then he wouldn't know who he was any more. He would have fought for nothing. And the thing he had done to his father would become . . . hideous.

'Otto, my brother,' he murmured, daring himself to speak out loud. 'I have done a terrible thing. I have to tell you, tell you so you can forgive me. But no. I can't. I can never tell you why I know for sure that Papa is dead . . . You will hate me forever. As I am beginning to hate myself . . .'

There was a rattle at the door. Erich and Klaus marched in. 'Door was wide open,' said Erich.

'Someone forgot to lock it,' said Klaus.

'How's the patient?' asked Erich, peering over to look at Otto.

'Sleeping like a baby,' said Klaus. 'But is he any better?'

'I don't think he is,' said Ulrich, his voice catching. He told them what had happened when he got home, missing out the bit about him losing his temper and how Otto had seemed quite delirious.

'*Scheisse*,' said Erich.

'Let's hope Helene arrives with some useful medicine,' said Klaus, and they settled down to peeling a handful of vegetables and preparing the stove to make soup.

Helene did not come home for another two hours. When she turned up it was well past seven at night and they had all begun to worry about her. She came in looking unusually happy and dashed over to Otto at once. But even seeing him in his sorry state did not wipe the look of delight from her face.

'So, did you find some medicine?' asked Klaus.

'So what have you got then?' said Ulrich. 'And did you find Holzman?'

Her face fell. 'No luck. No luck at all. Not even some measly antiseptic ointment. And I couldn't find Doktor Holzman. He must have been at work.'

'So what are you so pleased about?' said Klaus.

'I'll tell you in a second.' She went over to Otto's mattress again. He was in a deep sleep. 'He looks very pale,' she said.

Then she stood up, her face beaming again, and looked directly at Ulrich. 'Ulrich, your Papa, he's alive,' she said. 'I saw a note from him, on the wall by Charlottenstrasse. Isn't that fantastic!'

Ulrich stared at her. What was she talking about?

Erich and Klaus grinned and patted Ulrich on the shoulder. But there was also something slightly subdued about them. They were probably thinking of their own father, a war hero, dead in Stalingrad, buried in the cold, unforgiving soil of Soviet Russia.

'Ulrich, isn't this marvellous news!' said Helene. 'Aren't you pleased?'

Ulrich still stared at her; his mouth was open, but nothing was coming out.

'Are you sure?' he said finally. 'What makes you think this is the case?'

'You're a cold fish, Ulrich!' She grinned, taking both his hands. 'Your Papa, he's alive!'

'Yes, but how do you *know*?' said Ulrich. The news had left him feeling hugely confused. Now he was getting impatient.

'The message I found. Written in his handwriting. I can remember it exactly. "Doktor Friedrich Roth of Alexanderplatz Military Hospital seeks his two sons, Otto and Ulrich Roth, aged sixteen and fourteen. Please contact immediately if you have any information." That's got to be you. There can't be two Doktor Friedrich Roths with boys the same age and name, surely. We have to go to the hospital, see if we can make contact.'

Ulrich carried on staring into space but he stood a little straighter. He felt lighter, like he had been stooping for a very long time. He looked at Helene. 'I know exactly what we can do to get Otto some medicine. But I am going to do this on my own. No questions. Do you understand?'

'Don't be so dramatic, Ulrich,' said Helene. 'What on earth are you talking about?'

'You'll see,' he said. 'Tomorrow I will save my brother.'

Helene stared at him, clearly expecting an explanation. When it was obvious he wasn't going to say anything else she delved into her bag and placed the elephant girl clock back on the shelf above the sink.

Ulrich had a secret he was quite unprepared to share with anyone at Skalitzer Hospital. He had hoarded away a lot of the money he had made from Ernst's cigarettes. He had known the Werewolf resistance would need funds to bribe and to buy black market weapons and medicine. But now his Papa was alive! Ulrich felt free from the guilt he'd been constantly shutting out. The Werewolves – if they existed – could do without him. He didn't even want to find them any more. He had his real family back.

But he could not tell the others he had saved all this money and not shared it with them. A moment's revulsion passed through him. Seen in the light of this new beginning, it seemed yet another vile thing he had done – he had shared in their meagre rations while he himself had enough money to buy them a roast pig and all the trimmings. He would take that money and buy penicillin with it. That would redeem him.

He felt like his life had changed in an instant. Suddenly these people with him at the hospital were the most important people in the world. They would never forgive him if they found out. He was sure of that. But he could save Otto. That was something.

The next morning Ulrich woke early and took his bag out, quickly slipping the wad of money into his coat pocket. He would wait outside Dr Holzman's apartment building. Sooner or later the slimy creep would come out and he would talk to him. Holzman would definitely know where to get penicillin.

Fortune was on his side. Barely ten minutes after arriving, Holzman emerged from the apartment building with a young woman.

'*Herr Doktor*, I am hoping you will be able to help me,' said Ulrich with his most ingratiating smile.

'Ah, Elsbeth,' said Holzman to his companion. 'This is Ulrich, one of the young men of the Skalitzer Hospital gang. Now, what can I do to help you?'

'My brother Otto is terribly ill. He has been bitten by a rat and his finger has got very infected. Helene thinks he may have gangrene.'

Holzman had the decency to look shocked. 'I will come at once,' he said.

Ulrich did not want to have this conversation in front of the others. 'We are sure that's what it is. Helene saw plenty of cases on the wards when she worked as an auxiliary.'

'I will come and see. I have a shift at the hospital in an hour. I may be able to bring back a few things that will help.'

'Do you have penicillin?' asked Ulrich.

Holzman started. Then he laughed. 'My dear boy, here in Berlin penicillin is more valuable than diamonds. I cannot get that without considerable risk.'

'So there is a black market in the drug,' asked Ulrich. He was getting bolder.

'Yes, but it's terribly dangerous. The Russians will shoot anyone who steals it. The Americans and the British . . . maybe not a death sentence, but many years in prison.'

The young woman with him spoke up. 'It's true, young man. Two colleagues were shot last week for trying to smuggle the drug out of a Red Army hospital. Both of them were highly experienced doctors.'

'I have a lot of money,' said Ulrich boldly. 'Do you know anyone who will be able to sell me some?'

'This is foolish talk, Ulrich,' said Holzman. 'The cost is prohibitive. Now let's go and see Otto.'

Ulrich put on his most emollient voice. 'Doktor Holzman, please may I beg of you a favour? If you think the only thing that will save Otto is penicillin, please do not mention my offer to buy it in front of the others.'

That was it. He was completely at Holzman's mercy.

The doctor nodded. 'I understand,' he said.

Holzman said goodbye to the young woman and they went at once to the hospital basement.

Ulrich realised with some surprise that he had the measure of this man. He had admitted he knew about the black market in penicillin and he had understood Ulrich's desire to keep his money secret. That could only mean he was open to negotiation. This was promising.

Otto was fast asleep when Ulrich arrived at the basement with Dr Holzman. Helene was placing a damp cloth on his forehead to try and bring his temperature down. She looked up and smiled with relief. 'Thank you for coming to see Otto,' she said.

Holzman immediately took Otto's pulse and felt his forehead. Then he examined the swollen finger. 'He has a very high temperature, which is why he is so feverish. And yes, this is a very nasty infection, and it's starting to go gangrenous. If we were living in normal times I would order an ambulance and he'd be in a hospital within an hour. But a military hospital won't take him, and the civilian ones are chaotically overcrowded. No chance of getting him in one of those, even if we could take him ourselves.'

He paused and stroked his chin. 'I will go and get some antiseptic ointment, but we'll need to do something more than that to cure him. If this gets any worse I may have to amputate the finger.'

Helene looked horrified. 'The poor boy,' she said.

He returned ten minutes later with antiseptic and a fresh dressing. 'This will hinder the spread of the infection,' he told them, 'but it won't cure it. I will see what I can do and come back tonight.'

'We've heard of this drug penicillin,' Helene said. 'Do you think he needs that?'

Holzman told her what he had told Ulrich – that it was impossibly expensive and dangerous to get on the black market.

'I'll sell my clock,' she said. 'I had some good offers yesterday, but I'm sure I could push them higher.'

'I'm sorry, dear Helene,' said Holzman gently. 'That's just a tiny fraction of what it would cost.'

Ulrich's heart sank. Would his cigarette money be enough then? It didn't sound like it.

Erich and Klaus were looking unusually serious. 'So is it really likely to be amputation?' asked Erich.

'We'll see,' said Holzman. 'I know it sounds drastic, but if the gangrene spreads it will kill him. But amputating a finger, in these conditions, that could kill him too. It's difficult to control infections outside of a hospital ward. What's really going to kill him is blood poisoning from the infection.'

Holzman looked over to Ulrich and gave him a barely perceptible nod. Ulrich understood and left shortly after him.

He caught up with Holzman just outside the hospital.

The doctor didn't prevaricate: 'Tell me more about the sketches – the ones that are supposed to be by Dürer. You haven't mentioned them again. Has your friend found a buyer?'

Ulrich shook his head. 'I can't talk about that. He told me he would kill me if I mentioned them to anyone.'

Holzman dropped any attempt at charm. 'That's too bad. You need that drug to save your brother. But it's very rare, and very dangerous to steal it. You need to think about this. If those really are Dürer sketches, they will be valuable enough to trade. I will risk my life to get the drug. You have to risk your life to get me those sketches. Tell me more about them.'

Ulrich could not speak. He knew what Ernst would do if he stole them from him.

Holzman turned on his heel. Ulrich watched him go, wanting to punch him to the ground. Then in a single lucid moment he knew what he had to do. 'Doktor Holzman, wait!' he called.

CHAPTER 21

'Tell me everything you know,' said Holzman sternly. 'How do I know these sketches are genuine, even if it's possible for you to get hold of them?'

There was a steel about him now. That veneer of charm had vanished. Ulrich suddenly felt afraid.

'He told me he had taken them from Prague Castle,' he said, 'when he worked there with Reich Minister Reinhard Heydrich.'

Holzman found it difficult to hide his astonishment. Ulrich realised at once that he had told him something significant.

'And how does a man like that manage to stay free in Berlin?' he asked.

'He is a very resourceful soldier,' said Ulrich. 'He's hiding himself very well.'

Holzman gave him a smile that did not reach his eyes. 'And do you know where he is hiding?'

Ulrich stared hard into those eyes, wondering if he could trust him.

Holzman put a hand on Ulrich's shoulder. 'My young

friend, this might be easier to resolve than you think. Tell me, just in the vaguest way, where this man is hiding.'

Ulrich took a deep breath. 'In one of the parks,' he said.

Holzman's smile reached his eyes. He even showed his teeth.

'Excellent. That tells me he is not protected by powerful friends. He's out here on his own, a fugitive in fact. Now I know this, I know how we can come to an arrangement. Tell me more about the sketches . . .'

Ulrich tried to remember. 'They were of animals. I don't know anything about art. Ernst was convinced of their value . . .' Then he stopped, realising he had told Holzman his name.

Holzman reassured him. 'His name is of no importance for now. What sort of animals?'

'A parrot, an owl . . . and a stork, I think. He said they were four hundred years old.'

Holzman nodded. 'And where does he keep these drawings?'

'They're there in his hideaway. He showed me. He buried them beneath a floorboard.'

Holzman scoffed. 'Ulrich, you are trying my patience.'

'It's true. I swear on my life. He got drunk one evening after I sold a lot of his cigarettes and he showed me. I don't know why he did that. I wish he hadn't. The minute he had done, he was threatening to kill me if I told anyone about them.' Ulrich was gabbling now. 'Then he asked if I knew someone who could find a buyer for them. Then he changed his mind again . . .'

'Where is he hiding?' asked Holzman.

'Can you get the penicillin?' begged Ulrich. He wasn't going to give everything away unless he was convinced Holzman was going to help him.

'Ulrich. You are in a weak position here,' said Holzman, almost like he was instructing him on how to bargain. 'I can help you but you have to convince me your story is not a tissue of lies.'

'He's in Görlitzer Park. We can get there in fifteen minutes.'

Holzman nodded. 'Good. Take me there now.'

Ulrich refused. 'Why should I trust you?' he said. 'You help Otto and I will help you. I swear it.'

Holzman thought about this. 'Ulrich, you are finally displaying characteristics I can admire rather than despise. I will return tonight and help Otto. Then tomorrow, or the day after . . . you will show me where this man is hiding.'

'He's very dangerous,' said Ulrich. 'He could kill you in an instant.'

'I'm sure he could,' said Holzman.

He looked hard at Ulrich. 'I like your little friends,' he said. 'And so should you. They've put up with you with extraordinary patience. I have decided to help you. But if you are lying to me . . . well, I'm sure you can imagine what I will do.' And with that he walked away.

An hour later, Ulrich shivered in the late summer wind. He was drenched in an anxious sweat. He could not shake the feeling that what he was doing was abhorrent. He was

228

betraying a comrade. But he was slowly learning to think differently. Sweeping aside his anxieties, he took a deep breath and asked himself: *What would Papa think?* And he knew without a doubt that Friedrich Roth would think that saving Otto's life was a very good plan indeed.

He had an arrangement to meet Ernst that morning, to collect more cigarettes to sell. He would have to steel himself, try to pretend nothing unusual was going on. Ernst had been quite distant with him the last couple of times they had met. Ulrich wondered if he meant to harm him, but dismissed the idea. He imagined he was too useful to this strange man living in his hole in the ground. He hoped he was right.

Ernst sneaked up on him this time, and looked stern when Ulrich jumped. 'Better keep your wits about you, comrade,' he said. He looked more unshaven than when Ulrich had last seen him, and his white shirt was utterly filthy.

'Have you got any more cigarettes?' Ulrich managed to say without his voice shaking. It was hard to look Ernst in the eye, knowing that he'd just told Dr Holzman where his hideout was.

Ernst eyed him suspiciously. 'Keen to get going, are you? I risk death every night getting these and all you have to do is go to the market. You'd better not be cheating me.'

'No, no!' Ulrich babbled. 'Not at all.'

Ernst laughed and slung an arm round his shoulder. 'No. Because you know what I'd do to you, don't you?' He leaned against Ulrich, who could feel a knife handle under the filthy shirt.

Ulrich swallowed. 'Yes . . .' He could hardly breathe.

Ernst looked around, then swiftly handed him the cartons of cigarettes. He patted Ulrich on the back. 'Good, good. Soon the money will be put to use.'

Ulrich nodded and walked away as slowly as he could force himself to. His legs were shaking. He couldn't possibly steal the drawings. Ernst would know it was him. But how could he get the penicillin otherwise?

Back in the hospital, Helene stayed with Otto all day. 'He's too poorly to leave on his own,' she had said to Klaus and Erich as they left to forage. Ulrich too had vanished, as he often did.

For the whole of the day, as the shadow of the sun crept from one side of the room to the other, Otto drifted in and out of consciousness and was still running a high fever. Helene ensured he drank, and managed to feed him a little soup, and sometimes he was able to talk. He called her 'Mutti' a few times, which made her wipe her eyes. Most of the time, though, he drifted between gauzy consciousness and stupor, and occasionally he would look at his septic finger with fear and apprehension. She hugged him carefully, and whispered words of consolation. She couldn't bear it that her brave, kind friend was like a fretful infant. They had gone through so much together. He couldn't die of an infected finger. Not after facing Russian machine guns and those huge T-34 tanks.

As the day wore on, she realised that more than anything

else in the world, except perhaps finding her mother safe and well, she wanted Otto to stay alive. It was times like these when she missed her mother the most. She never entirely stopped thinking about her. She often dreamed about her, and even when she was drifting on the edge of sleep she would often spring fully awake, startled by the knowledge that she had no idea where her mother was, or even if she was still alive.

The twins returned with some little apples – crisp and sweet and quite edible once you had removed all the worm holes. 'Back garden in Treptow,' said Erich. 'Lovely little tree. Ballerina, I think they're called. They grow straight up. Produce apples every other year. Lucky us!'

Helene smiled to herself. 'You boys love your natural history, don't you?'

'We do,' they said together. 'When everything's back to normal, that's what we want to do,' said Erich. 'Klaus wants a job at the zoo. I'll stick to studying plants. Much more predictable.'

Ulrich returned soon after with cheese and bacon. 'The market was good today,' was all he said, though he looked paler than usual.

As good as his word, Holzman arrived at the basement in the early evening. He was still a little unsure about whether to trust Ulrich, but he had sounded convincingly desperate. A boy like that was not a born thespian. This whole performance had a ring of truth about it. And besides,

Holzman had a stash of penicillin in his apartment, stolen weeks ago, before the black market value of the drug became so high. Maybe this was the time to realise its worth. And swapping it for valuable artwork, with these kids, would be easier than trying to get a good price in the murkier end of the black market. It was a gamble, but if it paid off it would make him a wealthy man.

Back at the hospital Otto continued to deteriorate. They all kept a close watch on him, wondering what they could do to save him. As evening fell there was a loud banging at the door and Holzman called out to tell them he was outside. Helene rushed to let him in, delighted to see him.

'I have something for the gangrene,' he said. She was so pleased she gave him a big hug. 'What have you got?'

Holzman tapped the side of his nose. 'You'll see.'

He knelt down by Otto's mattress and spoke softly to him. 'Otto, can you hear me? I have two things to help you.'

Otto gazed at him with rheumy eyes.

'I am going to give you an injection to help you with your infection. And then I am going to treat your finger. That will be painful so I am going to give you another injection to put you off to sleep.'

Helene stood close by, with the others around her in a semicircle, watching him at work. Holzman took a small glass phial from his bag and filled a syringe, then injected it into Otto's hand. 'I will be back with another one of these tomorrow morning, and then in the evening. Twice a day for three days,' he said to no one in particular.

'Now we wait, see how that affects him.'

They stood in breathless anticipation.

'But I thought this was too expensive,' Helene said. 'How did you –?'

'Never you mind,' said Holzman with a brisk smile. 'Now, it will take a couple of days to have an effect,' he explained. 'In the meantime I have to cut away the infection. So I have something else for that.'

'Will you have to amputate?' asked Helene. Her throat tightened as the words came from her mouth.

'Not if I can help it. But let's try this first,' he said.

He filled the same syringe from another phial – this one clearly labelled 'MORPHINE' – and administered it to Otto.

Otto's restlessness left him, and within a minute he was in a deep sleep, a sweet little smile playing on his lips. Helene stroked his arm.

'Thank you, *Doktor*,' she said softly.

'That's the happiest he's been all week,' said Erich.

'So would you be if they pumped you full of morphine,' said Klaus.

'Helene, can you help me?' said Holzman. 'I need you to hold his hand steady while I work on it. And fetch me a bowl of water, and a towel if you have one. There will be blood.'

She was proud to be asked. 'I worked as a nurse at the end of the war – well, an auxiliary,' she told him.

233

He explained what he was going to do. 'We must wash the wound and then cut away the damaged flesh. I am hoping this will be sufficient and I will not have to amputate. You will need a steady hand and a steady stomach.'

'Oh yes, I remember this,' said Helene. 'It's called "debridement", isn't it?'

Holzman looked impressed. 'Well done,' he assured her. 'You should come and work with me. I will see if I can find you a vacancy.'

Helene smiled politely. She didn't entirely trust Dr Holzman, despite his kindnesses. She would have to see.

For twenty minutes they worked away, rapidly losing their audience. Even Ulrich could not bear to watch. Otto remained deeply unconscious as Holzman drained the wound of pus and then began the tricky process of paring away the flesh that had been irreparably damaged, with a scalpel. He slathered Otto's finger in antiseptic cream and dressed it tightly.

'Now we shall have to see if the treatment will work,' he said. 'If the injections don't drive away the infection then he'll not stand a chance. It's that simple.' With that startling news he got up and left.

As they settled down, Otto remained in a deep sleep. Helene lay down beside him, anxious that he might stop breathing altogether. Ulrich was restless, though. As Helene lay awake, listening to Otto's shallow steady breathing, she could hear Ulrich fidgeting and turning in his bed. When he did sleep he would murmur. Occasionally he woke with a start. Helene began to feel deeply uneasy. She had seen him coming and going with Holzman. She liked the doctor, but she wondered why he was suddenly supplying them with penicillin. She wondered if Ulrich had struck a deal with him and, if so, what it would cost them.

CHAPTER 22

Otto awoke the next morning to find Helene asleep in his arms. He had a thick head and felt desperately thirsty. He was cold and clammy and found the light from the window painfully bright. But he felt something he had not felt for several days: happy. For a moment he looked at Helene's sleeping face and instinctively squeezed her shoulder. She stirred and her eyes flickered open.

'Hello, Otto,' she whispered. 'How are you feeling?'

'Very thirsty and very dirty,' he said, his tongue like sandpaper. Then he winced and held up his bandaged finger. 'Oww, what on earth has happened here?'

'Holzman came round. Pumped you full of something and then we did a little operation on your finger. He thinks we might be able to save it. You had gangrene.'

'Gangrene?' Otto shouted, disturbing the others. They rose from their beds and gathered around his mattress.

'How is the patient?' asked Erich.

Klaus went to get him a pitcher of water.

'You know, I had the funniest dream,' said Otto after he

had drunk the entire jug. 'I dreamed that Helene came in and told us she had found Papa.'

'It's true, Otto,' she said, wiping away a tear. 'I haven't found him as such, but he left a note on one of the walls. He's working at the Alexanderplatz Hospital. As soon as you're better we must go there and find him.' She hugged him, carefully avoiding his damaged finger. 'Isn't that wonderful news!'

Otto couldn't believe it. They could find Papa! He felt light-headed with happiness. Otto looked over at Ulrich and his brother smiled too. But something wasn't quite right. Ulrich's smile seemed tight and forced, his eyes haunted. But Otto couldn't focus his mind on Ulrich for long. Whatever was wrong, Papa would put it right. He wondered again if he was dreaming, but the stinging pain in his finger, and his rational mind, told him he was definitely awake. To see Papa again! Otto sank back against his pillow in wonder.

Helene brought him a little cheese and apple to eat. Holzman came round soon afterwards to change his dressing and give him another injection. He refused to tell him what it was, but reassured him it was obviously working.

Holzman left and Otto marvelled at the news the day had brought. He still couldn't quite believe his Papa was alive. For a moment he thought sadly of his watch, so recently stolen, but now it didn't seem to matter any more. They would go and find Papa Roth as soon as he was back on his feet. But for now he was barely able to rise from his bed. Soon, he drifted off to sleep again.

The rest of them went out again to forage and barter. Ulrich had told them he had his own business to attend to.

Ulrich headed for Görlitzer Park and met Ernst Barth again. When he handed over money from his recent bartering he felt there was something of the snake about to strike in this man. He headed home convinced that Barth was planning to kill him. Holzman, too, if he didn't steal those drawings. He had still not worked out how he was going to do it; he was simply too scared that Ernst would catch him doing it. Either way, it seemed, he was a dead boy.

As Ulrich approached the derelict entrance to the hospital, Holzman was waiting for him there, leaning against the building. 'Ulrich,' he called out. 'I have a pressing need to talk to you.'

Ulrich swallowed hard. 'Yes, *Herr Doktor*.'

'Now listen carefully,' Holzman began. He had his serious voice on. 'I have given your brother three shots of penicillin and it's done a very good job. But with this treatment you have to complete the course, otherwise the infection will come back worse than ever, and almost certainly kill him. There are two more shots to come, but I would like you to fulfil your half of our bargain now and give me those sketches.'

Ulrich tried to disguise the fear he felt rising in his chest.

'I assume you retrieved them last night?' Dr Holzman said eagerly.

Ulrich shook his head.

The doctor's face became cold. 'Ulrich, I want those drawings. That is the price of the penicillin. We agreed.'

Ulrich stared at him unhappily. 'He is a very dangerous man, *Herr Doktor*,' he stammered.

'So you say. But he is just a man. If you are quick and you are clever, Ulrich, I think he will not catch you.'

Ulrich gulped. 'That is quite impossible, *Herr Doktor* . . .'

Holzman leaned over Ulrich. 'Who are we dealing with? You can tell me his surname, surely?'

Ulrich paused. Here he was taking a great leap into a dark pit. 'It's Ernst Barth, I think. Standartenführer Ernst Barth.'

Holzman blanched. 'God in heaven,' he whispered under his breath.

'You know him?' asked Ulrich.

'Not personally. But I served in the same sector of the Eastern Front and Barth was a byword for cruelty. I saw him once when he visited our field hospital. His men were terrified of him.'

Holzman stood lost in thought. Then he spoke, his voice reflective. 'So now he's hiding in a hole in the ground . . . Well, Ulrich, we have both bitten off more than we can chew with this one. But I need to know that those drawings are the real thing, and you are not deceiving me. You can understand, surely?'

Ulrich smiled. For a moment he almost liked Holzman for his frankness. But then he realised again what the doctor was asking him to do. 'If I take those sketches, then he will kill me. As far as he knows, only he and I know about them. It's as simple as that. I'll be dead and you won't have your drawings.'

Holzman frowned. Then, 'I have it!' he said. 'The police will know his name. They'll want to know where he is. Let's have him arrested first and then you will get the sketches.'

Ulrich stared at him, amazed that things could be so simple. If Holzman could have Barth arrested, that would solve his problems. It had simply never occurred to him to do this. Now he eagerly nodded. 'When shall we do it?'

Holzman sighed deeply. 'I am trusting you here, Ulrich. I have to give Otto two more shots – tonight and tomorrow morning. But then I have three days of very heavy work at the hospital. So . . . I'll go to the police on Saturday and they will no doubt pick up Barth as soon as possible after that.'

Ulrich flinched. Three more days to wait! In all that time, Ernst could kill him even if he didn't take the drawings. Maybe he should go to the police himself today? But no: he remembered Otto and Helene saying how dismissive the police were when they went to report Hanna as missing. He realised he had no choice. He had to wait for Holzman. He'd just have to pretend to Ernst that everything was normal until then.

CHAPTER 23

Early September

Klaus and Erich liked September. Their birthday fell in the middle of the month, and the crisp autumn weather that arrived at that time always filled them with a sense of purpose and excitement for the new school year. They had felt like this ever since they were five years old – and then especially when the war had begun in the September of their eighth birthday.

'I think we should mark the occasion with a very big explosion,' said Erich.

'We must seize the hour,' said Klaus, mimicking the dramatic style and shrill, insistent voice of the Nazi newsreels. 'Shall we ask Ulrich to help us?'

Erich shook his head. 'No, this is one for you and me. He's been a bit unpredictable lately, hasn't he? And I don't want him getting silly ideas in his head about using those rockets to attack the Yankees. But perhaps he will settle down when he finds his father again.'

'The church is still our best idea,' said Klaus. 'And I have a plan. To get those *Panzerfaust* rockets from Muskauer Strasse to Wrangelstrasse will be very dangerous. We must be careful. I don't think the Yankees will kill us if they catch us, not like the Ivans would have done, but they will certainly lock us up in prison. But I know how to move this box.'

Erich raised his eyebrows expectantly.

'Come and see.'

Klaus took his brother to the courtyard at the back of the hospital. There among the rubble and clutter was a rickety old trolley – four wheels on an iron frame and a long handle to pull it along.

'Perfect,' said Erich. 'All we have to do is bring some bundles and rags and an old mattress or two, and people will think we're just moving house! My brother, you are a genius.'

'Here, look at this,' said Klaus, pointing to a cello case wrapped in a coat that nestled in the corner of the yard. 'Never noticed that before. I might have a go on that one day. Remember those cello lessons I took when we were nine?'

'The noise was appalling,' said Erich with a smile. 'Don't go near it.'

The change in Otto was extraordinary. Although the morphine had made him sleepy for the next day, by the time Holzman had finished his course of injections he was restless and eager to be up and about.

'No wonder they won the war with this,' said Klaus.

'Miracle drug indeed,' agreed Erich.

242

Helene went out with the twins during the day to barter at the street stalls close to home, and they came back with enough to keep them fed for the next few days. She had agreed with Otto that the Tiergarten had become too dangerous and was thankful to have avoided that encounter with the thugs in the Flak Tower. Ulrich did not go with them, which was a shame as he was so good at selling and buying. He had a ruthlessness about him that Otto joked would make him a perfect salesman, once all this had passed and the world was back to normal.

'He's been a lot nicer since we found out Papa was alive,' he said to Helene. 'But he's still up to something.'

'Otto, Ulrich is being very useful to all of us,' she said. 'He's helped you stay alive. Let's not annoy him. If he wants to be secretive about things, we'll just have to trust him. I suspect he has dealings with people I would never want to meet.'

'But that's just it,' said Otto. 'I worry about him getting up to something he is too young to cope with. I worry about him disappearing one day, like Hanna.'

She agreed. 'But as soon as you can make the walk we must all go and find your Papa at the Alexanderplatz Hospital. I hope this isn't going to be difficult. Just think. A year ago all you had to do was pick up the phone, then hop on a tram . . .'

Alexanderplatz was a good hour and a half walk away. Otto did not feel up to that yet. Helene had asked Ulrich if he would go with her while Otto recovered, but he'd said he would wait and they could all go together. That was typically odd of him, they agreed. Although he was clearly pleased to hear his Papa was alive, he still seemed ill at ease with the world. He was pale and fidgety and startled at the slightest noise. Maybe actually seeing Dr Roth again would sort him out.

CHAPTER 24

On the following Saturday afternoon, as they'd agreed, Ulrich met Holzman outside the hospital and together they walked the short distance to the police station on Lausitzer Platz. Ulrich glanced at him nervously. Dr Holzman had worn his neatest suit, and looked entirely at ease with the world, certain he would be listened to. 'They know me here,' he said to Ulrich. 'I have done favours for them.'

And indeed, despite the usual chaos inside the station, as soon as they arrived, he and Ulrich were whisked into a room at the back of the building. Ulrich and the doctor sat behind a battered table opposite a harassed-looking senior officer, who was wearing civilian clothing. When Holzman told them he knew of the whereabouts of Standartenführer Ernst Barth they took him very seriously.

'He is in Görlitzer Park,' said Holzman. 'The boy here has spotted his hiding place. We will take you to it but we cannot be involved in the arrest. This must be something you do.'

'I understand, *Herr Doktor*,' said the policeman, meeting his eye. 'We all have to be careful these days. You never know who is still carrying a torch for the old regime. Now what does he look like?'

Holzman leaned back in his chair so that Ulrich could explain. Ulrich's hands were clammy. When he opened his mouth to speak, he stammered and coughed, his throat closing as he watched the police officer become more and more impatient.

'I have some pictures,' the officer interrupted harshly. 'Will you look at them?'

The Americans had sent a series of poorly reproduced mugshots of wanted war criminals, thieves and murderers. Ulrich flicked through and eventually came to a badly reproduced wire photo that sent a shiver of fear through him. Even here, in a smudged collection of dots and shaded lines, Ernst Barth's cold eyes were unmistakable.

'This is the man, *Herr Oberwachtmeister*,' he said quietly, looking away from the paper in his hand.

The policeman studied the image. 'Our American friends are keen to capture him. They suspect he was involved in a murder at a supply depot some weeks ago.'

Ulrich blanched at the word 'murder'.

The man rounded up three of his plain-clothes colleagues and left the station at a pace, with Holzman and Ulrich trailing behind. Ulrich had explained exactly where the hiding place was and they had assured him they would not need him to be there when Barth was arrested. They wanted them both nearby, though, in case they needed further assistance in finding the spot.

While the officers marched ahead down the ruined street, Holzman took a firm grip of Ulrich's arm, his hand biting into the thin material of his worn jacket. Without looking down at the boy or slowing his pace, the doctor hissed at Ulrich through gritted teeth, 'And once we have completed this public service, and this villain is locked away –' Holzman looked down and met Ulrich's eye '– you will fulfil your promise to me. You will recover those sketches.'

The police were in luck. Within moments of entering the park they had spotted Barth returning to his hideaway. They approached him, and one of them showed his identity badge. Barth brushed them aside and walked on, his pace quickening. But the officer they had spoken to in the police station called out again, and brought out a pistol which he pointed straight at him.

Ulrich watched from a safe distance, with Holzman by his side staring through a pair of army binoculars. He expected Barth to offer them violence, but he was surprised by how easily the *Standartenführer* gave himself up.

'There's almost a suavity about him,' the doctor said, keeping up a running commentary. 'It's like he's a business-man smooth-talking his way with officials come to arrest him on a fraud charge . . . He looks confident that there's been a misunderstanding and that everything can be explained and sorted out . . . Fascinating.'

Ulrich shivered. 'Do you think they might let him go?'

Holzman put down his binoculars and placed a reassuring arm around his shoulder. Ulrich shivered some more.

'Barth doesn't know what they know about him yet. They'll hang him soon, I expect.'

They watched as the policemen handcuffed Barth and then marched him away. Barth still offered no resistance. He still looked for all the world like he would soon be released once the police realised they had made a mistake.

'Now we must seize our moment,' said Holzman.

Ulrich led him to the spot and once more had to admit the man had done a superb job concealing his home. Holzman whistled, impressed too. Ulrich pulled back the cover and for a moment his resolve weakened.

'What if it's booby-trapped?' he said. His hands were shaking and he felt terribly clumsy.

'Then you will have a trained doctor on the spot to assist you,' said Holzman. He gave Ulrich a little shove. 'In you go.'

Ulrich carefully lowered himself down. In the dim light of the autumn afternoon he tried to remember exactly where Barth had hidden his treasure. It was not logical, but he expected the *Standartenführer* to return any second and his hands were shaking so much he could barely make them do what he needed to do. None of those policemen looked like they would be capable of keeping a hardened SS killer in captivity. Every one of his senses was screaming out that he should leave this place – every footstep or sound in the outside world was Barth returning to his hiding place. Holzman would certainly not be able to protect him. Despite the autumn chill, Ulrich was drenched in sweat.

But everything was as it had been on the night of vodka,

caviar and secrets all those days ago. There was the section at the end of the trench with the floorboard and the earth which had been smoothed over. He began to dig with his bare hands. Only when he was some way into his excavations did he notice a trowel hanging from a nail on the side of the trench. That made things easier and after he had dug down twenty centimetres or so he hit something hard and metallic. He pulled the gas-mask container out with some difficulty, scattering soil around the floorboards. The lightness of the container made him fear there was nothing in it, but when he removed the lid at the top he could see in the dim light that there were rolls of parchment inside.

Ulrich passed the gas-mask case up to Holzman, then hauled himself out, carefully covering the entrance behind him. Holzman had already opened the case and was admiring the sketches. He smiled at Ulrich, who was now shaking hard and trying not to be sick. Holzman rolled up the parchment pages and placed them inside the case. 'Excellent,' he said. 'They are either as you said they were, or brilliant forgeries. They certainly look as though they are four hundred years old. You have been as good as your word, Ulrich. Thank you.'

They hurried away, both scanning the park for any sign of Barth returning to his lair. By the time they reached the hospital and went their separate ways, Ulrich felt utterly drained. He had never felt like this in combat. Then there had been glory and purpose, and comrades to admire him. He missed the old certainties of the Hitler Youth and wondered if he would ever be as brave again.

CHAPTER 25

Later that afternoon, Klaus and Erich set off from Skalitzer Hospital, pushing their trolley towards Muskauer Strasse. Over the sound of metal wheels on cobblestones they could just about hear someone call their names. It was Ulrich. They stopped pushing. 'Shall we ask him to come with us?' said Erich.

'Go on then,' said Klaus.

When Ulrich was near enough to hear them, Erich said, 'We're off to do some mischief. Want to join us?'

Ulrich looked blank. He seemed unusually haggard, like he had been awake for several days, and his shirt was soaked in sweat. 'Not today,' he said and left without another word.

Erich shrugged. 'Please yourself.'

The twins marched on, ebullient and full of purpose. The late afternoon sky was a radiant blue with only a few wispy white clouds scattered across it. The brittle cold made Berlin seem cleaner and tidier than the shattered city deserved. For the first time since the spring you could actually see your breath in the air. When they got to the house they both had a sense that no one had been inside since they had discovered it a few weeks before. And no wonder. With its burned-out windows and charred woodwork it looked sinister, and a likely depository of gruesome secrets.

Klaus bowed low in the empty doorway of the house and Erich curtsied before stepping over the threshold. They walked together downstairs and were relieved to find the big wooden box in the basement, exactly where they had last seen it. 'What do you think?' said Erich. 'Shall we carry them up one by one or just take the box?'

'Keep them in the box,' said Klaus. 'Much less chance of us being spotted. Then we can cover the thing with an old blanket.'

'Think we can pick it up between us?'

Erich and Klaus both spat on their hands – a gesture they had copied from their father. 'Let's do it.'

They lifted the box with one swift jerk.

'Lighter than I thought it would be,' said Erich.

'Hang on, there's something catching on it underneath,' said Klaus.

They met each other's fearful eyes, both realising the significance of those words an instant before the box exploded, blowing them both to fragments and bringing the house, and the one next to it, down in a tall and sulphurous plume of dust and smoke.

The explosion rattled the windows of the cell holding Ernst Barth, waking him from an exhausted stupor.

251

He surveyed the room in the police station where he was being held captive with a strange mixture of contempt and intense relief. They were holding him in a room adjacent to an outer wall and the window looked like it would be hard pressed to survive a mild storm, never mind a man like him.

The policeman who had arrested him had carried out the initial interrogation. Barth could tell by the way his eyes darted around, and the thin film of perspiration that formed on his forehead, that the *Oberwachtmeister* was still intimidated by his rank. He was not surprised. After all, a lowly *Orpo* – the uniformed police of the Nazi state – would have spent his life in fear of the SS and Gestapo. Barth had of course fed the policeman a pack of lies about who he was and what he'd done – but both men were well aware that only a short time ago, Barth would have had the power to decide the life or death of a lowly police officer.

Barth thanked the gods it was the Germans who had arrested him, and not the Ivans or the Yanks. Maybe the days of Russians killing SS men on sight had passed, but he didn't want to put that to the test. At the very least, when they discovered he was an SS *Standartenführer*, he could fully expect to have his teeth kicked out of his mouth before being sent away to some hellish work camp. The Yanks would be just as bad, he was sure. Especially since the incident at the supply depot where one of them had interrupted his errand. They would probably hang him for that.

It was early evening now, and Barth expected the interrogations would begin again tomorrow. So far they had treated him well, but very soon he would be handed over to the occupiers. He had listened carefully from his cell as the staff had all gone home with cheery goodbyes, leaving a skeleton crew to man this makeshift station. They had handcuffed him by one of his wrists to a solid pipe on the wall, despite his protests, but had brought him a simple meal before the evening set in.

The room was cold but that suited Barth fine. If he had been provided with a blanket and a pillow then he might have been tempted to sleep some more. No, he would stay awake until one in the morning, then he would disappear. Some of the church clocks had started working once again, so he would know exactly how the time was passing.

The lining of his shirt held a small pin. It was more than enough for him to pick the lock on a pair of handcuffs. Especially one as simple as this. He smiled at the memory of him sewing it in, expecting that one day it would come in useful.

By the time the church clock struck its solitary chime there had been no noise at all in the police station for at least two hours. Barth was certain that whoever was on duty was asleep, quite confident that their handcuffed prisoner would not be able to escape. His comrades in the Gestapo had always held the *Orpo* in utter contempt and now Barth could see why. Using his free hand, he worked away at the pin concealed in the fold of cloth that ran up to the neckline of his shirt. It came out in moments, then he crouched on his bench and made quick work of the lock of the cuff.

Barth examined the window and quickly noted there were two locks at the side and that the wood was peeling, bordering on rotten. In another extraordinary lapse of security, the guard had even left the plate for his supper, complete with the metal fork he ate it with.

He worked away at the window locks with the fork, carefully burrowing around the screws in the soft wood. Within half an hour the locks were off. Barth sprang from the window and disappeared into the shadows.

He reached his hideaway twenty minutes later. As he pulled the tarpaulin over his head he knew in an instant someone had been in there. He lit a candle and immediately noticed a scattering of soil on the floor. The gas-mask container was gone. Whoever had taken those parchments had come specifically for them. Nothing else had been taken – not the stash of cigarettes or the bottles of spirits, or the tins of meat, or his combat boots. Even his MP40 submachine gun was still in its place. Somebody had known exactly where to look.

A cold fury swept through him, and he reached for a combat knife and placed it inside his belt, the hilt concealed by his baggy workman's shirt. He knew there was only one person responsible for this: Ulrich. He cursed himself and his vanity for trying to impress a mere child. Now how was he going to get away from Berlin? He couldn't buy forged papers without selling the drawings. And if he couldn't get forged papers, it would be almost impossible to leave

Germany. And now they knew about him. They would send him to the gallows if he was recaptured, he was certain of that. And now he could not even rely on the safety of his hiding place. When they came looking for him, they would almost certainly come here.

Barth had been up most of the night and he was exhausted. But he realised staying in his hideout was not a prudent thing to do. Ulrich must have told the police he was in the park. They must know too about his hideaway. Grabbing his heavy overcoat and knapsack he ventured out again into the night. He would find a safe spot to rest, and as soon as it got light he would go to Skalitzer Hospital. Ulrich had told him exactly where he lived.

Barth was in luck. There was an abandoned factory close to the park, recently cleared out by the Russians, and a small office partition by the deserted shop floor even had a couple of padded chairs in it, although he had to shake broken glass from them before he could sit down. He slept heavily and woke to find daylight flooding through the windows. He grabbed his belongings and began to walk purposefully towards his quarry.

It was far later in the morning than Barth had intended. The hospital was only a brisk walk away from the park, and when he arrived his strategist's mind immediately saw why it was such an impressive hiding place. The inside of the building was utterly destroyed, although its floors and walls were still standing. He walked through the entrance hall and searched for a stairwell to the basement. In the dim light he headed for the room they lived in – 'the orderlies' room' Ulrich had called it – the room with the door still on its hinges. It was obvious enough where it was. The other rooms had their doors open. He would never have done that if he was hiding down there. Every door would be closed.

He listened intensely, his ear pressed to the door. Nothing. He turned the handle and to his surprise it opened. But this only took him to a small vestibule room where a more formidable door lay closed before him. Again, there was no sound from within. Ulrich was unlikely to be there. Perhaps he had fled, once he had revealed the location of the drawings. He knew Barth would kill him. It was a shame. Ulrich was promising material. Barth had lost a useful ally.

Maybe the kid had hidden the drawings here? It was worth a look. Would he be that stupid? People were. Life had certainly taught him that. He pushed his shoulder with all his might into the door, and it did not budge a centimetre. He remembered seeing a few scattered oxygen bottles near the hall and went to fetch one.

A few brutal blows and the door flew open. He looked around with cold-hearted envy at the tablecloth on a large dining table, the mattresses over by the far wall, the cleanliness and comfort of the place. He noticed a beautiful carriage-clock ornament of an Indian girl on an elephant on a shelf over the sink and thought to cast it down to the ground. Then he cursed his stupidity. He would sell that for something, once he'd sorted out this business. He overturned the mattresses and opened a few cupboards, but if Ulrich had hidden his pictures here he had certainly not left them somewhere obvious. He would have to find the boy and winkle it out of him.

Then he caught sight of a series of other drawings there on a wall. These were the people Ulrich had talked about: the elder brother (a strong family resemblance, to be sure); the older girl (she was a beauty, wasn't she); the two twins who liked to blow things up (peas in a pod); and the little girl. Did she still live with them? He couldn't remember. Ulrich had said he was certain she was a Jew but Barth's skilled eye could see no hint of anything Semitic in her features. And of course there was Ulrich. The artist had caught his defiance perfectly. He plucked the drawings from the wall. He would be making enquiries about these children. It was a brilliant stroke of luck to have these images of them. He would hunt them down until he found them.

He placed the portraits in his bag, grabbed a couple of apples, and walked back out into Skalitzer Strasse.

CHAPTER 26

Hanna sat close between two people who terrified her. She tried not to think about the life she had had with her mum and dad, and those nice children who had rescued her from the shop. That just made her cry, and the people she was with beat her when she cried. The autumnal wind blew harsh across the square and through the shattered buildings around it, penetrating her thin coat and causing her to shiver. From bitter experience she knew they would be here all day and there was no point in complaining about it.

The man and the woman insisted she called them Mama and Papa, and when she refused they hit her. They called each other Marek and Roza, and from what she could pick up from their conversation, they were Polish survivors from some hideous place they called 'the camp'. It did not sound like any camp she had been to – her kind of camp was a fun place where you slept under the stars and had bonfires and outdoor feasts, went swimming in the lake, and played with other children until it got dark. Her memories of camp reminded her painfully of her real mum and dad, but this one sounded like somewhere you would go only in a nightmare. She imagined it was one the Russians had put them in. Hanna could not imagine her own German people creating such a hellish place.

Sometimes she tried to feel sorry for Marek and Roza because she could see they had had a difficult life. They were both painfully thin, with skull-like faces and many missing teeth. Even Hanna could tell they had not had enough to eat for years, rather than just the few months that she had been constantly hungry. The woman often wept and had terrible dreams, when she would scream and plead in her sleep. He, on the other hand, seemed quite numb and his face was a cruel mask.

They had taken her when she had gone to get water. She had protested, but they had scolded her and slapped her, pretending to be her real parents. When she had cried for help the other people in the water queue had just looked on with dull eyes. The woman, Roza, had shrugged and smiled. 'Come on, Lidia,' she had said in a sing-song voice, 'stop making a fuss. You are making Mummy and Daddy very ashamed of your behaviour.'

Now they chained her up at night and never let her further than grabbing-length when they went out begging in the day. And every day was the same. They laid out a ragged blanket and unloaded a bag of pitiful articles pillaged from the ruins. Today there was a small bowl, a hammer, pieces of crockery, a handful of nails and a few buttons. They would call for customers in German, but with heavy

Polish accents. Sometimes they would make a little money and sometimes there would be food.

Hanna had tried to escape, of course, but the second time, when she ran down the street soon after they had gone out for the day, Marek had caught her and threatened to cut her eyes out, waving a sharp knife in her face. 'We might get more money if you were a blind girl,' he had told her.

Sometimes the woman showed her kindness. She hugged her and said, 'We make more money with you, little Lidia.' When Hanna told them her real name they just said, 'You are Lidia now.'

Business had been slow that morning. But this afternoon she could see a man eyeing them from the other side of the square. There was something about him that reminded her of Marek – both men were tall and lean, and bristled with the threat of violence, like a dangerous animal. When the man strode over with an insolent swagger, she felt a shiver pass between them.

'I don't like the look of him,' Marek said to Roza from the side of his mouth. 'He's a die-hard Nazi if ever I saw one. Why hasn't he been rounded up by the Russkis?'

Then the man was there in front of them and they put on their business faces, ready to bargain.

Hanna noticed several sheets of paper half folded in his hand. They were sketches of a girl who looked like her and for a moment she thought she could see Otto there. Her heart leapt. Had he come to rescue her? She looked up and smiled but there was only hate in his eyes.

'I'll give you a Chesterfield cigarette for the lot,' he said to Marek with a crooked smile.

'Go screw yourself,' spat Marek, his eyes flashing with anger. Hanna felt Roza bristle with indignation.

'You can have the bowl for a cigarette, *Scheisskopf*,' said Roza. Hanna had never heard words like that when she lived at home. Now she heard them every day.

The man reached for something on his leg that wasn't there. It was an odd gesture that made them all very anxious.

'Such intemperate language, and in front of a child, too,' said the man. Hanna was puzzled. He seemed to be speaking up for her.

Marek stood up, his eyes brimming with hate.

The man did not seem perturbed by his hostility. Instead, he stood before Marek, staring straight into his eyes. Hanna was breathless with anticipation. She wondered again if this man had come to rescue her. Then he opened his coat a little to reveal his service dagger – enough for them all to see the Nazi eagle and swastika that separated the handle from the blade. 'Sit down, *Untermenschen*,' he said in a contemptuous whisper. That was a word Hanna had heard a lot before the war ended, in school and on the radio. It meant the people of the East – the 'subhumans' they called them.

'You've had your day, you Nazi *Arschloch*,' spat Marek. But then he did something very foolish. He reached for his own knife and in an instant the man had whipped out his dagger and stabbed him through the heart. Roza screamed as Marek fell silently to his knees, then toppled over their meagre wares.

Now Hanna felt sick with fear. Her heart hammered in her chest. She had wanted the man to rescue her, but she hadn't expected him to kill Marek. Roza was looking at him too, horror in her eyes. In an instant she pushed herself to her feet, knocking Hanna back, and took to her heels.

Instinctively Hanna did the same, fleeing in the opposite direction. As she ran she looked over her shoulder. The man was still standing there, looking at Marek's body and slipping his knife back into his belt.

Hanna ran until she could run no longer. When she stopped to catch her breath she had not the first idea where she was or what to do next. An elderly German woman approached her. 'Are you lost, *mein Schatz*?' she said.

Hanna wasn't going to let anyone else grab hold of her. She bolted off away from her, hoping to God she wouldn't run into Roza.

Barth kept a careful eye on passers-by, hoping to spot the little girl again, but his luck had deserted him. He returned to Skalitzer Hospital in little under an hour and went to look inside the basement again. The scene was exactly how he had left it – they had not yet returned. Now he would find a spot to watch the comings and goings around the hospital. He would stay there until Ulrich came back. If the children had fled this hiding place, then he still had the little sketches and they would eventually lead him to Ulrich.

Across the road was an abandoned baker's shop. The store front had been completely destroyed, and shattered glass still lay on the floor. This was as good a spot as any to await their return. And to plan.

CHAPTER 27

Otto and Helene had been out foraging and had agreed to meet with Ulrich at four thirty that afternoon, at the end of Unter den Linden in the centre of Berlin. They all arrived early and in good spirits. Otto and Helene had sold enough to buy bread, and Ulrich too had found cheese and, amazingly, *Pfannkuchen* – jam doughnuts.

'We can share the doughnuts with your Papa, boys,' said Helene. 'How amazing. People are making cakes. That is a sign that the world is getting a little bit back to normal, isn't it?'

'I haven't had jam doughnuts for at least a year,' said Otto.

'Too bad Klaus and Erich aren't here to eat them too,' said Helene. 'I wonder what those silly boys have been up to.'

No one had been particularly worried when they didn't come home last night. Like Ulrich, they had always come and gone as they pleased.

Now they intended to go to Dr Roth's hospital. They thought he would be busy during the day and if they turned up later in the afternoon there was more chance of finding him in what was bound to be a chaotic situation.

As they all approached Alexanderplatz their mood darkened. 'What if it's been a misunderstanding and there's another Doktor Roth?' said Otto. 'What if he's caught a disease from a patient and died since he left the note?'

Helene batted him gently around the back of the head. 'Otto. Don't be a misery. We will find your Papa and he will be so pleased to see you and Ulrich.'

Ulrich remained silent. He seemed deep in thought.

There was a desk near the main entrance which looked like a reception. A Russian woman of middle years sat unsmiling as they approached. She wore an army uniform and eyed them sternly.

Suddenly Otto felt tongue-tied. Ulrich looked similarly stricken, now they were so close to finding their father. Otto gazed pleadingly at Helene, who nodded.

'Excuse me, do you speak German?' she asked.

The woman nodded.

'We are looking for a Doktor Roth,' Helene said. 'These two boys are his sons.'

Otto and Ulrich both instinctively stood a little straighter.

The woman's face changed in an instant. 'I am so please,' she beamed, her forbidding manner set to one side, almost like a hat. 'You both look like your Papa! Herr Doktor Roth, he is good man and a great value to wounded soldier. But he carry terrible loss. Wife, and you boys. He thought he lost you all. We spend many a nightshift talking,' she said. 'I too lost a husband and a son . . .'

For a moment she looked terribly sad, then took a deep breath and beamed at them again. 'And your good *Doktor* help me greatly with German speaking, yes?' She turned to Otto and Ulrich. 'Your Papa, I am so pleased! But he not here now. Gone to his quarters. I don't know where. He never tell me.'

Otto's heart sank. Not here? 'Do you know when he will be back?' he asked.

'Tomorrow, he work eight until six. Straight through. You come, here, six in evening. I tell him expect big surprise, yes?'

Helene bit her lip and turned to Otto. 'But what about the curfew tomorrow?' she asked. 'We won't get back home if we come at that time.'

The Russian receptionist laughed. 'It not problem,' she said. 'We find you somewhere to stay in this great big building. We find you something to eat too. No problem!'

They thanked her profusely and began the long journey home. Otto was now convinced nothing was going to go wrong. The woman had even said they both looked like their father. It must be him!

Helene looked at Ulrich and nudged Otto. 'You look like you have had a great weight lifted from your shoulders,' she told Ulrich. 'Or have you met a nice girl you haven't told us about? Is that where you've been sneaking off to?'

He smiled but said nothing. Otto thought he looked much happier than he'd seen him for a long time. He beamed at his younger brother, then felt a pang of sadness. If only they could be a family of four again, then it would be perfect. But that was impossible. Mama was gone forever. They would never be four again.

As they walked they talked about how the hospital had water and heating, and wondered if the staff there were given priority accommodation.

'Perhaps Papa can find us somewhere better to live,' said Otto. He put a hand on Helene's shoulder. 'All of us, I hope.'

Helene looked wistful. 'Don't get your hopes up, Otto – your father is a doctor, not the Medical Chief of Staff for the Red Army. And even if they did find accommodation for you two boys, I can't imagine they would let a waif like me come to live with you.'

'Then we shall remain at Skalitzer Hospital,' said Otto decisively.

'Nice idea, Otto, but that place is going to be hell in the winter,' said Helene, and squeezed his hand.

Otto nodded. 'Yes, you're right. Papa will have to tell the Russians you are his daughter. Then all three of us will be able to stay together.'

'Well, let's see what happens,' said Helene. 'My next task is finding my own mother. I know she's out there. And I know I'm going to find her. Maybe your Papa will have news?'

Otto smiled, trying to keep the doubt from his face. He had a feeling he and Ulrich had been extraordinarily lucky. But maybe Helene would be lucky too. She deserved to be.

'And what about Klaus and Erich?' said Helene. 'We can't forget them. They'll be back soon enough. Let's just see what your father says tomorrow.'

It had turned into one of those glowing, misty afternoons, and the sun was warm enough to keep the autumn chill from the air. Otto felt light-headed with relief after the terrible week he had had. Now they had found his father, they had a reasonable chance of finding somewhere better to live, and there would be far less to worry about.

A few blocks from Skalitzer Hospital Helene declared that they deserved a treat. She stopped to barter a cigarette with a street trader for a jar of strawberry jam. British, by the look of it. She gave it to Otto to pop in his large coat pocket. If they got home before someone else stole it from them, that wasn't going to last longer than this evening.

They arrived back at their basement just after six. 'I'm starving, let's eat at once,' said Otto.

Across the road a lone figure hidden in the shadows of a derelict bakery regarded them with barely suppressed fury. Seeing Ulrich had ignited a murderous rage in Barth. As angry as he was with the boy for betraying him, he was also angry with himself for telling him about those drawings. He felt the shape of his dagger under his coat. That boy had taken away the future he had planned for himself. Vengeance was moments away.

Timing was everything. He would let them arrive and discover their home had been violated. Then he would surprise them as they began to panic. That would catch them at their most vulnerable. He recognised the two teenagers with Ulrich, but they didn't look like trouble. They were frail enough to snap in half.

CHAPTER 28

It was obvious something was very wrong the moment Ulrich saw the door had been forced open. Although it still hung on its hinges, the lock and handle had been badly damaged. 'Who's there?' Otto called, and they all held their breath expecting a hostile reply.

As they spilled in, several things struck them at once. The sketches were gone; the mattresses had been turned over; in short, the place had been ransacked.

Ulrich was trembling with fear. 'He's been in here. I told him where I lived. We have to go at once.'

Otto rounded on his brother. 'Who did this? Who the hell are you talking about, Ulrich?'

'There's a soldier hiding in the park. I have been helping him . . . but I . . . but he's turned against me. But he's been arrested! Oh God . . . It's complicated to explain . . .'

'I'll bet it is,' Helene spat. 'Why would he do a thing like this? He's obviously looking for something, Ulrich. Have you stolen something from him?'

'Never mind that now,' wailed Ulrich, his hands on his head. 'We must go. He'll come back any moment . . .'

Helene visibly gathered herself. 'Look, Ulrich, calm down, you're not making sense. You say this man was arrested, so it can't be him, no?'

'Could he have been released? Or escaped?' said Otto. 'But we don't know for certain it was this person.' He stepped towards his brother 'Look, anyone could have done this.'

Ulrich was grabbing blankets and crushing them together to take with him, his heart pounding. 'I know this man. He is extremely dangerous. We have to go *now*.'

'Where are we going to go, Ulrich? Are we going to sleep overnight in a bombed-out building? What if Klaus and Erich come back?' Otto was shaking with anger. 'What have you got us into?'

There was a creaking at the door. They all looked round to see a lean figure blocking their exit. Ernst Barth closed the door and held his officer's dagger in front of him. His eyes darted around the room as they all froze in terrified silence.

'Ulrich Roth,' he commanded. 'Come to me.'

'You'll do no such thing,' said Helene in a hoarse voice.

'Stay silent,' snapped Barth. 'I could kill you in an instant.'

Ulrich stayed rooted to the spot. Barth moved with a swiftness that surprised them all and grabbed him, dragging him by the neck back towards the door where he held him with the dagger pressed against his throat. Ulrich could feel the sting of the blade, pressing into his windpipe. Barth smelled strongly of dirt and sweat. There was something utterly animalistic about that smell – almost like the tigers at Berlin Zoo.

Otto and Helene tensed, ready to spring forward.

Barth shook his head. 'Stay very still and some of you will still be alive when I leave. Ulrich. You have something of mine. Where is it?' he crooned, twisting the knife slightly.

Ulrich struggled to speak. Barth held him so tightly round the throat he was on tiptoes. The *Standartenführer* relaxed his grip a little.

'Please, Ernst,' begged Ulrich. 'I don't know what you are talking about.'

'Of course you do. The drawings. They have been stolen. You were the only person I told.' He pressed the point of his dagger into Ulrich's windpipe, drawing a thin trickle of blood.

Ulrich gasped. He knew then he was going to die. 'Why would I be so foolish? Please, Ernst. You have to believe me.'

Barth paused, deciding what to do.

'I will count to five. You will tell me or I will slit your throat. One.'

His grip tightened around Ulrich's throat and he held him off the ground.

'Two.'

Ulrich's eyes began to bulge.

'Three.'

His hands scrabbled at Barth's arm, but he couldn't loosen it.

'Four . . .'

Barth relaxed his grip, allowing Ulrich the chance to speak.

'I don't . . .'

The door behind suddenly burst open, hitting Barth hard in the back, knocking the dagger from his hand. Hanna burst in, shouting, 'Helene!'

Before Barth could recover his senses, Otto grabbed the jar of jam from his coat pocket and threw it directly at his head. Glass and jam exploded in a bloody mess on his forehead. A moment later, Helene snatched the heavy elephant clock from the shelf and threw that with all her strength at him. She missed his head but caught him a glancing blow on his shoulder. Ulrich wriggled free and grabbed the dagger from the floor. He twisted round, plunging the long blade blindly downward.

Ulrich caught Barth on the back of his hand, pinning him to the floor with the knife.

Instinctively Otto grabbed a heavy spade propped against the entrance and brought it down hard on the soldier's head with a hideous, splintering sound. Barth lay still, a trickle of blood oozing from his temple.

A terrible silence fell on the room. Ulrich had blood streaming from his neck. Otto and Helene stared at each other in disbelief.

Hanna sprang to her feet and ran to Helene, hugging her tightly.

'That horrible man, he killed the man who snatched me away,' she said.

'Oh, *Mausi*, so that's where you've been,' said Helene, stroking hair away from Hanna's face with shaking hands. 'You're all skin and bone. I'm so glad to see you!'

'It took me *all day* to find the hospital again,' Hanna wailed.

Her story poured out. 'Some horrible people took me off. They seemed nice at first but then they kept telling me they would kill me and eat me if I tried to run away. They made me sit with them while they begged and tried to sell things. They wanted people to think I was theirs . . .'

'Ulrich, are you all right?' said Otto.

Ulrich was kneeling on the ground, still staring at Barth. He nodded numbly. 'I have glass in my hair, just a few slivers.'

Otto went over at once to examine Barth's prone body. 'So this was the soldier,' he said. 'Well, I hope we have killed him.' Even as the words came out of his mouth he felt a dull surprise that he could say such a thing so casually.

Helene glanced up at Barth. 'There is no further bleeding from the head wound. That must mean his heart has stopped. Thank God for that. I certainly wouldn't have the courage to hit him again.'

'I would do so immediately,' said Ulrich a bit shakily, grabbing the spade. But then he looked at the still, prone figure, and paused. Could he really be dead?

'So what are we to do with him?' asked Otto.

'I have an idea,' said Ulrich quietly. All three turned to look at him.

'I have a *Panzerfaust* that Klaus and Erich were planning to use to blow up a building. I propose we take him further down to the other side of the courtyard. There are basement rooms there where we can light a bonfire around this rocket. We'll leave him next to it and the explosion will bring down the roof and bury him. Anyone who hears it will think it's just an old bomb or shell going off.'

'Good idea,' said Otto. 'It's far enough away from where we are here.'

Shakily they bundled Barth on to an old stretcher that had been propped up in the corridor. He was quite a weight and it took all three of them to carry him – Otto at one end, Helene and Ulrich at the other.

'You wait for us here in the room,' Helene told Hanna, but she clung to Helene.

'Don't leave me!' she cried.

Ulrich remembered then what she said Ernst had done. This was the second killing she had seen that day. He was surprised to find pity rising in his chest. All of a sudden, he felt ashamed of the way he had behaved towards her and had to look away.

Helene stroked Hanna's hair. 'OK, you can carry a bundle of sticks for kindling.'

'We need Erich and Klaus at a time like this,' said Otto, trying to take their minds off the grisly task they were about to perform. 'I wonder what's happened to those two.'

Ulrich looked down at Barth's lolling face in the stretcher. He could swear he was still breathing, but it was difficult to tell with the way he was jolting around on it.

At the far end of the basement corridor, on the other side of the hospital's central courtyard, they found a suitable room. This one was small and full of debris. It even had a door you could close – better to concentrate the blast. They laid the stretcher down and cleared the floor, making a perch for the *Panzerfaust* with stacks of bricks. Otto and Ulrich quickly began to make a fire under the weapon and within five minutes they were ready to light it.

Ulrich threw the last kindling on to the bonfire they had built underneath the *Panzerfaust* and swallowed hard.

Otto looked over at him. 'Do you want to say anything?' he asked.

Ulrich looked at the man he had all but worshipped and a terrible sadness came over him. He had spent his life in thrall to men like Ernst Barth and now he bitterly regretted it. 'No.' Then he paused. 'Only that I was a fool to put my faith in someone as evil as him.'

Otto struck a match and applied it to the straw, mattress stuffing and kindling, and when they were confident that the fire was going to take, he and Ulrich closed the door and hurried down the corridor.

'I'll give it five minutes,' said Ulrich. 'Let's go and wait in our room.'

Back in the basement room, Hanna was nestled in Helene's arms, chattering about how pleased she was to be back. She was unusually animated for a child who had had such a frightening day, but being reunited with her friends had seemed to make up for it all. Otto looked at Ulrich, clearly hoping for a quiet chat, but Ulrich turned away. He could never tell Otto the full story about Barth. He didn't want to ever think about him again.

As they waited, Helene looked sadly at the shattered remains of her clock. 'Well,' she shrugged. 'It saved us from a monster, so it was well worth keeping until . . .'

The explosion came earlier than anticipated, cutting off her words and making them jump. Ulrich stirred himself. He wanted to be sure. When the smoke had settled he ran down the long corridors and peered into the room. The ceiling had collapsed all right, but he could not see anyone tangled up in the wreckage. Then he noticed the door, open and undamaged by the explosion.

A heavy blow hit him from behind, and he fell with a terrified cry. Otto immediately ran down the corridor towards him. The soldier was standing over Ulrich, swaying unsteadily, an iron bar raised above his head. 'You are a grave disappointment to me, Ulrich,' he said, a slur in his voice.

Ulrich had frozen with fear on the ground. Barth was invincible! And now he was going to kill him.

Otto launched himself at Barth with all his strength, knocking him off his feet and slamming his head hard against a concrete door frame. Ulrich heard a sickening snap and Barth fell limp to the ground, his head at an unnatural angle, staring ahead through blank, dead eyes.

Ulrich grabbed the iron bar Barth had attacked him with and hit him again.

'Look at him, Ulrich,' said Otto. 'He's dead for sure.'

Ulrich and Otto walked back to their basement room, Ulrich's head was pounding. He put a hand to the wall and looked back over his shoulder.

Otto took him by the arm. 'He's definitely dead now,' he said gently. 'Come and rest, Ulrich. Make sure you are OK. Are you bleeding?'

He was, from Barth's final blow to his back.

Helene and Otto dipped a couple of rags in one of the buckets, wrung them out and pressed them against the ugly weal that was forming where Barth had hit him.

'Nothing broken, at least,' said Helene. 'Will you be all right to walk to Alexanderplatz tomorrow?'

Ulrich nodded. 'Thank you, Otto,' he croaked. 'Thank you, Helene.'

They patched up the door to their basement room the best they could, salvaging screws and hinges from other mangled doors. Anyone could kick it in if they wanted to, but it still looked shut now and that might be enough to deter a casual snooper. And Klaus and Erich would still be able to get in with their key when they came back. 'If they're not back by tomorrow we'll leave a note,' said Otto. 'Tell them where we've gone. We'll have such a tale to tell them . . .'

Then Otto and Helene went to fetch water from the pump, wondering if this would be the last time they would stand in this particular queue for water. 'Let's clean ourselves up – try and look a bit less like rats from the sewers!' said Helene. 'Make ourselves presentable.'

As they walked there, she put an arm around him. The dying light of the afternoon made even the rubble on the street glow gold. 'It's been a terrible day,' she said, choking back a sob that caught in her throat. Then she smiled and wiped away a tear. 'But Hanna is back, we're still alive, and tomorrow we will go and find your Papa.'

Otto put his arm around her, and this time they stopped for a moment and kissed.

FACT AND FICTION

Although the characters in my book are fictitious, I hope I have depicted their thoughts and circumstances realistically. Some of the locations, especially Skalitzer Hospital, are also fictitious. The Zoo Flak Tower in the story was demolished in 1947 but you can still see the remains of two other Flak Towers in Berlin. The 'Werewolf' resistance was minimal. There are recorded instances, though, of boys blowing up shells and bombs for fun, as Klaus and Erich do here.

I grew up admiring the bravery and tenacity of the Russian people and am very grateful for their extraordinary resistance against the Nazi regime. It pained me to depict the brutality of the Red Army when they arrived in Berlin, but I hope I have offered some explanation for their behaviour.

PAUL DOWSWELL is a prize-winning author of historical fiction. Among other awards he has twice won the Historical Association Young Quills Award, and also the Hamelin Associazione Culturale Book Prize, and for non-fiction the Rhône-Poulenc Junior Prize for Science Books. Paul is a frequent visitor to schools both in the UK and abroad, where he takes creative-writing classes and gives illustrated talks about his books. Away from work he enjoys travelling with his family, and playing with his band in the clubs and pubs of the West Midlands.
www.pauldowswell.co.uk

ACKNOWLEDGEMENTS

Special thanks to Bloomsbury's Rachel Boden and Vicky Leech for their suggestions, patient editing and enthusiasm. Thank you too to Isabel Ford, Nick de Somogyi and Bronwyn O'Reilly for their additional help with the manuscript, my agent Charlie Viney for his support and advice and James Fraser for the evocative cover. On the home front I'm always grateful to Jenny and Josie Dowswell for their support and Dilys Dowswell for her boundless encouragement.

I also wanted to thank again my Berlin friends Katinka Nürnberg, Stephan Roszak and Kati Hertzsch whose hospitality on previous visits to Berlin enabled me to develop some familiarity with this fascinating city.